2 CROWS
in the
SHADOWS

a novel

M.D. NEWTON

ACKNOWLEDGMENTS

Special Thanks to everyone who helped in this process:

My girls, Mak, Karsyn Mac, and Boom (Elise)
you are the light of my world. I am so proud of
the young ladies you have become. Roll Tide!

Mom, you have always been the rock and
foundation for everything I do.

To Weh Koh Hees – you saved my life three times
and never gave up on me.

The pain in my backside Midgett – LW.

Special thanks and gratitude to my friend
Alyssa Fawn Hoffman. I could not have done this
without your guidance, input, and inspiration.
I will be forever grateful to you Lilah.

Eric Shaw for providing the framework,
and dialog for the original work.

"MaTa MaCiLan Ni Ma TiuPia.
NaMe Kwax Ni MaTiu."

Ninj O'Ha Wa Sok

"Don't remember the man of the past.
See the man of the future."

2 Crows

Chapter 1

29 MARCH

Now that doesn't mean anything to anyone except a select few friends and family but if you decide to read to the end, then you will understand.

Lightning flashed across the cool November morning and thunder rolled in the distance from the passing storm. It was just before dawn, as we took our spots in the cover of the dense underbrush of the old-growth forest I grew up in. The day star would soon breach the eastern rim of the hill and cast the morning light across the sky eliminating the shadows and the things that lay hidden from sight. The tent of the cool night sky slowly breaks as the warming rays cast outward over the land and last night's rain lingers as only as a kiss of the dew on the fall leaves. The repeated drip, drip, drip from the canopy above is the only sound until the silence is broken by the unmistakable sound of urp-urp-urp a short distance away.

No one moves. Shortly, the sounds of crunching on brittle multicolored leaves strewn on the forest floor could be heard along with the occasional branch breaking loudly as something was closing in on our hideaway. Something big. Another tending grunt, urrrrrrrrp, confirmed our hopes. I glance to my right and nod at Little Bear and Running Fox, my two young cousins' eyes wide with excitement, we were all ready. We could hear him but not see him as the changes of the autumn brush hid the beast with its hide, head, and ears all camouflaged in tinsel browns. Waiting, breathing, anticipating, and......Zip, an arrow broke nature's silence, followed by two more zips of our bows. The buck bowed low and bolted into the brush and disappeared, but I saw the pink mist, and I knew he had been hit.

As we stood, we saw him cresting the small berm 30 to 40 yards in front of us. The chase had begun. Up we sprang and started to sprint, zig-zagging around trees both large and small. Leaping, one by one by one over a great fallen tree of years ago, we were quick with the pace to catch our prey. Through the underbrush, and around trees, on we sprinted the warriors were on his trail. As we crested the berm, we spotted the blood trail and upped our tempo. Sweat began to shadow our faces and breathing heavily onward we went. In the narrow opening just before the giant field there he was. An 8-point buck with an arrow stuck in the hindquarters and one directly behind the heart, the kill shot.

I lay my bow down, watched his solemn eyes, deadpanned and something I would get used to seeing, and kicked the buck to make sure he was gone to the afterlife before getting within an antler strike or kick. I knelt beside him, pulled my knife from my boot, and drove it into his chest cavity rearward of the shoulder. As I tore open the cavity, I found what I was looking for and made two cuts, one for the veins, one for the arteries, and connective tissues to release the still-warm heart free of the cavity.

"Great Spirit, I said as I raised the heart skyward, with fresh blood running down my arm, "this is in your honor, and we thank you for the blessing of this great beast you have bestowed upon us. Hear me as we kneel before you, one of your many children, we are small and weak. Your strength and wisdom we seek. We need strength, not to be superior to our brothers but to fight the greatest of enemies of all, ourselves. This fallen warrior will nourish our bodies and make us strong and we give you thanks."

With that, I took a bite of the heart and handed it to Little Bear, who in turn took a bite and then handed it to Running Fox. Our first kill without the elders, boys becoming men.

Chapter 2

THE DAY BEFORE YESTERDAY

I was orphaned by the career choices I made that left me trapped in the shadows. Invisible to everyone except the ones I wanted to see me, a double-edged deadly sword. I was two distinct and yet separate people. Normal to everyone on the outside and a deadly warrior to my enemies and maybe myself.

Carrying a gun and badge, balancing right and wrong all the while representing the most displaced people in American history, Native Americans.

My mind is always swirling, going back and forth just trying to keep up, and speed up my thoughts to reach the end, but there is no end. There was no black and white, there was no finish line, and this warrior will never sleep.

I grew up as part of the Powhatan Confederacy on the Algonquin Reservation in the middle peninsula of Virginia. The old ways are kept vibrant through our rituals, language, and engagement with the land. Stories were handed down from father to son, with little variation, through countless generations.

I learned the habits of the birds and animals, the voices of the winds and waters, the flickering of the shadows, and the mystic radiance of the moonlight. We know sacred things are meant to be quiet things and treated with reverence. We walked through the sacred fields and learned the secrets of the shadows. We stared into the fire but saw through the light. It helped me keep the peace with my present—even as they've focused my ferocity on the past. My ferocity. I didn't live in the black nor did I live in the white, I lived in the shadows as a warrior.

For I am 2 Crows, and this is my story.

Chapter 3

TODAY

My name is Montgomery Maxwell Knight and I live in King George County, Virginia. It's an unincorporated area of about 4,000, with ranch homes on big lawns. A few gas stations and strip malls entertain us, and it's about an hour southeast of crime ridden Washington DC. I've been here for over a decade, since my first career ended with the Drug Enforcement Administration (DEA). I needed the amenities: clean streets, few strangers, and no weirdness anywhere and it was close to the Reservation.

Ceremonies and feasts were a vital part of Algonquin culture, like all cultures. We celebrated special occasions throughout the course of the year and rejoiced in the changing of the seasons with ceremonies that reflected our respect for nature. We also performed sacred rituals to commemorate the life phases of birth, puberty, marriage, and death. In traditional ceremonies of old, our people painted their faces to express emotions. Red symbolizes life, black means death or eternal grief, and purple signified royalty or marked a momentous life event. Sometimes everyone wore masks in ceremonies that were intended to cure illnesses or ward off evil spirits. Sacred beads called wampum, made from small shells also played an important role in rituals; wampum was used in ceremonial jewelry, belts, and sashes for bartering and trading.

Of course, as Native Americans, we had our rituals of violence just as Asians, Hispanics, Blacks, and Whites do, but the bitter days of war with the U.S. government are long gone, and we need to look elsewhere if we want a righteous cause.

On this warm summer Wednesday, I drove to Dutch's Mart, an old-style filling station just two miles from my house. It sits at the cross of Route 206 and Indiantown Road. That name, 'Indiantown', is just one more echo of the maneuvering of Virginia's variously colored citizens—which can haunt everything in the state.

The 206 is a two-lane road that's busy twice a day—when commuters belch back and forth headed east or west—from their bedroom communities to the Navy Base and back. The Navy is the jumbo-sized employer in the county, and it is about 10 minutes from my house.

When I hit Dutch's, it's usually with no shirt, and never with any shoes. Growing up the elders always told me our strength comes from our connection to the earth's energy, our life force to nature, and the world around us. We walked barefoot in summer and wore leather soled shoes when winter's dark and cold bite covers the land. I grounded myself in Mother Earth's dust on my feet, her storms on my face that changed my direction, while I followed faithfully, knowing the past and blindly keeping my spirit connected to her will and my future.

As a people we know grounding supports our circadian rhythms, helps with sleeplessness, and many major illnesses, and more. Our people are sensitive to our surroundings and inner energy and intuitively remove our shoes because it feels right.

I pulled into a parking spot with my dog Rosie and we were listening to Red Line by Geordie Kieffer and I have to smirk at the lines:

"I come from a long, long line of denim jean
Cut beside all types of fiends
I robbed the DEA and overdosed
Spend the cash on guns and coke
I am the warmonger, more crazy strong
Droppin' drones inside Iran
I am the big, bad, super-charged sex machine
All-American, extra lean
If you lose your cool, Baby, I'll lose mine
You draw the redline, I love crossing red lines"

If that doesn't sound like me, I am not sure what does. You draw a redline and I will see you on the other side, I can promise you that. Let's make a drug deal.

I jumped out of the truck and stepped quickly to the store over warm asphalt and concrete pebbles and enter the store with a ding of the door.

"Mr. Bossman, you are looking good, how are you doing?" Gina asked looking over her reading glasses.

"Hey Gina, are you still cheating on me with that ol' husband of yours?" I mentioned as I headed to the back

"You know I am", she smirked shaking her head.

I grab a tea, beef jerky, and tell Gina to take care, then head back to my pickup. As I was getting into the truck, a very attractive brunette was headed towards the store, so hot most guys would hump her shadow casting across the parking lot. Our eyes lock and she gave me a long once over and then cast her eyes toward the ground but not before tossing her long black mane back and forth, knowing I was watching the best view of her walk away. Hell, I am not called the Sassy Kitty destroyer for no reason.

"Yep, I am still sexy." Looking down at Rosie, who only cocked her head. "How in the world did I miss seeing her before?" as I got pawed to hurry up and break apart the beef jerky.

Breaking the jerky into pieces, I'm lazily watching a Chevy pull into a spot a few spots over from me, because it's just there, and I notice it has Maryland plates. We've had trouble with Maryland folks crossing over the 301 bridge and creating problems here in Virginia. and I'm thinking about that as a Black dude with a baseball cap turned sideways, leaves the driver's side, and rolls up to the store.

"Rosie maybe I should get you a hat so you can half cock it and look like a fuchtard......naw, you got too much sense." As she just stares at me.

Our eyes don't meet, but nothing about him makes me think of rose petals and sugar plums dancing around us at the prom. A minute or so later he exits, not having bought a thing and goes and gets back in the car. Maybe he forgot his wallet.

There's a beat, then a second guy exits the passenger side after an extensive conversation with his driver.

Now, I'm interested.

In my former line of work, I was taught to pay attention to the little things folks do, and it seems odd to me that any two hombres would go into a store separately, one after another. Usually, if just one goes, he's gonna say, hey, man you want anything? Or like most females, they go in pairs, especially to the bathroom. Maybe this is an exception to the rule, but did the first guy just case the place?

Enough is going on with the second fella to make me sure something is not right. He's wearing a camo-patterned safari hat with a mesh crown, the brim pitched low over his eyes. As he approaches the door, he puts his chin on his chest as he gets close, sum bitch is concealing his face from the camera. He pulls his right shirt sleeve over his hand to open the door. He seems to be making sure his fingerprints don't touch the haft. And, as he leans forward for this awkward act, his shirt-back pulls up, and I see a pistol in his belt, between his butt cheeks.

The thing I have kept hidden from everyone, including my wife and children, stirs and the shadow warrior awakens. Hell, maybe he wants to make a drug deal, his weapon for his life.

That's a stupid place to put a pistol hard to yank out quickly. But his whole plan is stupid because I'm going to follow him. I feed Rosie, the remainder of the jerky.

"Rosie, if I don't come back, bite the hell out of that sum bitch, ok girl and if not you, Leann should pulverize their kneecaps."

The bell dings as I enter, and the man looks me over mechanically. I've got a high and tight haircut like a lot of jarheads, and maybe he notices but maybe he doesn't, but I'm not sure he cares and I sure as hell don't. He steers his gaze down, then mucks around the racks and cold cases, waiting for me to leave. I walk to the ATM with a view of the whole store and pretend to press buttons. I'm wearing polarized black Oakleys that conceal my eyes even when you're close. I can tell he knows I'm watching him, but I don't give a rat's ass. He finally grabs a pack of gum, and coke and walks to the counter. I walk out from the ATM and set myself six feet behind him.

I've got my Smith and Wesson .45, open carry, on my right hip, in a stretch-spandex holster that holds two extra magazines. I am wearing shorts, so the holster and weapon are visible and, in my left pocket, I've got a little KelTec 380.

I'm a bit concerned because my left side faces the door, and If scumbag number two decides to join the swing party I could get flanked by the other guy. I'll gamble that this first session will be just us two and number one is the getaway driver.

I can see from her facial expression; Gina was scared with wide saucer eyes, but she was trying hard to stay calm. Maybe she saw the gun, too, but I lift my left hand and pull down my sunglasses just enough to give her a wink and a smile—she sees it, but it doesn't seem to affect her mood. She still freezes her eyes open and tries to squeeze her body behind the cash register like she's scared.

I click the safety off the .45. It doesn't make much sound, but I know something he doesn't, the ferocity that was getting ready to be unleashed upon him like the sound of thunder announces the imminent danger of the approaching storm.

"Hi. How are you doing?" Gina asks nervously. Nothing from scumbag number two as he throws the goods on the counter – an iced tea and a pack of Trident gum.

"Can I get you anything else?" Nothing again. He looks at the register and pays petulantly.

"Would you like a bag?" He angrily grabs the items with a swipe, and he storms out.

What a little candy ass piece of garbage. Of course, I follow. I'm sick of people coming and disturbing my neighbor's peace. My wife and kids come to this store almost every day and I want this nonsense to end.

I should tell you right now, I'm a tribal son of a bitch. A Redman's blood guides me, and something twitches in me when some warrior from the other side of the river hunts on my land. Old instincts guide me, the shadow is growing. Respect your enemies, but beat them off with every thought, word, and deed.

Maybe because old ethnic wars and clan skirmishes still burble in my blood, I've always fought thus, and as hesitantly as I put on my morning pants. Once in the arena, I battle with wit, abandon, and especially without holding back. The politically correct ways of the non-natives seek to bleach out the perceptive matrix and vital impulses my battle sense feeds on it seeks to dull my trickery, to press me into habits of conformity that offer no advantage to any man or woman, but the effort's a lost cause. I don't take kindly to carpetbaggers—whether red-faced, pale-faced, or black-faced.

I'm as tree-hugger as a hippy and as cognizant of categories as any social justice warrior, but I fight with all the tools at hand. I fight with the recklessness of the old days. There are shell games. There's laying bait for your adversary's mind. And there are weak ways to play this game and strong ways. I watch my words through a system that's not determined by fashion. I enjoy politeness; however, bullets are cheap, and lives are expensive. When hunted, I'll be mean. When a scout from a stalking tribe cast his shadow on the land of my heart, I don't hesitate to throw words like bullets and don't hesitate to throw bullets that function better than the arrowheads of old. I'm a nice guy, who knows the advantages of being a bad man. Mr. Honorable Adversary steps to the car and looks back, and I shout, roughly.

"What's up, Motherfucker?" growling. Maybe you see where this is gonna go. I've got my hand on my .45 and lifted just a hair from its holster. I lock my gaze on him as he turns, then cock my head, and spit.

"Y'all ain't bringing your ass over her and robbing this fucking store," I warn. He's halfway in his comfortable seat in his luxury piece of shit with 22s on it.

"Bitch boy, I guess you didn't hear me, you fucking forget something?" As I am slowly walking directly at him.

"You talking to me mother fucker?" he shouts as he turns around.

"Let's make a drug deal, ditch digger."

"Man, you gonna get fucked...." he stops mid-sentence, when he realizes I have a weapon half drawn and I am not just standing there, I am moving forward and closing the gap. Scumbag number one is shouting to get his ass into the car. He opens the door and slowly gets in, but he is still talking crap.

"Get out of the fucking car, ditch digger, you got heat stuffed up your ass so it's a fair fight." I've got my voice toned up, but I'm also cool as Cochise. I'm ready to drill both these bitches, so let the drug deal commence.

I know these fellas steer clear of the practice range. I know they hold a pistol sideways and spray and pray. You hear about the overlong gunfights in Baltimore, Chicago, and LA, and people just getting winged. They might put a hole in me if their gods smile on them, but I'll dispense a special kind of justice that will add several more breathing holes to each of their foreheads.

"Fuck you whiteboy, I will knock your cracker ass out." and professes his love for me. He doesn't know how wrong he is. Flailing, he won't get my goat, but it's child's play to get his.

"This ain't the place for you, brother." I guarantee the hand of the Great Spirit will double-tap both, center-mass, back into yesterday and this drug deal will end in a terminal situation for both comrades one and two.

"Now, let's do it, ditch digger and your bitch boy driver or tuck your shit-stained jammies back in your saggies, and fuck off."

He kept shouting, but I'd pierced him. He had no cards to play—with insults or bullets. He ran his mouth, but it was weak, and he shouted from a shut car door. 'Cryin like a bitch', he rolled up the window, and they shot off like a stream of piss.

I waved, to their backs, "Bye-bye, mother fuckers." As I gave them a little version of my moonwalk, that would have made "Mikey Jackson" proud.

"Bye." As they drove away, I went back inside Dutch's and Gina ran to me and hugged me, and, broke down crying.

"You are my hero," she said as she sobbed.

"Gina, calm down. I am no one's hero." I muttered knowing the truth, as I held her to calm her down. I got her a drink, called Old Man Johnson, who owned the store, and he was on his way. I waited with Gina until the police arrived.

"Gina, things happen." as I sat her in a chair at the corner table where I could watch the door.

"What if you hadn't been here?" she said as tears streamed down her face.

"There are a lot of ifs, honey, a lot," I said as I saw the first of the dragon land.

Once the police got there, I went back to my truck and looked at Rosie and she knew I wanted to fight, needed to fight. I felt alive. I justified protecting the innocent by potentially killing someone and it felt good. The dragons looked on and smiled with delight because they knew they were drawing me back in.

The shadow I tried so hard to hide in my private life had awoken the ferocity of my past.

Chapter 4

TRIBAL INITIATION

Maybe I was a bad seed even as a boy. I wish I could say that I wasn't a narcissistic sociopath, but that would be a lie - especially since I've been diagnosed as one on several occasions. It says in the *Diagnostic and Statistical Manual of Mental Disorders,* people like me "consistently show a lack of regard for others' feelings or violate their rights." Psychiatrists tell me I might not recognize this, but I do. I know I'm a shit.

Maybe my mom held me too much, or not enough, or I ate with a golden spoon that turned into a crack pipe. I have no intention of getting up every morning and being sexy, it just happens. Hell, what do I know?

In the last analysis, I am different, because I do feel empathy, and I do feel love. But, yeah, I'm madly egocentric, so it's not that deep, deep love other folks say they feel. When I get tired of someone, I just move on. I don't want to hurt people, except the ones I thought deserved it, but I don't think much about that. I just see myself as your normal conflicted human.

Like you, gentle reader, I abide by the limited counsel found in my skull case, and—friend—sometimes I'm so wild, I can't even listen to that.

Life is composed of high points and low. As a kid, I was just reacting to the world, but I did so with a passion for play that probably wasn't normal. I liked fooling people. I liked playing the fool. But all that got more serious after my tribal initiation in 1980.

My inner trickster didn't go away, and my inner sociopath wasn't exorcised from my soul, but a mature sense of self did settle in. Some part of the boy burned off in the heat of the Great Spirit's burrowing eye, but some aspect of the boy in me has retained its feral purity, too. Maybe you could say my craziness sweated its way toward holiness during that five-day ordeal.

I came out from the trees, grasses, and rivers into the world of concrete, televisions, and cars with sharpened instincts for how "2 Crows" (my Native nom de plume) could swim in that wide world. I realized there was a place for my style of seriousness and my style of wackiness. I was Algonquin and would always own whatever earth wiggled under my feet— because I practiced an obligation to it. It was all there for me to take care of—in Virginia, in Texas, in Colombia —in whatever outrageous way I found for myself. The initiation went down in June of that year.

To reach manhood, Algonquin boys, were taken to an isolated place and put inside elmwood cages and put through a series of "exercises" meant to strain them both mentally and physically until exhaustion. How far can you be pressed before you give up and quit?

Years later I was told a story about a guy training in the Seal Water Challenge Test or Drownproofing test. This guy wanted to be a seal his entire life. He excelled at everything, well except the drown-proofing test. He had failed the challenge multiple times, and this was his last chance before being booted from the program. As hard as he tried, he was running out of time and more importantly air. The last thing he remembered was being almost there. He was dragged from the water and immediately given CPR; he had drowned for what he wanted to become. Luckily, he was brought back to life, and when his eyes opened and it a half a gallon of water from his lungs, the first thing out of his mouth!!!!! "Did I pass? Did I pass?"

You see the test wasn't about how quickly you finished the test or even if you finished the test. The test was how far were you willing to sacrifice yourself for the team.

The drill instructor looked at him and said, yeah. Anyone willing to die for this team and this country sure as hell passes. That man gave his life to be a part of a team and a tradition. Self-sacrifice for others.

On a bright sunny morning, next to the Pamunkey river on the Res, I was shouting to one of my fellow detainees.

"Little Bear, ...John!" I yelled as I took a husky breath of morning air. One of my closest buddies and cousin, Johnson 'Little Bear' Knight, occupied the cage next to me. My head was swimming with cold—and with a drug called Wysoccan that whacks your sense of the present, future, and past. Wysoccan is a powerful, yet potentially dangerous, that caused hallucinations. The whole goal of the ritual was to force the memory of childhood out of our minds and focus on becoming warriors. If the elders deemed that you had not ascended to manhood you were turned, given another dose, and forced to suffer a second time.

"Little bear! You OK!?" I yelled as I shivered.

"Yep. Just waiting to feel the old ball sack again," he responded with a smile.

"That should be a very, very small task to get the feeling back in those tiny peanuts." I laughed. "I think it's day five."

"Yep. We're through."

"Fuck, yeah!" I pumped my fist in the cool late spring air.

I was 14, a year older than the other boys. Here I was, at the cusp of a new decade, shivering in this smart cage constructed of rough-cut wooden slats with four 13-year-olds. I was under a thin blanket on a dirt floor atop a bed of straw. We'd been going hard every day—swimming in cold pools, baking in a sweat-dome, getting whipped with elm sticks, hunting, living off raw meat and forest plants or living off nothing at all, dancing with the older men, and then coming back to these little cages for "sleep" after each day's artfully curated gauntlet.

We were taught and expected to carry on the knowledge that was handed to us. From learning the cleansing song and dealing with the elements and effects of performing the ritual. It represents our connection to Mother Earth and the four elements: earth, water, air, and fire. Sage represents the earth. The shell represents the water and holds the ash and spent wooden matches that will be buried underneath a tree. The smoke from the burning sage represents the air. The fire from the burning match – we only use wood, and it represents the fire of course. Smoke from the sage burning presents the air. Our cleansing ritual completes the detox of our darkness and then watch it depart as if a dream that is carried away on a wingless, sage-stained fog.

We made our medicine bags of deerskin that each warrior had killed, skinned, and prepared the leather. What we place inside the bag is personal and relates to our own experiences, expectations, and a vision of both our past and our future. It can contain, herbs, stones, animal relics, etcetera but we own it. It was late spring right before early summer in Virginia it wasn't hot but with the heat of summer and a couple of weeks off, we would be facing the change as warriors.

It wasn't the Algonquin initiation from the past either. They'd made this trial both simpler and more complex from year to year—just like the DOD does with special forces training. Indian time might not move as fast as White People's time, but it moves. Yeah, it was harsh, but we knew why. Compassion was flowing from our handlers all through the strain. All four of us boys were being tried by five older, shrewder men in this ungainly, harrowing process. There was just enough light to see. The men would be coming for us in minutes. They'd jab us with poles, and we'd run, barefoot, through the woods to the big camp.

In the outside world, the Iran Hostage Crisis had just drawn to a close, and Reagan had become president. Here on the res, this hostage crisis was winding down, and we were all about to feel like kings.

"I feel good," I said to Little Bear.

"Me too," he said. "Soon, rabbit and squirrel meat will be but a memory ...." Little bear talked like a fox. I laughed. He always had a way of mimicking nature.

At that age, our bodies could bear the punishment of every kind and spring right back. I began to laugh more, and then John, Carter, and the last boy, Warner, joined in too. We all felt good, next to that river, breathing chilly air, with whip marks still bleeding, and the lifetime visible scars I bear to this day, smarting all over our backs. We'd made it through, and if there was anything whiney in us, it'd withered.

It felt good to be strong. It felt good to see things more as a man. It felt good to feel I was taking my place in the world. My Native name, "2 Crows," was anointed by my mother. We were at Virginia's Smith Mountain Lake when she anointed me. I was in the stroller, and a pair of crows dropped through the lake air to perch. It was the sky's affirmation sent from Mother Earth that she'd hit it right.

Since that day, crows have shadowed me in most places I go. Girlfriends and new friends catch it shortly after we start going out and other outside friends as well. Crows again. Pointing to a telephone wire, in a tree, or flying over. Usually, the birds are jabbering away up on a high perch and when my mojo's flowing, they come more and talk louder.

"Montgomery" is the legal label. Not a fan. I'm wedged in my birth line between Justin, Running Deer three years older, and Odessa Ludwella, three years younger. Asked my mom once about the source of Montgomery for my name.

"I had a dream 2 Crows, that I would name my son Montgomery," she said with her southern style and soft accent. My 12-year-old brain found the explanation wanting.

"Uh, I have an older brother," I said, "Could've stuck him with it."

The men dragged us out and fed us cooked meat and vegetables a surely welcome change and then we danced, carried on, and felt alive. Our bodies were painted up as we gathered in a circle while the elders were in the center of the wheel of life. A drizzle started, symbolizing a cleansing by Mother Earth, as Warner's father, our Medicine Man, called me to the middle and repeated my name:

"Ninj O'HaWa Sok, you are 2 Crows. Quietly you will endure. Silently you will suffer. Patiently you will wait. For you are a warrior, and you can dodge raindrops."

I didn't know what the hell he meant by all that. I stepped away, sat back in the circle, and my chest was heaving as I cried, but not out of fear or grief. The girth of some reckless courage was creeping into me. I was comprehending that I was one in a lineage of men who didn't live by fear—who wanted more from this life—more pain, more change, more insight.

An appetite for what was real had made its way into me during those days, and maybe because I lacked some moral faculty, that lust encompassed everything—both good things and bad things. The painful/ecstatic play of polarities in the world seemed acceptable, right, and alluring—as I squatted in that light rain, at age 14, marked with red, white, and black clay—the bloodied marks were now turning to scabs from elm whacks. I proudly wear the scars as a badge of courage, honor, and endurance. My face was a wet sock because I felt nobility—the nobility of my family, my tribe, and the complicated country that held my larger sense of self.

Yeah, I was an outsider. I was Native.

My spirit forebears were blinking in and out of the shadows thrown by this sunrise, and they were telling me the White Man's government war wasn't for me anymore. I was an "American" Indian. I cheered for this nation's soldiers, athletes, and mothers like everyone else. Hell, I'd likely kill for Dad's alma mater, the Alabama Crimson Tide. Roll Tide.

I felt adulthood rising in me while we danced around fervently with the spirits while the fire pit drumming reverberated throughout my being. I exulted inhaling the fragrance of grand pines, cedars, and oaks with the air of freedom. Tears flowed silently down my cheeks, my heart, broken open by the decency of the men who'd dragged me through this week. I comprehended their motives and the motives of every elder before them. Through ceremonial rituals, striving and prayer a boy became a man.

The nobility of those who'd sacrificed for the great turning of the world wheel descended on me—and some spirit of mission came to me in that hot minute, too. When the cloak of night descended upon us in the cages, and the cloud of fog disrupted our vision the wheel continued. When you reached the bottom and nowhere left to go, the wheel continues.

Thinking, quietly you will endure. Silently you will suffer. Patiently you will wait. You are being turned and burned, torn, and whipped, all the while being molded by the wheel. When you have lost yourself, your ego and now childlike in its form, but fighting for autonomy, you will turn as if at birth, and give your soul to the Great Spirit. You now understand that his will be done through me as his instrument.

Like the impressionable 14-year-old that I was, I thought about the headlines. I thought about those eight dudes who'd been blown to bits or burned up in Operation Eagle Claw—President Carter's stab at saving the Iran hostages that fizzled with the crash of a Sikorsky Sea Stallion in the Iranian desert in April, just a year before.

I saw myself there. I could jump from a 'copter. I said to myself. I could catch bad guys. I could shoot as many people as necessary to preserve the law and not feel guilty.

I would unleash the shadow warrior to unheralded success and private torture.

Chapter 5

THE POWHATAN PEOPLE

The Powhatan people refer to any of the indigenous Algonquin people that are traditionally from the eastern part of Virginia. In Virginia, six tribes make up the original Powhatan confederacy and we all speak Powhatan Algonquian while others further north speak a traditional Algonquin and different variations much like today with 'CA''' for car in Boston, a 'yous guys' in New York and 'y'all' in Alabama and all over the south.

Between the time the Spanish arrived in 1570 and the English came to stay in 1607, Powhatan originally from the Patawomek Tribe which lived at the mouth of Aquia Creek established control over many - but not all - tribes east of the Fall Line which is recognized as the Rappahannock and James Rivers.

The Algonquin-speaking tribes in Virginia are often treated as if they were all part of Powhatan's "paramount chiefdom." However, the Manahoacs and Dogue were groups north of the Rappahannock River which Powhatan did not control and he grew up and lived. The Manahoacs rejected his control and sold Powhatan's daughter, Pocahontas, to the English in 1613. She had been in the area ensuring the corn tax would be paid to her father but ended up instead as a captive sold for a copper kettle.

Powhatan inherited control of just four to six tribes from his mother rather than his father, which is in accordance with the cultural tradition. While men and women have their designated roles in our culture, they equally held power. He conquered another 30 or so and exerted control over many Algonquian-speaking Native Americans in Virginia when the *Godspeed, Discovery,* and *Susan Constant* sailed between the capes at the mouth of the Chesapeake Bay.

Those Algonquian-speaking tribes were all located east of the Fall Line near Fredericksburg, Virginia. Powhatan ruled between the Falls of the Rappahannock and James River (today the site of Richmond) and the Atlantic Ocean. Powhatan dominated tribes on the southern part of the Eastern Shore, which could be reached only by canoe until the Europeans brought the new technology of sailing ships. Powhatan's power extended south to the Blackwater River and today's Virginia Beach, and north to Potomac and Aquia Creeks.

Further north in Virginia, from the Occoquan River to the Falls of the Potomac River, Powhatan exerted no power. He tried to block the English from dealing with those tribes outside his control, so Powhatan could set prices and keep the Jamestown settlement dependent upon him. The Algonquian-speaking Dogue Tribe were allied to Piscataway and other

Maryland tribes rather than to Powhatan where their Chief was located.

Many of the place names in Virginia are based on the names used by the Algonquian tribes, such as Chesapeake, Occoquan, Accomack, Rappahannock, and Potomac Rivers. Such names are common east of the Fall Line, but tribes belonging to the Siouan and Iroquoian linguistic groups dominated the area west of the Fall Line.

Native Americans are renowned for their medicinal plant knowledge. It is rumored they first started using plants and herbs for healing after watching animals eat certain plants when they were sick. In order, to protect these plants from over-harvesting, the medicine men used to pick every third plant they found. The Native Americans had a spiritual view of life, and to be healthy, a person had to have a sense of purpose and follow a righteous, harmonious, and balanced path in life. They believed some illnesses were life lessons the person needed to learn and that they shouldn't interfere. Many modern remedies and medicines are based on the Native American knowledge of the different plants and herbs they used for thousands of years.

Native Americans, like many other indigenous tribes that lived off the land, practiced a sustainable way of living. They hunted, fished, and cut down trees to provide food, fuel, and shelter, but we can see that they had a need-based lifestyle, not a pleasure-based one.

The great reverence Natives had for trees, mountains, water bodies, and even the animals they killed for food, protected the world around them from exploitation. It also helped subsequent generations to continue with their traditional way of life.

The Native American tribes maintained a unique relationship with trees. The associations they drew between different types of trees and divine forces, or ancestral spirits bear evidence of that. Among living things, trees grew taller and stronger with every passing year, outliving several generations. They provided almost everything the people needed.

Trees were a reliable source of food for many Native American tribes. While berries and other fruit were seasonal, pines, pecans, walnuts, and other nut trees provided year-round nutrition. Oaks were valued for acorns. The leached flour made from acorns was a staple of Northern Californian tribes of Miwok, Karok, Yurok, Hupa, and Pomo. These tribes are known to have cultivated orchards of these useful trees. Pine trees that grew abundantly in the northern regions provided pine nuts, and tribes even used their bark in times of scarcity. The Adirondack tribe of upstate New York earned its name, which means "bark eaters" in Iroquois, from its consumption of pine bark. Early European visitors to the continent found large stretches of pines with the bark stripped, but it should be noted here that it was done without killing the trees. Birch, spruce, slippery elm, tamarack, and balsam fir are some of the other trees that provided edible bark.

The indigenous people of America met most of their medicinal needs with herbal remedies that included the use of leaves, bark, and other parts of trees. Willow bark tea is the most famous among their concoctions. This potent brew of the 'toothache tree' is effective in bringing down fever and relieving headaches and arthritic pains. This is not surprising, since the tree contains salicylic acid, the ingredient that gives aspirin its analgesic effect.

Chapter 6

HOMELIFE

On December 3, 1976, I turned seven and received my first weapon. We were in our little settlement built on land my family had occupied for centuries. In the houses to the left of us, 1-2-3, lived my great aunt, grandmother, and my great uncle, Mac. My maternal great-grandfather lived across the street, and all of this had once been his land.

We ate meals of venison, quail, and other game as well as steamed Maryland crabs in the summer together. We had dinners of duck and goose where we had to spit the lead shot out. After my brother and I joined the hunt, you could always tell which bird my brother shot because the breast was splattered with lead shot.

"Damn, more lead, obviously another kill shot from Running Dear," I mentioned.

"Shut up and keep stuffing your piehole," he barked at me. Wasn't my fault he was the second coming of Ray Charles. My father and I were much better with weapons, and we always had headshots. No lead in our meat. I grew up with a family who had shotguns and I was more than ready to shoot, too.

I smiled at my mom and dad and tore the gift wrap off a single-shot 20-gage shotgun. It would be more than a year before I could hunt dove, duck, or geese with it, but I started stalking rabbit, turkey, and quail that winter.

I walked across the warm room and gave Mom and Dad a hug.

"Thanks," I said proudly sporting my weapon.

"Remember 2 Crows, this is a tool that is a deadly resource that can be used in a good or bad my father stated firmly. "Remember to use it wisely and carefully."

My bloody initiation was seven years off, but now I had the instrument that partly defined my dad, uncles, and gentlemen's cousins. I wasn't going to shoot just cap guns and squirt guns anymore. I wasn't just going along for the ride on hunting trips. I thought of myself as a real tribal killer who could supply food for the family meals.

When I got older, I'd stalk elk, deer, and bear, but there was a middle phase that had more meaning for my future career. When I was 6, Dad gave me a BB gun, and right on through my adolescence—I learned to hunt those who hunted me.

Out there in King & Queen County, Virginia, a stone's throw to Charlottesville, Richmond, or New Port News, there were whole herds of boys galloping like bobcats through the woods, figuring out things on our own, while living out dreams of Nazis fighting Yanks or the Lone Ranger fighting the Redman on TV.

My friends and cousins, Little Bear, Warner, Carter, Marlon, Emerson, and others would kill birds and make hare traps and eel pots for our camping excursions and roasted our kill on open fires that fed us the same way our people had survived for generations. We never wasted anything, feathers, and fur for decorations whether headdresses or dream catches. We were using the skills we learned and imitating our elders that would help us excel in life.

Whether it was a question of Apache, Cherokee, or Comanche (the tribes with top screen billing), we all wanted to play Indians (not Cowboys) if the Wild West was the rude conflict of the hour.

We gathered in the center of the wooded area south of the tribal center, on the side of a tributary that fed into the Chesapeake Bay. We'd flip a coin, before heading out in both directions on 100-plus acres of trees and grass all around us, and the loser would have to play the paleface.

I flipped the coin.

"Tails," Little Bear belched. Of course, it was heads, so I was the Native Chief and Little Bear was the head of the double tongues.

"Ok, you five pale face bitches go west and the 5 of us godless heathens and the favorites of Mother Earth will head east," I said smiling ear to ear.

I called us heathens, a name which haunted us in our past because outsiders believed since we did not believe in their gods and had strange rituals that surely came and manifested from a dark and evil place. It is funny that we bathed when they did not. We cleanse ourselves of evil spirits and the past when they did not.

Standing Bear said, "For us, there was no wilderness, nature was not dangerous but hospitable, not forbidding but friendly. Our faith sought the harmony of man with his surroundings; the other sought the dominance of surroundings based on his feeling superior to God's design or plan for the turning wheel. We believed in prayer and faith while the others believed in force.

"Who was the real heathen with limited beliefs instead of limitless beliefs??

The first afternoon was hot but settled into a cool evening when we camped for the first night on the edge of our territory; the same land my ancestors had roamed. Our cherub death squads were learning strategy, via our ancestors and Rogers Rangers, as we crept through the brush, then rose, mowing down foes in a fusillade of BBs—which stung like yellowjackets and 'killed' if you got hit in the head or heart.

We didn't wear goggles like the paintballers of today, and we never put out an eye. God knows how. I watched as we marched in single file, I didn't care if they tracked our initial movement. The pale faces, led by Little Bear, spread out to ford the stream, just as we were taught. It is harder to spot one track going into, through, and out of the water than a single file line that stirs up a lot of sediment. "Little Bear might be more of a challenge than I anticipated," I said to Warner.

"His emotions will get him 2 Crows." It didn't matter within the next several days they were all getting a dirt nap.

We knew the rules capture or be captured, it starts on a Friday evening and wasn't done until late Sunday afternoon unless no one was left to kill or captured.

I gathered the other four at the farthest point east of the center. See we natives like to enter from the east and I knew the pale faces would likely attack from that direction. We had our BB guns and hatchets as instruments of death and our packs.

"We will make camp here tonight, up well before dawn, and make sure we don't leave anything in the camp that can be stolen and make sure that we don't forget anything."

We had time to adorn ourselves with war paint made from berries, charcoal, and an abundant amount of orange clay, mixed with animal fat and water. I used my normal crimson strip above my eyebrows, charcoal across my eyes anchored by another line of crimson that went from one side of my skull to the other. Gathering the team together,

"When we start, Ben take point 20 yards ahead."

Looking at Warner and Marlon, "You two take our left and right flanks."

"We got it," said Warner with a wink.

"Emerson, you got my six and I will take middle" I got your six is a military term taught to me by my father. It means I got your back figuratively and physically it corresponds to the hours on the clock, where 12 o'clock noon, and six o'clock is directly behind you. Thus, anyone behind you is "at your six" so you must trust that person or you will get drilled in the ass.

First attempt at growing into a leadership role that I learned from my father. I learned to trust my instincts, especially in battle, and later in life to discover ways to beat the system I was saddled with or at least make it work in my favor.

I dug a hole as Emerson found stones and bigger rocks while the others gathered firewood for the night. The crickets and other bugs were serenading us with a buzzing and humming chorus as the first chill and mist crept onto our camp. We all understood this as being in sync with our higher spirits which we began to feel as a larger presence in adolescence... like a God of the Hunt. Our group was gathered and preparing for the impending storm. it was the quiet before the looming firefight and tensions would rise. Only one thing Little Bear and the other pale faces were about to learn, I was the storm, and I would have no mercy on them for treading on my land.

We had a nice fire going and were ready to start cooking our venison, duck, ears of, corn, and beans on the hot rocks which also provided a radiant heat long into the night. As we cooked, we told stories of old.

Before her passing several years ago, my great-grandmother, Shadow Dove, was sitting on an old rocking chair on the front porch, said, "2 Crows, I am afraid our traditional Indian ways are passing like a warm summer breeze waiting for winter." It was like a whisper, so no one else could hear.

"Why do you say that Nana?" I asked purposedly.

"When I was but a little girl, I would rise before the sun and stoke a fire in the fireplace for warmth and to get ready for cooking," she said looking down at the creaking wooden deck.

"At daybreak, my brother and my older sister would run to our fields of corn, squash, and beans and sing our corn and bean songs for a great harvest as we tended to the plants of the fields. No one sings our songs anymore," she said as a matter of fact.

"Nana, we still celebrate and sing our songs," I said almost pleading but I knew what she meant.

"In the evening, I sit here, listening and watching, in the shadows I see again the days of old. Our village with smoke swirling upward from our huts, I hear the warriors' voices and the children's laughter rising from the Pamunkey River as the fish jump skyward." I sat and listened in silence.

Nana continued, "Now, an old woman, the shadows rising from the river have been silenced, our traditions, our fires, warriors' voices, and our Indian way of life. It is only a distant memory never to return." At that moment I knew what I had to do to make sure we all carried these dreams forward.

An hour before dawn, I put the last of the wood on the fire and we made our plan.

"Carter, take point 20 yards ahead, Warner and Marlon left and right flanks, Emerson, you got my six, and I will take the middle. Brothers do your jobs and show no mercy."

We walked slowly as the waxing moon was fading from the night sky and the brilliant colors of the dawn began to awaken all our senses. The jasmine and honeysuckle floated through the air, the chill was fading, and the hunt had begun.

We sprinted west for several hundred yards before slowing to a jog for another hundred. Then we turned hard due north, to the southeast wind and we would be able to pick up their scent just as a deer could smell us. We came to a crawl and pretended that with each step, heel to toe, we were stepping on twigs that would crack and give us away. This slow, meticulous stroll lasted for a couple of hours before Carter gave the balled fist. Everyone down. The pale faces had closed the gap quicker than I had anticipated.

My dad always told me about Murphy's Law – "Anything that can go wrong, will go wrong."

Emerson indicated that their flank side was to our left and signaled me with a low bobwhite call. A bobwhite quail, also called a Virginia quail, makes a call that sounds like, bob-white then a pause followed by "are your peas all ripe." Hence making it a distinct call but also very common in the woods at daybreak announcing the sunrise.

I sprinted in that direction for 20 yards or so before finding shelter in a low dense shrub that likes to grow underneath the loblolly pines that stretch and reached toward the Great Spirit and our ancestors with its thick, rough bark that we used to treat both external and internal conditions. There on top looking down upon me, were 2 crows, squawking in delight and I knew instantly, we were going to be just fine.

I crouched and waited until I could see Winston, Little Bears' brother crawling on his stomach in my general direction. He was so intent he was within several yards before our eyes met. Unfortunately, he was staring into the barrel of my gun as I squeezed the trigger, and it was over.

"2 Crows, squeeze the trigger never pull it." My father always said that there is a difference. Squeezing is like closing your fist softly and well, pulling is like pulling your pudd.

I felt exhilarated and moved forward, constantly scanning and listening for bird calls that signaled for the pale faces, as I took his weapon and extra ammo. The killing had always seemed to come naturally and while it was not real this time, I felt no remorse even if it had been because I had a job to do and that was to protect my brothers at all costs.

We kicked their ass within 24 hours 5 to 2. Marlin and Warner paid the price by not following what they were taught. Let the enemy come, let them get so close till they are almost close enough to touch. Let 'em have it and finish 'em with your hatchet so as not to sound off where you are located. They forgot to duck.

My father always said the two biggest motivators in life, are fear and pain. Not money as most people would guess but fear and pain.

From a young age, Mom and Dad didn't turn off the TV when *Cry Blood! Apache!*, *El Dorado*, or *Ulzana's Raid* paraded across the screen, despite the wooden depictions of us 'injuns' by Hollywood. We got the daily dose of violence our little eyes lusted after, and we took lessons in the ways big-screen braves exhibited resolve, whooped, or shouldered a gun. We were resourceful, cunning, and unstintingly loyal. We were devoted to the tribe—a sensibility I carried into grown-up life when I committed to defending the constitution. Early on, we brothers saw ourselves as savage, yet honorable men.

A few years later, I was in college and my grandfather, Walking with the Wind, was in a very serious car accident on an old country road we all had traveled a thousand times. I was the first to the hospital. I entered and asked for my grandfather and was immediately admitted to a side room. I was met by Dr. Rodgers before entering his room.

"Are you the grandson?" he asked with a very concerned voice.

"I am."

"He is very stubborn and has multiple wounds from broken bones to internal injuries but won't discuss pain levels and areas where he hurts. We will know shortly via x-rays and CT scan, but please tell him to talk to us." he pleaded with me.

"I will, but he doesn't trust the white man, I am sorry he just doesn't."

My father, Night Owl, had a different path and was determined to live in play in a world outside the Res. He was the first to go to college in our family and expected us to follow suit. He was not bitter at anyone; he earned his respect by getting a higher education and working harder than anyone else. He saw himself as a human first, an American second, and a Native third. He was determined to make it in this world with the vast opportunities that are available to all of us. He always told me if want something, you must pay a price. When you want to do something, there will be a price to pay, and you have to be willing to pay it. It is true in every step of our life.

I entered the room to a man whose body was broken but not his spirit or his will.

"U'Ra. (grandfather)

"Ninj O'Ha Wa Sok, you are here," his voice was horse.

"U Ra, listen, you have to tell them where it hurts and how bad, they are trying to help you," I told him.

"Ninj O'Ha Wa Sok, listen to me, our land was not discovered, it was invaded, never forget that."

"But......," as I was interrupted by his grasp of my collar.

"Live, fight and die as a warrior Ninj O'Ha Wa Sok, make our ancestors proud," as he passed out on the table. Those were the last words he ever spoke to me.

Walking with the Wind was medevacked to a major hospital in Richmond, Virginia where he had multiple surgeries but succumbed to his wounds three days later. There was a long funeral procession, and he was laid to rest with the rest of our ancestors and others on a small plot by a small country church surrounded by nature and the trees he loved so much. Walking with the Wind was now truly walking boundless.

It was December and I found myself walking a street in downtown Ashland, Virginia, home of my college. I should have been home in Fredericksburg with my parents or back on the Res with extended family but here I was. It was cold and rainy, and the street was bright with lights for 'The Blessed Day of the Child that is coming,' in my Algonquin language that is how we say 'Merry Christmas' because like a lot of words we speak to the old version and don't have a translation for it as translated by the elders' years before.

I was anything but happy. I walked slowly staring off into the distance and felt alone, weak, and looking for the guidance a young warrior needed. The chilled drizzle dotted my face. I knew Walking with the Wind was now on a different path, a spiritual path, and standing with our ancestors and the Great Spirit. but I missed him. As I nodded my head, I remember the first-time saying goodbye to an elder, early in life alluding, to a discovery that all things, both good and bad, will eventually disappear to travel a different path.

I snapped to attention when I was struck with the cold driving, sleet upon my face like the hand of Mother Earth speaking to me. What the hell, then it all came flooding back like it was yesterday.

You are 2 Crows.

Quietly you will endure.

Silently you will suffer.

Patiently you will wait.

For you are a warrior, and you can dodge raindrops.

If I can dodge raindrops, I sure as hell can dodge sleet and now it was time to stop mourning a physical loss and start celebrating the life. I will see you again, Grandfather.

Chapter 7
LESSON

My Dad, Harmon, or Night Owl was DEA.

Mountainous at 6'5" and 250 pounds, he was the Drug Enforcement Administration's by-the-book Chief of Security Operations, and his love for the Law wasn't only for public consumption. If sufficient evidence was presented to Number One to establish his second son's guilt, Daddy wupped you as needed. You didn't want those big meat claws hitting you.

"The most essential element of combat is competent and confident leadership" Dad screamed in my brother's face after he messed up royally during one of our warpath raids. Elders were always watching and reporting and trust me it didn't end when I left the Res.

"But", my brother, Justin tried to feebly mumble.

"There is no secret sauce, follow what you have been taught, Running Deer." When dear old dad called you by your native name it is the same thing as your mom using your first and middle name, shit was going to hit the fan.

"Leadership, Orders, Contingency, Actions, Communications, and Native Creed," my old man continued.

Later in life and formal training, we added SERE – Survival, Evasion, Resistance, and Escape. My ancestors knew it as life and it was taught to us from the time we could crawl. For our ancestors, it meant survival.

Soon enough, I got to be 6'3". I sent my legs and arms churning on football and lacrosse fields across the middle peninsula and the whole damn state. I made myself into an educated heap of muscle. So wuppin' was no longer daddy's option. That said, both of us still knew who the boss was, and old Monte still got a dressing-down when court cases didn't turn out his way. And there were always a lot of cases on his docket about said defendant.

I loved making trouble and didn't mind facing my mother or father—despite his ferocity. Him, I'd provoke—while getting away with murder. Her, I'd impress—while doing the same. No other Knight kid grew up with the same "special relationship" with the 'rents'. I was Pop's special pain in the ass, and I was Mom's n'er-do-wrong superchild.

While Dad tromped around the house—head of security in both our planet and our kitchen—I absorbed his attitude toward work. The truth is, you grow up intuiting how to handle the career of your ma or pa. Their vocation puts its teeth in you; 'cuz you're close enough to it to get bit.

In my house, it was my dad who dutifully trudged into the world to bring back bacon. I didn't know it at the time, but I smelled the DEA on his breath, I heard it when he shouted at the dog, and it wagged my bones when he piloted our fart-ing, '70 Ford over potholes on our dirt-pack roads in King & Queen County in the middle peninsula of Virginia.

In 1989, I graduated from Randolph Macon College and later from Georgetown University. My girlfriend, Constance Marie Wigginton, at the time was a sweet southern girl from south Alabama that decided to attend Randy Mac, a cute name for Randolph Macon of all places.

"Roll Tide," I said I soon as I saw the Crimson A on her white shirt.

"Roll Tide," she quickly fired back, brushing her long black hair behind her ear. "You're a Tide fan?"

"Sure am, as is my dad and my grandfather." I shrugged.

"Are you from Bama?" she looked at me with those puppy dog brown eyes.

"Naw, I wasn't that fortunate, but I am smart enough to be a fan, I am Monte by the way," I said as I closed the gap between us and extended a hand.

"Monte, interesting name, I am Constance," raising from her seat on the side of the fountain in the middle of campus. "My friends call me Connie," she said with a smile.

"Yeah, I think my mom was thinking of Monte Hall, the gameshow host of Let's Make a Deal when I was conceived." she laughed so I knew I was in. That Southern drawl was always a killer for me, plus she was wearing cowboy boots a and sun dress and it was lust at first sight, I got lucky she had a Tide shirt on. As pretty as a sunset when spring shakes off the cold of win-ter and the bucks go into rut so to speak and we had a great 3

2 CROWS *in the* SHADOWS

years before I headed to Georgetown. She once asked me why I didn't love her enough to stay and my plain and simple response was, I tried. I really did. I wanted too but those emotions were hard to define and difficult for me to understand.

My old man always told us if he could have stayed in college and gotten paid as he would have chosen that path just to learn. Of course, he had a photographic memory, so no use in me trying to spread my bullshit to him, and he loved learning. Spent all his life learning something new. I always wondered about that until I got older, and I understood. Sleep in, go to class, start the day drinking, chase ass, repeat and if you got paid, well, yee haw, count my backside in for that career.

Boring ole Monte, I got a Business Admin degree and a Master's Degree in fucking around, and it's probably what saddled me with a desk job my first year at the DEA. Truth was, I needed to learn the ropes and inner workings of an International Law Enforcement Agency.

Yep. I got hired on Daddy's farm. Most folks inclined toward DEA agenthood must creep through mud, swim rapids, and fly through thunderclouds to win the rare job interview—and even then, they might still be remanded to some other sector of the economy. It is a really hard process because they wanted the best of the best.

It was one more instance of me getting my way again. Dad was in, so Monte was too.

Chapter 8

LEAVING THE RESERVATION

I went to the Res before I was scheduled to leave to stay with my grandparents in a house that I had been to 1000 times before. While my parents had moved away when I was little, we spent the summers and winter break on the Res. I wanted to walk the lands and cross the streams, swim in the river of my ancestors one last time before I left not knowing what lay ahead for me and if I would ever return. The elders had spoken, and I knew I was leaving and wanted to tell everyone face to face.

Walking I took in the sights, sounds and smells of where I grew up, a boy to a man. I sat and watched a sunrise rising across the river evaporating the misty fog in late summer. Watched the sun sitting amid the flies and gnats over the large pond with crickets and bullfrogs providing a steady cadence along with the quails with their familiar "bob white" calling. I wanted to remember the smell of the smoke rising from chimneys and campfires floating through the air that spoke of the coming of fall and the beginning of the hunt. The smell of lilacs, and mountain laurel, Virginia Bluebell in all its over-grown glory and the hint of honeysuckle. I watch as family members harvested pond grass, cattails and bark and stored in sheds for later use. Most of all, I wanted to remember that this was my home and speak to my family and friends, not to say goodbye, but to say I was going on my journey.

The final night, before leaving the Res, I lay in the bed, with the windows open and listened to the winds as they presented the familiar smell of the approaching thunderstorm. It began to drizzle and picked up quickly and started a drumbeat rhythm on my grandparent's tin roof. Lightning flashed and lit up the sky as well as my entire room followed by the crack and boom announcing the storms presence and power in the distance. It reminded me of a cleansing. The storm was not there to disrupt my life, it was there announcing that it was clearing a path for my journey and my life to begin. It would start tomorrow, with a hard discussion with my cousin, more like a brother, Johnson "Little Bear" Knight.

In the morning, I went down to the river to check the shad baskets. Little Bear, tried to sneak up on me, but I heard his breathing.

"WinGaPo, O'Ha Wa Neh Ski," he shouted as if he thought it would scare me.

"WinGaPo U Rah," I said without turning to face him. Peyak MeNot CaHam.

"It is full of shad, I see."

I turned and faced and sat on the ground, KaHa Pis."

"Ok, what's up?"

"The elders say my path is different and I must walk the path they have foreseen for me. Little Bear, I do not fear the journey and as a warrior, I will stand tall and accept my fate just as you will one day. I will leave the Res and explore the world." I said calmly.

Little did I know then I would visit foreign lands and fight a war that is never-ending, and one we can never win. Leaving a path of destruction both internal and external for myself and others along the way. Always looking to make the next drug deal.

"Mom told me, but you want to leave all this?" he stated half joking half serious. We both laughed.

"2 Crows why are you always breaking my balls and saying bullshit like this?" he frowned at me.

"Well, they are low-hanging fruit but very hard to hit because they are soo-o-o small," I pushed him back.

"Fuck off." As he pushed back. Nice but I didn't expect anything else, but I know he was hurt, and I knew it.

"Yeah, I will have to cut the kitchen strings for a while and return when the Great Spirit tells me."

"Where are you going to go?" he looked at me with a squint.

"I joined the United States Drug Enforcement Administration (DEA), follow in my father's footsteps and I will try to stop the flow of drugs into communities like ours."

"That is the White Man's war, not yours, and Night Owl did the same thing and it changed him." He said angrily.

2 CROWS *in the* SHADOWS

"They are men's wars, Little Bear, not just whites, you know that."

Looking down, Little Bear gave pause, as if I had pierced him. Again.

"I know and you know I didn't mean that about Pops," he said sadly.

"I know you didn't." comforting him as I saw the disappointment and the look of despair on my young cousin's face.

"Little Bear, my path will lead me back here to our home or to rest with our forefathers and I will sit at the Tribal Council, but I will always be by your side." I wasn't saying goodbye because saying goodbye implies forgetting and tears are for the sad, but my soul is happy and forever linked to my past and to the Res.

Then looking toward the distant bay, opposite to where the mid-November sun was starting its descent, there it was. A perfect rainbow and what lurked in the shadows below; the Shadow Warrior I was about to become. I will first figure out the game and then I will play it to the best I can. I will chase the Sun across the sky and when I return home, I may be burnt but I will be wiser.

"Oh, when I am gone do not forget to water my plants." I always had a thing for plants. Everywhere I went they were my connection to nature, Mother Earth, and the Res, my home. The fall after getting that fateful Business Administration degree, and Master's degree, I was off to Quantico, Virginia for DEA Basic Agent training.

Chapter 9

DRUG ENFORCEMENT ADMINISTRATION (DEA) HISTORY

Prior to 1995, the American Drug Enforcement Administration (DEA) was a largely unknown law enforcement wing of the Department of Justice (DOJ) which carried little respect and very little name recognition. That all changed when Its Mexico operation, supervised by Special Agent Ed Heath, functioned as more of a data collection mission than an actual counter-drug trafficking organization, as the DEA were considered guests in a foreign country. Fighting drug trafficking fell to the notoriously corrupt Mexican Federal Police, the Judicial Police, State Police, local police, and the infamous Federal Security Directorate (DFS).

DEA Special Agent Enrique "KiKi" Camarena conducted his own investigations into the growing Guadalajara Cartel and discovered a massive 2,500-acre plantation, yes, a plantation, in Chihuahua, Rancho Bufalo, which was run by Rafael Caro Quintero with the consent of the DFS. During his undercover visit to the ranch, he spotted DFS commander Juan Jose Esparragoza Moreno supervising the operation. The ranch had barracks for 7000 workers, state-of-the-art irrigation systems, a mess hall, warehouses for processing and storage, and vast swathes of marijuana fields.

Just a couple of months earlier a joint Mexican-DEA operation destroyed the Marijuana growing operation during Operation Condor. DEA burned down all the marijuana fields and a major victory against the Guadalajara Cartel. Soon, the other DEA agents were convinced to initiate their own fight against the cartel, although their efforts to capture Caro Quintero or the organization's "Boss of Bosses", Miguel Angel Felix Gallardo, were stymied by corruption within the Mexican police.

However, Guadalajara station supervisor Jaime Kuykendall discovered that the aerial reconnaissance photos provided to him by the Mexican government were years old, and, when he sent Camarena with the Mexican pilot Alfredo Zavala Avelar to take new photos, they confirmed the existence of the mega-plantation. Kuykendall and Camarena presented these photographs to Ambassador John Gavin and Agent Heath, the latter of whom was infuriated that they had proved the field's existence, as he was opposed to undertaking any new operations against the cartels, lest the US public find out that the DEA had been ignoring Guadalajara's operations over the last few years. Ambassador Gavin and Agent Kuykendall convinced Heath to authorize a search-and-destroy mission to eliminate the mega-plantation and thus prevent the plantation from making American headlines.

Once the operation was executed and the gunfight ended all the civilian workers were evacuated, the force cut down the cannabis from their stalks and placed them in heaps, doused with oil to fuel massive bonfires destroying marijuana profits. A total of $8 billion worth of marijuana was destroyed in the raid and the Guadalajare leadership vowed revenge against DEA and it allies. On 7 February 1985, Camarena was kidnapped on his way to meet his wife for lunch by the DFS. Special Agent Enrique "KikI" Camarena was tortured and murdered two days later. Three leaders of the Guadalajara drug cartel were eventually convicted in Mexico for Camarena's murder. This ignited the never-ending war on drugs.

Red Ribbon Week was established as a tribute to fallen DEA special agent Enrique Camarena in 1985. It is an Alcohol, Tobacco, and other Drug and Violence Prevention Awareness Campaign observed annually in October in the United States. Red Ribbon Week is the nation's largest and longest-running drug awareness and prevention program.

I have been fortunate to give a couple of speeches at my children's school and the Res about KiKi, rest in peace brother.

Chapter 10

DEA SPECIAL AGENT TRAINING

DEA Special Agent Training is an 18 Week school on the grounds of the US Marine Corps base at Quantico, Virginia. Special Agent in Training (SATS) where you are paired up with roommates. I drove myself to Quantico and met my parents at the building I was going to call home for the next 18 weeks.

"Monte, this is a big moment that will set you on a path for a successful life, try not to fuck it up." Ya know, it wasn't a win one for the Gipper-style speech, but I knew what he meant.

"Roger that, pops." man he had a way with words.

"Monte don't listen to the grouch, you will make us proud as you always do, love you." Mom always had the lightest of touch like a butterfly kiss and administered it with southern style and grace.

"Love you too," as I turned to walk away into a brand-new life.

I entered the building that would change my life and soul forever. I wondered if I would trade my passion for glory as if

I knew it would eventually be put to the test but nevertheless, an interesting thought passed like a butterfly kiss into the air.

At orientation, you get all the necessary information about where to go and to whom to talk, an introduction to the Dorm Daddies, and a special number to call if you needed anything. I also got to meet my roommate, none other than Mr. Special Agent Trainee Roberto Adolph Genovese, IV. Yeah, I can't make that shit up. He was built like a fire hydrant, squatty with wide think shoulders and hands like a baseball glove; thick and powerful. The jet-black Italian head of hair, steel jawline with a nose that was askew from who knows how many bar fights, street fights, or fun fights back home on the streets of Staten Island. His grandparents got off the boat at Ellis Island. Ellis Island is a federally owned island in New York Harbor that was the busiest immigrant inspection station in the United States. From 1892 to 1954, nearly 12 million immigrants arriving at the Port of New York and New Jersey were processed there under federal law. Today, it is part of the Statue of Liberty National Monument and is accessible to the public only by ferry.

"Special Agent Trainee Genovese." as he stuck out is ham hock of a hand. Fuck tard we are going to be roommates and work colleagues so get over yourself was my initial impression.

"Monte." as I extended mine.

"I am from Staten Island, you? Really, with that accent, I was thinking of West Texas.

"Virginia, not too far from here." nodding south not that he knew which way was up much less south.

"Oh, yeah, your father is a big shot around here, right." In a very condescending and arrogant kind of way.

"Yeah, something like that." I shook my head.

"So that's how you got in?" and almost offhandedly and "you're the Native." Damn, this dude is full of shit with himself, but he did do some homework prior to class.

"Correct on both accounts, seems like being a Guinea got you advancement as well." Now, he didn't like being called Guinea.

Raising an eyebrow "Hey, you know that isn't a nice term to call an Italian?"

I had to counter with. "Would you prefer Wop?" As you can see, we were great roommates and friends.

"Just mind your fucking business and stay out of my way, we clear?" he stated firmly.

"Clear as mud, Guinea." or should have said bitch boy.

"Whatever-r-r Redskin."

"Hail to the Reskins, Hail Victory, Braves on the war-path……." As I did the tomahawk war dance in the middle of our dorm room.

I called him Guinea and he called me Redskin for the rest of the academy; eventually, everyone started referring to me as Bossman. In his Italian heritage 'Guinea' is deemed to be a negative slur much like heathen to our people. At first, it was too close for him to see, but he was embarking on an experience he never knew existed with no clear destination. It was a frail gesture, a word meant to control him while I wanted him to embrace the word, be proud of his heritage, and most importantly, cut the puppet strings of those that used the word to control people, everyone should get over it. Cut the strings.

I was always told that I had natural-born leadership qualities that even when we were kids, both older and younger followed my lead. He graduated first in our class and was a first-class shooter and a good man all the way around, unlike his roommate. However, I think he cheated somewhere along the line, just saying. I was the best man in his wedding and as a great best man made sure he will never forget passing out on the top bunk and pissing all over himself and dripping down onto me. Nothing like a golden shower among friends.

Day one began with us dressed in our issued "uniform" polo shirts and pants or non-distinct gray jogging suits with our names on our backs. Two camp counselors are assigned to each class, they are former DEA agents who are the support structure, which normally starts with 30 SATS, both men and women, give or take a few.

A few of the guys, and one special young lady, that I became close to and still friends with to this day are Rodent, Knuckles, Skip, Barbie, and of course Mr. Special Agent Fucktard.

As for the rest, first up and in no particular order is Rodent, Alphonso Jefferson Beckford. Rodent was the same age as me, but he is black, long, and lean and I am a Redskin. He is ugly as homemade sin, and I am pretty and easy on the eyes sexy. He smells like a rhino's crotch in August and my farts remind people of roses opening on a spring day. He got the nickname Rodent because when his grandmother first saw his ugly ass, she had to feel sorry for him, he had big ole ears, like a Rodent so, Rodent it was and it stuck, plus he always left an afro sheen pillow stain from the jerry curl on every pillow he laid his head on. Soft and cuddly he was not. Excellent at hand-to-hand combat, a shitty driver and golfer but great at diving through a moving car's window, especially in downtown DC, and an expert marksman.

One day after work, we decided to stop at a strip club in Crystal City, in northern Virginia on our way home from HQ. We met a guy from out of town that wanted to see something other than pasties and G-strings. Only one place to go, Good Guys where the ladies are bare ass. We convinced him to drive because we were all a little buzzed on suds. We had a great time, made some great memories, and had way too much to drink, but we got in a car anyway. Yeah, I know smart.

Well, when we pulled out of a parking spot after a couple of hours of T&A, Mr. Out of Town Guest, miss judged it a little and sideswiped a parked car. Now, I was looking out the passenger side door and kind of down because we were elevated, yep elevated.

"Hey buddy", I don't remember his name, "I think we might have a slight issue."

Rodent said, with a shake of his head, "You are on the side of a parked car."

"I got this," he said as he shoved that bitch into reverse and stomped the gas. Well, all that did was make us go up and down, with a loud screeching sound like a prehistoric 4,000-pound screech owl was sitting on the roof of the car. Not that anyway and everyone within a 20-block radius, in downtown

Washington D,C was looking right at us but this didn't discourage what's his name whatsoever. If anything, it motivated him, and this mother fucker turned into Mario Andretti right there. He was working the stick like my shaft in a whorehouse, shifting between reverse and drive and gunning that bitch like he was in the back straight away, heading for the checkered flag. We were going up and down like popcorn in an oven and screeching like hell.

I looked back over my shoulder at Rodent, "Let's get the hell out and see if we can push this bitch."

"Roger, Roger."

Rodent and I got out the other side and a bystander had to yell out," what the fuck are you two, of course, he had to use racial slurs, of course, he did.... Dude, I know I have a tan but. Well, that got said asshole an ass-whooping in front of his girlfriend no less. As we were doing our duty to instruct the gentlemen do not use bad words in front of a lady, our ride unattached himself from the parked car and took off, headed down the street. He left a hell of a lot of paint to boot.

Rodent punched me, "Bossman, our ride is leaving town HOT".

We both turned and sure enough, the sum bitch was moving and took a right and slowed down only because of DC traffic. Don't forget half the damn town is staring at us, as we sprinted down the street, like we had robbed a bank. Thankfully, I had rolled the passenger side window down, Rodent dove into the back window and I in the front window and ended up face down in Mr. What's his name smelly crotch with my feet sticking out the window. Now, I don't mind being face down in a crotch, I just prefer it to be a smoking hottie and not chowing down on some pork and beans.

I straighten myself and looked over, "Hey buddy, I think you might have dented your car a little."

Rodent leaned forward and said, "You think?" Well, he didn't seem to mind.

"It's all right." Well, ok then, not my car. We directed him to DEA HQ and he dropped us off the guard at the gate looked at us and said what the hell happened to that guy's car. "Don't know, wear and tear, I guess. Rodent, the poor bastard, is still ugly, still stinking, and still stalking the hallowed halls of headquarters in Arlington Virginia.

Up next is my man, Stephen Marion, aka Knuckles. He got the nickname because the dumbass lost a portion of his hand playing with fireworks in his hometown of Huntsville Alabama; can I get a Roll Tide yell. Really just his pinkie and half his ring finger on his left hand. Little ironic that the Federal Bureau of Investigation's (FBI) Explosive Device School (EDS) is in Huntsville, Al, and Knuckles did eventually get to attend the school and somehow become a certified Explosive Ordnance Disposal (EOD) tech.

Do not let the name confuse you. Those sum bitches know how to blow shit up too. Later in years, we changed his name to Sugar, Sugar. See Knuckles was teaching a class at EDS, yes, the dumb shit that tried to blow himself up with homemade, manipulated fireworks, Bubba Hold my beer scenario here, was leading a class. Fact is, you can take 50% sugar and another substance that you can find in any grocery store and combine them in a 50% to 50% ratio and get a mixture that is just as volatile, if not more so, than gunpower and is great in scenarios when you need an improvised explosive device. During a demonstration, Knuckles (aka Sugar Sugar) tried to show the class that when you mix 50% sugar and 50% of the other compound it would ignite, and BOOM.

Well, after several tries and no success, a kid in the back of the class raised his hand, "Sir, I think you mixed 50% sugar with 50% sugar."

"Well, damn, you get an A in this class" he quipped.

Guinea, Rodent, Barbie, Leann and I busted out laughing and the whole class turned and looked at us. We excused ourselves but to this day, it is Sugar, Sugar, not Knuckles.

Now we have Skip or Vincent Ellsworth Summerford III (what the hell is it with the Second, Third, and Fourth at the end of everyone's name in this class). He was a certified boat captain and grew up in a small town in Reedville, Virginia. An avid hunter and fisherman, he could track the tiniest creature through the marsh, mud, or wetlands. Expert marksman, tracker, and could Pilot anything from a swoop to a 100-foot yacht and everything in between.

Skip invited me and the lovely Ella Beth, one of my girlfriends at the time, out on a weekend overnight sailing adventure. The first thing I look for in a woman is her heart, it's not my fault her breasts get in the way, and I like titties what can I say. Plus, size matters not but hers rank in my hall of fame as perfect, small, pert, and eraser length, you will put your eye out kid kind of thing.

Lounged out on the bow of the boat, Ella Beth looked over, "This was an amazing day, thank you for inviting me along for the ride." This wasn't the only ride I was going to give.

"Of course, I am glad you could make it." "Skip, as I glance back over my shoulder, where are we docking this thing?"

"A nice little secluded area called Mobjack Bay" he shouted back. Mobjack was on the western shore of the Chesapeake Bay in Virginia and between the Rappahannock River on the north and the York River on the south.

We dropped anchor and broke out the bourbon, red wine, and beer for me. I stay away from the white man's fire water, as my grandparents called it. We had a great time grilling out, drinking, and dancing on the boat, and later in the evening some horizontal bunk bouncing below deck.

Sunday morning, we awoke to a beautiful sunny early November morning. When skip tried to pull the anchor, we discovered we had a problem, or should I say I had a problem. While everyone was sleeping or fornicating, the rope attached to the anchor spun around the prop. Yes, sailboats have a prop so you can move when there is no wind.

"Bossman, we have a problem," Skip looked over at me.

"You mean, I have a problem." It was suggested that since my nickname was 'Bossman', and Skip made sure that Ella Beth knew the designation, I should be the one to jump into the frigid November water and untangle said anchor line. Well, sum bitch. If I ever wanted to get laid again, I had, just had to jump overboard, and save the day. I dove into the water and bam, major shrinkage and my voice went up four octaves, my teeth were chattering so bad I couldn't hear shit.

Skip yelled, "Swim around the boat to warm up."

"Swim around the boat he says, it will warm you up he says", standing on the deck in a nice winter jacket, the fucktard. I did swim hard and got warm enough to go under the water and untangled the line. It only took me three or four attempts before we were free. Once completed I sprung up to the surface and climbed back on board on the port side, that's the left side for you land lovers.

"Oh, you must be freezing, sugar, let me help warm you up?" Ella said opening her coat to expose a beautiful matching Vicky secret outfit. Looks like Christmas came early.

Later in life, Skip became a commercial fisherman with a small fleet and retired in South Carolina as a sport fishing guide. A good man, reliable and trustworthy, and his two sons are boat Captains as well.

Barbie, Lucretia Jackson Stonehouse, was a Poarch Band of Creek Indians in Alabama, and a striking 5'9" powerhouse of a woman, with a petite frame and killer body. She hated that I dubbed her Barbie, but it stuck, and she has never let me forget her disdain for it even to this day. I first laid eyes on her, passing in the hallway, with her long black flowing mane and legs as long as a country mile. As usual, things got off to a great start. It was the first day and still in civilian clothes, here she comes down the hall with her roommate.

"Hey, baby," I said with a wink.

She stopped, turned, and with a straight face, said, and I quote, "It's not baby, it's bitch" and at the same time told me I was number one, a reoccurring theme throughout my entire career, especially from her.

I might have just fallen in love if not for the fact that Guinea had to chime in with, "I see you have a way with women."

"Guinea, you couldn't pick up pussy if it had two handles," I said as I kept walking all the while smirking. This is going to be fun.

Barbie was a hell of an athlete, an expert marksman, loved to hunt and fish, a former Miami police officer and could drive circles around Guineas' dumb ass and wait, just wait for it, yes-s-s she was Native. No wonder she was a BAB; Bad Ass Bitch. I didn't know it yet, but she was going to be one of my closest friends and married a great guy who just so happened to be number one in his class also, Karl Weisman. Hell no, not Guinea's dumbass, Barbie wasn't a bottom fisherman or woman.

We were Basic Agent Class, BA 113. It is like graduation from High School great memories that follow you for a lifetime along with the men and women you served with. Agents never forget their class number and the fellow members of their class even the dumbasses like Guinea.

Looking around, I said, "You realize gentlemen 30 years from now we will be sitting on the back deck sipping a mint julep and smoking a Cuban stogie saying how great this experience was."

"We are making great memories" Guinea quipped.

"Don't get all teary-eyed on me, we won't be playing grab ass and sure as hell won't be holding hands at graduation, that is reserved for Barbie," I said with a wink in her direction.

"Ahhh, how about fuck you, Bossman." as she told me I was number one again. Barbie had a way of whispering sweet nothings in my ear again. Such a Princess.

Knuckles chimed in, "Ahhhhh, are you two light in the loafers?" A reference to Sanford and Son in case that flew over your head.

Skip wanted in on the action, "that's a distinct maybe."

Rodent didn't say anything and only gave a shrug.

The training is broken down into three categories - Classroom, Firearms, and Defensive Tactics. In the classroom, you learn about federal violations along with a major focus on narcotics investigations and programs of instruction such as Practical Exercises, Drug Identification, Evidence Handling, Surveillance, Undercover Operations, Interview and Interrogation, Confidential Sources Surveillance Operations, and Wiretapping to pursue narcotics dealers and traffickers. In other words, some badass guys are the most dedicated people in any profession.

Your classroom instructors are experienced FBI, DEA, and, Marine educators. You have regular exams and anything lower than an 80, you get to retake once. Fail again your ass is gone. Legal is an exam that covers advanced criminal procedures and constitutional legal bullshit, as far as I was concerned but a lot of people fail by tripping up on the small stuff.

"Gents hate to tell ya but got a 90 on Legal 1, baby."

"Damn, I got an 81." Knuckles lamented. Surprise from the sum bitch that nearly blew his own hand off.

Skip, "88 for me."

"Read 'em and weep, got a 98, bitches." with that fucking smart-ass wop smirk.

"93 and above everyone except the cutie" Now that jab was directed at me because Guinea and Rodent could have been twins and both would be the northbound end of a southbound mule, I will let y'all figure that out. The Bitch, Guinea, not only ended up being number one in our class but was a cocky asshole to boot. I was starting to like the sum bitch, in an annoying little brother kind of way.

Usually, half your day is spent in a classroom. The other half is spent either on the firearms range becoming an expert shooter with your semi-automatic pistol, shotgun, and M-4 rifle or practicing Defensive Tactics in the gym or outdoors learning how to arrest someone without getting killed. Boxing, wrestling, handcuff techniques, compliance holds, running and tackling, and obstacle courses are all part of this. All the things I grew up doing on the Res. Still can't believe I was third overall and Guinea cheated, just saying. In other words, working your ass off, putting in long days but having a hell of a lot of fun all the while developing lifelong friends.

On the range, and all exams, you must always score at least an 80 on the pistol qualification course in order to graduate on time with your class. Physical Training (PT) exams are given throughout your training, and you must not only meet the basic requirements for timed runs, push-ups, sit-ups, and pull-ups, but you must also show steady improvement. The first few days everyone is getting to know each other and you interact with other Special Agents in Training.

The Academy was a multi-jurisdictional cluster fuck with a rigid cast system. Headed by the Department of Justice (the mothership), the FBI was the golden child. What does that mean to me you ask? Let me rejoinder. The FBI, Secret Service, ATF, and even CBP owned their own goat lockers, own galley, and clicks, and that left DEA at the bottom of the bilge – Navy term for the shitter.

We ate last. We showered last. We shit last. Maybe it was intentional, and maybe it wasn't but I still took it as a slight and made sure the team felt the same way. We developed our own clique and I gradually changed from Redskin to Bossman among my peers. We bunked together, PT'd together, swam together, studied together and I wanted us to chow together. Not squeeze ourselves into a leftover chair, like the last fuck-ing guy picked at kickball. I wanted to be the skinny kid at fat camp. A Native leadership style was emerging. After visiting the mess hall twice on the first day I came up with a plan to make sure my buddies and I would aa sit together at one table.

"Hey Guinea, this is what...." I started before the I was rudely interrupted during my thought process.

"Listen Redskin, no one put your heathen ass in charge of anything," he decided.

Fucking moron, he would come around to my way of thinking, I just needed him to think it was his idea...just like

Miss Priss Britches. I am going to hang out with my wang out, just saying.

The technique I developed was simple and effective. We'd walk into the mess hall and fill our trays to overflowing from soup to nuts and all in-between smashed on the same tray. Then squeeze my ass into a seat.

"Good morning gentlemen", I said nodding politely. Guinea plopped down across from me.

"Hello, friends and family," he added as genteel as a virgin on her wedding night.

Followed by Skip and Knuckles. and Barbie. Pleasantries we exchanged all around. Of course, Barbie drew the most attention, yeah, I wonder why.

"May I borrow your knife?" Guinea asked politely to a well-manicured pussnuts of an FBI trainee.

The FBI guys had an air of superiority and high flatulency about them. They should, they were well educated and mostly attorneys and accountants and not like the knuckle draggers I was hanging with.

"Sure." Guinea proceeded to spread whatever type of butter, ice cream, or yogurt he got his hands on, onto a sandwich, steak, eggs, or anything else he thought might make them puke.

Knuckles followed suit. Half these sum bitches have never eaten outside of a building much less taken a bite from a still-warm deer heart that was cut from a fresh kill. This was the declaration that we live by, Let the Flag Fly, and let out a Roll Tide Roll.

Guinea chowed down as if he was Bluto from animal house and trust me, he would have made him proud. Shit was on his chin and chest, and he sprayed particles as he spoke. You know, everyone has a friend, the fucking guy that spits on you when he talks. So, stand back folks.

Barbie decided to take her finger and take a nice big swipe of spuge, no not that kind, off Guinea's chin and seductively sucked on her finger. Trust me that didn't elude anyone's attention, especially mine, damn Native girls will get you every time. Wasn't long before our other academy classmates stopped referring to him as Guinea, just puke. Me on the other hand I liked to snort food and wouldn't you know it Skip was the same way. Especially pasta it was small and slimy enough to snort up my nose.

"Hhhhmmmm ummm, good" Chef Boy'r dee style, as I snorted one after another as Skip followed suit. "Gotta watch the spicy marinara sauce, it will bring tears to your eyes"

"Tracking, Bossman." Believe it or not, most of our classmates thought it was funny; well at least the first time. Guinea, Skip, Knuckles, and, I had a little chat that night and decided that If being subtle didn't work, well, maybe crass would, I am a half-bread after all. The next day, we all strolled in and paired off to cover two tables. Might as well spread the love, especially since I have been trying to spread my love my whole life.

"Coffee, tea, me, or Barbie, Mr. Guinea," I politely inquired.

"By all means, coffee Mr. Redskin", what no Bossman, the asshole

"Cream?"

"No, thank you, Mr. Redskin." I could get used to that Mr. stuff, especially from his wop ass.

"Sugar, tea, or me?" yeah, redundant but effective.

"Again, I will have to pass on the sugar and tea but….."

Not to be outdone, Barbie chimed in "boogie anyone?" Well, she hocked one up and spitted from behind the arch it deposited like a drop shot style into the coffee cup. "Three pointer at the buzzer" Knuckles doing his best Dickie Vitale impersonation.

"Excellent" as he sucked the concoction down in one gulp. I looked at Barbie, "Guess fair is fair."

She gave me an elevated eyebrow look. "What?" "At least you did the spitting" Again, with the one-finger salute.

In other words, hyper high school Hijinx was designed to make the stuffed shirt panty waste recoil. It took about three days before we discovered that word of our performances had spread, all we had to do was walk in the room, and before we could even try to get a table, everyone had cleared out and I lost the moniker of Redskin and it was Bossman full time to all my DEA classmates and asshole to everyone else. My career with that dichotomy was just getting started. Of course, you can imagine my little bitch of a roommate didn't adhere to it, yet.

"Listen Redskin, you aren't the boss, got it."

"Yeah sure." I capito, which is Italian for I understand but he didn't speak Italian so I think it would have fallen on deaf ears.

If everyone at Quantico knew, I wonder who else might know. Probably addressed that question a tad late. Didn't take long before I got my answer. Coming back from PT, Big Daddy was standing in the dorm room. Before any salutations were exchanged, it started.

"Goddamn it, 2 Crows," Pop growled. How the fuck did he get in our dorm room?" Ok, stupid question.

"I can't leave you alone for three fucking days before you pull this High School stunt bullshit and…."

"Well, we…" before I was rudely cut off.

"Shut the fuck up!" and then turning to Guinea, "before you decide to open your fucking mouth," he glared. "I will kick you so hard in the piss pump you will piss blood for a week. Understand me?"

Guinea just nodded.

"I already know you are about as smart as boiled fucking horse shit following the lead of this ass hat." Referring lovingly to me I guess.

Beseeching a return to decorum, I say, "let me introduce you two, Guinea pops, pops Guinea."

Pop screamed but, he really did love me. Seriously, I think, well maybe, sorta kinda, anyway.

"Why does your name come up in the Administrator's mandatory morning meetings?" pops fumed.

"Just lucky, I guess?!?" That went over like a turd in a swimming pool on a scorching hot day in the middle of August.

"Shut the fuck up" Let's just say, it went downhill from there.

Besides the ass chewing, Guinea, Skip, Rodent, Knuckles, Barbie, (yes, they got it too), and I got all kinds of extra duties, like cleaning toilets, mopping floors, well you get the drill. It was just my old man's way of secretly saying thank you for the performance that got all the DEA guys and gals to bond together. We suffered in silence, but we knew why he did it. Loyalty to the Tribe. loyalty to the team, selfless service, and personal sacrifice had been drilled into me since I was a kid back on the Res.

Dorm life became a daily routine of rising early, chowing down, training, studying, physical training, classroom training, practicals, and more studying. It's like college life with the only thing missing being alcohol and chasing ass. Training and more training until it was reflexive like gunslingers of the old west.

"Guinea, guess what today is?" Yeah, I was laughing.

"Yeah, yeah pepper spray." he sounded defeated.

"Yes-s-s-s it is-s-s-s, what is that I smell, yep spearmint, you candy ass sum bitch." This was too easy.

Guinea says, "You know I have sensitive eyes."

"You know I have sensitive eyes," I responded with a downturned mouth while pretending to wipe away a fake ass tear. Bitch, go ask Leann to help.

You do need to understand what it feels like to use that spray on someone while you are trying to control them and breathe at the same time. The introductory pepper spray course involves two components, a lecture, to tell you this is going to suck and a practical application in which students practice using pepper spray or are intentionally exposed to the chemical to understand its effect on suspects. Luckily for us, we would receive a refresher training course that would also incorporate a lecture portion and a practical exercise portion. Got to love those practical exercises.

"Special Agent Trainee Genovese, close your eyes." The instructor belched. Get ready for the kicking of sand into your eyes and the inability to counteract the pain immediately. Now, take off running, even though you are blind, and try to engage a target and perform simple takedowns. Why? It allows you to understand what to expect, and how to adapt and overcome.

Once the spray is administered, "how many, how many, how many?" Screams the instructor until you answer correctly. Always guess three. The question forces you to open your eyes to see how many fingers the instructor is holding up.

"Three, I see three," Guinea shouted.

"Go, Go, Go." still more screaming.

Now Guinea takes off in the wrong direction and splats face down on the gravel. "Get up off your ass and turn around agent and go, go, go." And more motivation via screaming.

That night we crashed into our makeshift bunkbeds and Guinea passes out from all the hard work we all had been putting in for weeks. Of course, a little gravel to the face and you might think it would help you get a restful night's sleep. Well, I woke up around 01:00 to a drip, drip, drip from the top bunk. Now I know, I am not on the Res and this isn't raindrops floating down like in a vaginal ease itch commercial nor were they tears from the pepper spray.

What the fuck, was he still shedding tears like a bitch? Nope he had pissed himself and it was soaking through, and

I was getting a golden shower. Of course, I never told anyone. Well, I did wait until the morning.

The Academy is a great experience.

Chapter 11

FIREARM TRAINING
SAFETY, SAFETY, SAFETY

Firearm education and safety is paramount! Let me repeat that, firearm education and safety are paramount!! Almost all training and instruction are somewhat based on the National Rifle Association (NRA) protocols and procedures and century-old lessons learn from the military. How to handle a weapon whether it is hot or not.

I have been around firearms all my life and my granddaddy, and my dad always said never to point a weapon at something that you do not intend to kill. I remember I went quail hunting with my granddaddy, Walking with the Wind. We took the old ford pickup, with Susie the bird dog, and headed to a local farm owned by Leann Winkler one afternoon to do some quail hunting. The fall leaves had brilliantly changed to bright yellows and reds, fluttering in glorious death to the earth where green grass now turned brown. Nights were getting longer and days shorter and cooler. We needed Susie because the summer grass was now tall and brown and gave perfect camouflage to the birds. You could almost step right on them and never know it. Let them get so close you could touch 'em.

Susie would run left, then right then back to center, and stop. Slowly moving and crouching as she moved slowly alerting us to her prey. Once she was spot on, she stopped, lifting one paw, with her black and white spots, tail pointed straight back, and we knew the birds were straight in front of us. She would press forward, spring and the birds would take flight.

On the way home, we were following along in some traffic at a pretty good speed, and we were pulled over by a state boy.

"Damn it, I wasn't the only one speeding," he said to no one.

"License and registration, please," The officer asked.

"Why did you pull us over?"

"You were speeding, Sir."

"There were several cars right in a group. What made you decide to get us," My grandfather countered.

"I see you hunt" he mentioned looking at the two shotguns in the back window of the pickup. Oh, the good ole days of riding around with loaded weapons.

"Yeah, we did some quail hunting today, me and my grandson."

"Bird, hunting?" the officer stated.

"Sure do, among other types."

"Let me ask you a question," State boy commented. "When a group of quail jump up, say 4 or 5 of 'em, how do you decide which one to shoot first?" This guy was good, really good.

"Give me the damn ticket," Granddaddy quipped.

We got to the cow pasture and unloaded. Walking with the Wind, pull out my shotgun and handed to it me.

"2 Crows, this is an instrument, plain and simple, nothing more and nothing less. It can feed you or kill you. Watch where you point it, and never shoot low." he reiterated. That meant, the dog will stop, point and slowly move forward. The quail will jump quickly and start an upward flight don't shoot low and hit another warrior and give the birds time to ascend.

Briefings. Part of our daily briefings were the pre-brief for the gun range. At first, you go over which end of the gun is the smart end and the dumb end; the dumb end is the one with the trigger. We trained on shotguns, rifles, and handguns. In 1989, FBI Special Agent Urey Patrick wrote, "… no law enforcement officer should ever plan to meet an expected attack armed only with a handgun." This tactical principle is not limited to law enforcement officers, however. In anticipating danger, the first choice should be a shoulder weapon — a service rifle or repeating shotgun. The handgun is, primarily, a reactive weapon; its purpose is to be immediately available and carried to repel unanticipated violence. Regardless of whether its primary duties consist of domestic law enforcement, intelligence gathering, counterterrorism, or overseas military operations, each U.S. government entity has had a need, at one time or another, to issue a sidearm to its personnel." Very smart guy.

The FBI was the Department of Justice's golden child, (just I was my mom's best-looking and favorite) I truly respected all the men and women who served and represented the great organization. The folks in charge over there, had issued its field agents several different handguns over the years, and we always followed suit, but a significant doctrinal change occurred in the aftermath of the infamous Miami shootout of April 11, 1986, which left two special agents dead and five seriously wounded. Facing off against two heavily armed bank robbers, one of whom was armed with a .223-caliber Ruger Mini-14 rifle, the agents found themselves severely outgunned.

Special Agent M. Platt (February 3, 1954 – April 11, 1986) and Special Agent W. Matix (June 25, 1951 – April 11, 1986) rest in peace and two of the many heroes of the FBI and to all the heroes of Law Enforcement that have lost their lives in the line of duty. You are honored and you are missed. As a result of this incident, the Bureau decided to retire its revolvers and begin issuing semi-automatic pistols. After evaluating several weapons, establishing new guidelines, and conducting a series of tests, the FBI selected the Smith & Wesson 1076 chambered in 10mm Auto as its new sidearm in 1990. Fortunately, we were trained on this weapon and carried them.

The M16 rifle officially entered service in 1990 and we were fortunate enough to be trained on them at the DEA/FBI academy. The M16 rifle, officially designated Rifle, uses a caliber 5.56 mm, and is the United States military select-fire adaptation of the AR-15 rifle. The rifle was adapted for semi-automatic (3-round bursts) and full-automatic fire through the use of selector lever or the fun switch lever. The weapon has a fully adjustable rear sight. Again, fortunately, we were trained on the newer M16 rifle.

Our instructor was a long-legged brunette that had every man standing at attention if you know what I mean.

"My name is Sara Smith, and I am the lead firearms instructor of DEA, I started my career with the LA Police Department and have sat in the exact same seat you are in right now." She stated as a matter of fact.

I turned and leaned into Guinea. "At least we know she will beat the shit out of us if we don't get it right."

"Special Agent Trainee Knight, do you have something you would like to share with the class?" looking at me like mom holding a stick.

"No ma'am."

"Ok, good, because next time you make a smart-ass comment like that, I will beat the shit out of you, "Clear?" not really a question but a command.

"Yes Ma'am, we are crystal clear." Of course, I know damn well she thought I was sexy, how could she not.

First, we carried the bright orange guns that we wore everywhere we went to get used to carrying a weapon. What if you are color blind, never mind. The first part of the course was going over the weapon, cleaning it, and basic aiming. Most people don't realize that you must practice often to maintain your accuracy. And we did practice, a lot. Started out at 7 yards, moved to 14 yards and a standard success of 21 yards. You want to pass, blister the target at 21 yards. It didn't take very long before everyone knew who number 1 and number 2 were in our class.

"Special Agent Trainee Genovese, excellent shooting." Ms. Smith commented.

"Thank you." He said smiling at me with that dumbass smirk he always had when he scored an A on a test.

"Special Agent Training Knight, Perfect. Best shooting I have seen in years." she wanted some of me.

I looked past the hottie and gave Mr. Special Agent first in our class a one finger salute. It's Bossman now.

When aiming, look at a target with your thumb. Close one eye, then the other. When the target remains in your eyesight directly on the target and hasn't moved, because one will, that's your strong eye. I know right now you are looking at a picture on the wall and saying damn Bossman is right.

Then you have the rear sight, the front site and the target. Always squeeze the trigger and never pull the trigger. The difference is squeeze like you are milking a cow or for your ladies like milking something else as opposed to jerking it hard and fast. You get the same reaction, but one you miss the target. Just ask Miss Smith and yes, we did have dinner a couple times later in my early years and yes, she does know how to squeeze the trigger.

Then, obtain the target, find the front site, via the rear site. Think and totally focus on front site, front site, front site and gently milk the trigger. If you can concentrate so hard that when you squeeze the trigger the rapport from the weapon surprises you, you will eventually become an expert marksman.

Nothing to it, well until someone else is shooting back and then not only following the instructions above, learn how to get shit stains out of your britches. We also trained with shotguns and long rifles. While we both qualified as expert marksmen, it was very clear, no one in the class could touch me with a weapon in my hand. In the not so distance future, I would prove it and the ferocity would begin to grow.

Chapter 12

POOP TRAINING OR PHYSICAL TRAINING (PT)

Of course, intermixed, and overlayed in everything we did was Physical Training (PT). You wanted to get out of trouble just as fast, if not faster than you got your backside into trouble. We were led by and trained by or should I say the Pastor oversaw and pushed our reckoning every morning at 04:30.

Let me introduce you to our Pastor, none other than Gunnery Sargent Maurice Sparks, United States Marine Corps, our Physical Training (PT) friend from hell. Having a Marine PT grunt made sense, because we were at Marine Corps Base Quantico, Crossroads of the Marine Corps. Hundreds and I mean hundreds of pull-ups, sit-ups, up-downs, squats it we did it. Now, you have all types of people in all types of shape, so it started off easy but progressed quickly. One thing we always pushed and helped our 'battle buddies' and there is no "I" in team as the Pastor said. Always, always KISS. Keep It Simple Stupid.

"Guinea he is referring to you and the sow, female hog for you uneducated in farm life, you left back in new yack" I guided him.

"Listen, Lorretta is just big boned," Guinea stated.

"Ah, yeah, was it not the name of someone in Charlotte's web?" I said looking at him.

"Damn how stupid are you, it was Wilbur and a boy."

Agreeing, "k" which really means, whatever-r-r. From the picture I saw she was a very attractive Italian lady who wasn't big at all, but it was Guinea. Enough said.

The Pastor, this sum bitch, Gunny was a one-of-a-kind, true Louisiana Coon Ass. A heavy set, giant of a southern born and raised black man with a thick tongued muffled Southern accent. You must be physically fit to maneuver not only in a combat situation but on the streets of DC, Chicago, LA or back home in a small town.

"GentaMENS, GentaMENS, ..oorah!! you must always enter the field of battle prepared for anything...AND NEVAH, I say NEVAH...UNDERESTIMATES, your enemys and the elementzzzz of SUUprizzzz..."

"Oorah, Gunny, oorah!!"

"What the fuck did he just say Redskin?" Guinea looked me with eyebrows raised high.

"I think he is preaching the gospel of being prepared not to get shot in the backside when you are hauling ass out of a tight spot. I reckon."

"The Elemenczzof SUUprise, Oorah."

"Oorah gunny." Didn't know we were Marines but what the hell.

"What?" "Boy, whats yo name?" directly in front of Guinea's grill.

"Special Agent Trainee Genovese, Sir." Ok, this time he was saying sir, probably a good idea.

"I jus tolds you what the fuck I means, does I need to shovel ya dumbass!" I don't think that was a question but....

"Well Guinea I think that was crystal clear" Again with the one-finger salute, I was getting used to the adoration. Hopefully, my head wasn't getting big.

"Always remember, anything worth shooting is worth shooting twice, bullets are cheap, and lives are expensive."

Every morning we lined up in our standard Physical Training formation. "Your left, your left, your left, right left, your left," well you get it. Double time as we went for a jog. Now we "learned" all kinds of cadences, but my personal favorite was Casey Jones. Gunny Sparks would yell out the first part and the rest of us sum bitches would repeat it as a group. Watch the movie Stripes, you will get it.

"Casey Jones was a son of a bitch."
Chorus Repeat!
"Parked his train in a whore house ditch."
Chorus Repeat!
"Walked in the room with his cock in his hand."
Chorus Repeat!
"Said lookout women, I'm a ladies' man."

Chorus Repeat!

"Lined a hundred women up against the wall."

Chorus Repeat!

"Swore that he could fuck them all."

Chorus Repeat!

"Fucked 98 until his balls turned blue."

Chorus Repeat!

"Backed off, jacked off, and fucked the other two."

Chorus Repeat!

"Your left, your left, your left right left."

Love it, miss it, and want some more of it, as Zubyk used to say. Feeling good as hell and letting out a Roll Tide yell. First Sargent Sparks was on the PT course finishing up the weeks of physical training, school, and overall instruction. We had a pass for the night and that meant Saturday night off and a Sunday to relax or get over the hangover we were going to receive. Of course, for Guinea and, I it meant cleaning more toilets.

"GentaMENS, GentaMENS, I know you are off to the Fais Do DO" (cut loose and get wasted in Coon ass speak) . I only knew that because he said it about 1000 times because he felt like running the soles off our feet Fais Do DO. It is pronounced Fay doe doe.

"And Ca C'est bon" later learned it meant you are crazy.

"What the hell is that?" Guinea opened his yap again.

"Guinea, do I look like I speak coon ass, maybe it means get ass, which I did plan on finding some mud for my turtle tonight."

"jus' you remember this when you gets distracted by some Majestic Mammaries…use what is between your ears and look for a woman with a heart of gold…it took my 3rd marriage to know what matters and meanwhile the wrong women will clean YOU'ALL GLOCK at the same time she cleans your wallet." sound logic if you ask me and I like that, Glock, because we were all carrying glocks in our holsters. This is my weapon and this is my gun, this is for killing, and this if for fun, yeah I know that the army says that but it just seemed to fit right here.

Gunny told us one time he was "so black he was blurple" and that if you put salt on his face, he would be a starry night, we laughed but the warning of the wages of sin and overall passion for the corps and life, the guy we called Pastor had his shit together and we all had affection for him and respect for his training and the man himself. A man I will remember for the rest of my life especially after the night with Ashton.

I always tried to run into as many Majestic Mammaries as I possibly could throughout my career just to make sure they didn't have any lumps. Protect and serve is my personal code when it comes to boobies.

"Guinea, I know you didn't do well but I led a lot of ladies to speak to God," I mentioned in passing.

Looking at me like I had three heads, "What sane woman would believe you are a man of god?"

"Well, I only know that they said Oh, God, Oh God, harder Oh God a lot when I was around."

"Idiot." shaking his head.

"What?" Always the pessimist.

Chapter 13

DRIVING SCHOOL

You will also take the Emergency Vehicle Operation Course (EVOC) and learn how to operate your car at high speed and curves all the while maintaining your composure. The academy had a racetrack so to speak where we all were taught vehicle dynamics. There is a similar facility in Summit Point West Virginia among others around the country to train all levels of Federal, State, and Local Law Enforcement.

Walking into the room, "I am Special Agent Ross, and I am your driving instructor, and I am going to teach you how to get out of trouble just as fast as you got your ass into it." Now, I liked the sum bitch from the get-go. Sounded like Gunny Sparks. Exuded mastery of his skill of expertise and certainty. However, I wasn't going to run, "I wanted your scalp."

Understeer, oversteer is the worst feeling in the world, it is really a shit feeling. It is the more common of the 2 slides we would train to correct when it happens to you, not if! Once you get in the car, you can tell, you are steering, not turning you are steering. You get on the brakes too early and try to make up for it by pushing the gas. Then of course you run out of track and your ass ends up in the grass because it wants to keep going straight. Now you know your lap time is in the shitter, so you must roll off the throttle, drag the break a little, unwind the steering and bring the weight of the car back to the front of the car. The tires can start doing their job and allow the car to turn and keep your ass off the grass…read the sign!

Oversteer. Guinea's favorite. That sum bitch could barely drive a bicycle much less a high-powered car specially designed to be driven hard. Sitting in the car with Guinea at the wheel, Agent Ross in the suicide seat and me with Barbie in the backseat in all her majestic mammary glory.

"Hey Barbie, want to try a side swirl in the backseat for your horizontal boogie test and evaluation?"

Not even glancing in my direction "Idiot." Again with the idiot.

Flying into the first curve, I could see it coming, dumb sum bitch had way too much speed and once the ass end of our hooptie started to go, instead of turning into the oversteer he cranked the wheel at the same time let off the gas, and guess what? Yep, FUBAR.

"Damn dipstick, drive much?" I questioned.

Special Agent Ross turning to look directly at me, "Special Agent Trainee Knight, allow him to drive and me to teach, ok?"

"Yes sir, but he needs to hit the throttle not let off."

Then came the glare from Agent Ross that told me to shut up. Yes mom, but we both knew I was correct and after several trips around the track and feeling like we were in a washing machine.

"Well Mario Andretti, it is your turn," Ross said looking at his clip board and scratching something about the non-driving Italian Stallion.

Opening the car door, "About damn time," I blurted out without thinking.

"Excuse me?"

"About damn time, Sir."

"If you weren't so good, you would just be another annoying jackass." Damn, I wonder if he already spoke to pop?

I got in, fired her up, and let that bitch eat. "Buckle up bitches, time to put the women and children to bed" Oversteer, understeer, I rode that horse like I wanted to ride our shooting instructor and put her up hard, tired, wet and of course wanting more. A natural talent I was born with. See I practiced what we were taught, Correct, Pause, and Recovery. Hell, I started this when I drove the farm tractor bailing hay back on the Res around seven or eight years old, not to mention when I took pop's car out, in the secret of course, at night when I was 14. Remember, I was initiated and was a man at 14, so I should be able to drive, right?

Then a light rain started, and it was time to show off more of my driving skills with a display of drifting around the track. Drifting is getting the back end of the vehicle to slide around a curve. Drifting is easiest when you have a car with rear-wheel drive so kinda difficult to do on a tractor that is all-wheel drive and low-end torque but not hard at all in my mom's Triumph

Spitfire, a British front-engine, rear-wheel drive, two-passenger convertible sports car.

To start a drift, you must find a way to make the rear wheels lose traction. The easiest and most common way to do this is what they call the 'through the power over technique' method. You must turn the car's wheel to throw off its weight. There are other tricks you can use with or separately from the 'power over technique', like a 'handbrake slide', which a tractor also doesn't have. Or with automatic cars or a clutch kick with manual cars. When done properly and safely, drifting with these techniques can be a very thrilling trick to pull off and I gave them a proper show and the thrill of drifting only because we had some drizzle, and the track was a little wet. My passengers didn't need to know even though Agent Ross gave me a smirk and "Smartass" under his breath. Told you I loved the fucking guy.

Then just to show what I could do, I slammed that bitch into reverse, put the pedal to the medal and reached with my right hand all the way over to the left of the steering wheel, cranked it around and the car spun a 180 and as soon as we straighten out, I shifted into first gear and the acceleration pinned them to the back of the seat and we were off in the opposite direction.

"Now that, ladies and gentlemen is what you call a J turn." I received enthusiastic applause from the backseat Barbie, a shaking of the head from Ross 'like how the hell can I keep a grip on this dude?' from my front seat shotgun and the Italian sections groaned, "wat go smart ass."

Women, weapons, or cars, I got this, and don't threaten me with anyone of them because I will take each. We Let the flag fly, make a drug deal and of course, Roll, Damn Tide.

Barbie finally got her chance and did exactly as I expected. Perfect form, excellent execution and did what she was taught; Correct, Pause and Recover. Miami police department had taught her well, but she was also Native and smoking hot, so maybe I was a little biased. She was a BAB after all and not just because I wanted to introduce her to MTL, Monte Turbo Loving, but because she was good, a professional and fearless when it counted.

Chapter 14

OUR FIRST NIGHT OUT

Coming to the end of our 18 weeks of training, our class was awarded a kitchen pass. Now, this didn't mean we could go anywhere in the United States or back home, we had strict orders to stick to Q-Town and not deviate from the plan.

Let me set the stage for Q-Town. It is the only town in the entire United States that sits smack dab in the center of the United States Marine Corps (USMC) Base, Quantico. Ok, not in the middle but you get my drift. It does sit on the scenic banks of the Potomac River that runs down from crime-free Washington DC finally ending miles away in the beautiful Chesapeake Bay. It is like stepping back in time and features all the traditional shops with a look at America's past of white picket fences, full-service filling station and a barbershop where Floyd will cut your hair.

When I first visited Q-Town, it was a flashback to riding my bike, along with my cousins, to Miss Hudson's store at the edge of town. You entered to old squeaky wood floors, a pot belly stove with a fat tabby cat, named Linus sitting on top. A couple of old-timers hunkered over a pickle barrel playing checkers and smoking cigars. Suspended from the rafters were horse collars, lanterns, and milking pails. Boots, overalls, and cured hams were hung with ten-penny nails.

Entering the mart, "Little Bear, grab the cokes, I will get the peanuts."

One the old timers looked over at me, "2 Crows, do you know how that pairing came about, coke and salted peanuts." It was a small town, and everyone knew everyone.

"No sir, we just like it."

"The story goes, in the South, workers performing manual labor could pour individual packets of peanuts into Coke bottles and keep working without having to wash their hands to eat." Just like the folks in Q-Town, hardworking country folk.

I convinced the 14 of us that we could head a little further north up Route 1, Jefferson Davis Highway, or A1A to you folks from Florida. Route 1 goes from Key West all the way to Maine even though the names change a few times, it is still the same road and still Jefferson Davis to me. Major highways that go north and south are odd numbers and highways that go east, and west is even numbers. Think Route 66, east to west, I-95, and, Jeff Davis north and south.

Our destination was not Q-Town it was a nightclub called Uncle Julio's. Yep, he was not my uncle but maybe one of his attending ladies could be my friend. We piled into 3 cars and were on our way. We got stopped at the door, ID checked, and asked if we were Marines, for the first of many times that night.

We entered the bar, in mass, like a bunch of hobos looking for the first boxcar to hop on. Not me, I was selective. Shit who was I kidding it had been a couple of months since entertaining a lady and vice versa.

We split up and started doing the intel on the place, from the start you could tell, a target-rich environment. I turned to Guinea, "you know what burnt pizza, frozen beer, and a pregnant woman have in common?"

"Fuck no, but I am sure you are going to inform us."

Smiling I said, "Some poor sum bitch that forgot to pull it out."

Barbie shook her head, "how in the hell do you come up with this dumb shit?" This has been a common theme throughout my life. I guess it is like how a comedian comes up with jokes? They don't know, they just do.

Approaching the bar, 'What can I get y'all jarheads?"

"Three miller lites, one with a nipple for him." nodding towards you know who.

"You are marines, right?"

"Nah, Federal agents." Well, he didn't need to know that technically we didn't have the diploma, credentials, or the gun. Guinea approached and pulled a pack of cigarettes out of his pocket, lit one up, pulled a hard drag and let the smoke blow out his nose.

Looking at him with a WTF fact, "Aren't we full of surprises, you know those damn things will kill you."

"Yeah, but it tastes so good."

"I don't date chicks that smoke." I looked at Guinea.

"Really, why not?"

"Makes my dick smell like an astray!"

"Can you be any more of an ass?" Barbie had to chime her sexy ass into the conversation.

"Yeah, I sure can if you think it will help me get some mud for the turtle?"

"Bossman, why don't you just wear a shirt that says, I never want to get laid" she said, "that way you won't have to open your pretty mouth and smile before she tells you to fuck off" I have to admit, Barbie was turning me on more and more each day, and it was kinda funny. Kinda.

They were all kinds of people and like at the Academy I wanted to make our presence known. Why you ask? Same reason as before to show unity. We weren't a gaggle of poorly, low flying geese stumbling drunk to defeat at the first sign of resistance. No, we were highly trained professionals looking to roll over an ever-fleeing enemy or sexy hot target in this case. Barbie had a boyfriend, so she was the chaperon. I gathered all 14 of us together and squeezed our asses in front of the bar, sound familiar?

At the top of my voice, "barkeep, hay for my horses, beer for my men, mud for my turtle, and 14 shots of Jack Daniels." As we slammed the empty shot glasses down, oorah rang out.... not what I expected nor what I wanted. I wanted attention, not attention that we were just graduated Marines looking to use our newly acquired skills on the townies. I wanted to draw the attention of the female persuasion. I turned, scanned the bar, identified a target, and nodded in that direction, then pushed at Guinea to get his slow ass moving. We walked up to a table and introduced ourselves and were immediately blown off.

With a disgusted look on her face and I quote, "We don't date military guys and we sure as hell don't fuck enlisted marines."

"Damn, you are in luck, we are well diggers and have long equipment to work with and you look like you need a good drilling."

"Fuck off." She shrieked in a raspy chain-smoking voice and then turned her back.

"Sorry, you can't be first, but you could be next was my parting shot."

You must accept your losses gracefully and this was obviously Guinea's loss. Yes, I went there. We were going to take more losses as the night went on. Now some of us would hookup, or even desert us as car number two and three did, they were getting nervous and headed home. Candy asses. That left five of us. No reason to try to talk the traitors into staying and rejoining the ranks. We would bury the dead, bayonet the wounded, and keep moving on to the next target, with or without them. We drifted to the back of the restaurant bar to a quieter room with a bar away from the loud thumping of the club music on the dance floor. Guinea pointed out two love-lies, with an open mouth drool coming down one side, like my granddad's hunting dogs when they got on a scent.

He was all nervous and shaking, "Damn, dude calm down, and how about wiping that smirk of desperation off your face."

There she was, a statuesque, raven-haired beauty will her back against the bar, 5-inch heels, perched on the rung of a bar chair, cigarette poised between her bright red nail-polished fingers. Without breaking her gaze at me she reaches back placing her tumbler on the bar. The barkeep must have a routine established with her as he scoops ice into the tumbler followed by a splash of Jack Daniels. She picks it up, still not looking back, and, lifts it to her glossy, red lips, and gives me a salutary toast. I can tell this will be a contest of wills to see who breaks the gaze first and it won't be Moi. Did I tell you; I speak a smattering of French the Indians in this region were well exposed to French explorers, and traces of our lexicon is scattered with French expressions as well as some Spanish and Portuguese.

Guinea and I approach as I extend my hand, "Hi, I am Monte, and this is Guinea. He is a wop from Staten Island." I state nodding in his direction. "I am from Virginia."

"Guinea?" She looked a little shocked and glanced in his direction, before looking back at me. Didn't I tell you I would win the eye lock, war of wills contest?

"I know what that means," She says, "But isn't that derogatory?"

"Naw, it doesn't offend me at all, what are you ladies drinking?"

"Ah, wow, ok, I am Ashton, and this is Betci," She says gesturing toward her cherubic, faced friend with a halo of spun, golden hair echoed by a golden yellow, low-draped blouse.

"Would you guys like to join me in a Jack, I am buying." She offers in a deep whisper causing me to lean in toward her.

We passed small pleasantries and she says, "So, you are the one the guys call Bossman." Accentuating Bossman.

"Well, technically, I am not the boss of anyone…but yes, people have been known to refer to me as that."

"Why is that?" She smirked the question.

"Stick around and you might be lucky enough to find out."

To which she rejoined in her smoky, deepening voice "Well, Baby…you could be my Bossman anytime you like." This young lady was in desperate need of some MTL and since I am Monte, I was just the man for the job.

Drinks arrive and Guinea and I raise our glasses to the ladies as I say, "Thank you, and here's to Jack Daniels."

A couple of things, first, she noticed the sexy Kitty Destroy, and second, after hearing me referred to as Bossman she was still talking to me and laughing, and finally, she bought us a drink all while playing with her long jet-black hair. Odds on favorite, we were going to be bumping uglies tonight and I would get to see her mad Oh, God& face.

I was intrigued by Ashton's quippy, confident, and, controlled delivery. Her commanding presence calmed me in a way I had not experienced with a woman before. Having grown up on the res watching 40s and 50s noir classics with Mom-and-Pop right before being sent off for bedtime halfway into the finale…Ashton reminded me of the old-fashioned 40s and 50s movie stars…was it Bacall, Russell, Bergman combined with my favorite recent crush, Demi Moore, from tuning in with Grandmother to her favorite soap, General Hospital. And she had Demi's deep, raspy low voice that made me hang on every syllable. No matter, realizing she was a combination of all that mesmerized me about women before I even fully understood, she now had my undivided attention. Later I discovered Ashton's lashes were so thick she never wore eye makeup just a smidge of essential oil and put her dark crimson lipstick on in two movements, a slash of the tube from left on the top and without pausing a slash in the other direction on her bottom pout, from right to left. Which I adored watching, as it was her war paint and meant she was now ready for battle if you know what I mean. And she knew I enjoyed taking this gesture in and always looked back straight into my eyes from her dressing table mirror when she did so. I am pretty sure I wore more of her war paint than she did, at least between the sheets.

Back to the present time, Guinea moved alongside Betci, giving me Ashton all to myself as the Bartender brought another round of JD shots.

"Are you a Marine?" I heard Betci asking Guinea. Marine again, pretty sure we met some of her friends earlier.

"No, we are twins and work milking ink from squids for an International multi-conglomerate fish and seafood company," Sarah told me to use that.

"That's funny but don't lie, you look like a marine and you said 'oorah' earlier and I don't date marines."

Holding up three fingers, "Scout's honor" which I think is really a girl scouts sign, "I was never a scout but always wanted to be and that should count for something, and no I am not a Marine." Well, that got her laughing again.

As the night wore on, we drank, danced, and overall had a great time. All the while I noticed several guys just eye-balling Guinea and me. Not sure if my high and tight or my suave sexy outfit was attracting their attention. The girls got up and excused themselves and needed to visit the little girls and they always go in pairs, maybe for comfort or safety. My secret admirer approached Guinea and me, with three compadres.

"Listen, jarhead," Here with go with the Marine comment, again.

"Actually, I am not..." before I was rudely cut off.

"I don't give a shit who you are, you are sitting with my girlfriend, and I am going to beat your ass.

Guinea chimed in at the right time, "listen we don't want any problems, we are just here....."The rest never left his mouth a because he was knocked off the chair by a sucker punch from one of the lead miscreant's friends. Bad news for him, Guinea liked to fight and received his weekly scars on the streets of Staten Island and elevated to his feet with an uppercut that both surprised and knocked his ass out. One down three to go or so I thought.

I ducked meat heads initial thrust and claw-handed a throat jab that sent both hands to his throat and flat back on the floor. You would think this would bring everyone to their senses. Nope, these two had to be a special kind of stupid. Play stupid games you don't get stupid prizes as they say, and you get knocked out. Both were dropped with extreme violence. I grabbed a bottle, busted it on the bar, and stood over dickhead.

and was going to deliver the knockout blow to meat's head on the floor when I heard,

"Monte, stop, please don't, please!' she screamed.

I looked and saw the terror on Ashton's face, I let the bottle slide down my hand in a stay of execution to a vanquished foe. But I didn't want to, I felt weak, it pained me, and hurt to my core for not following through and delivering the last blow. He was in my world and the Shadow was growing stronger. My ferocity was screaming at me.

Looking at her, "Ashton, do you know this guy?"

"Yes, I went out with him a couple of times, but he was such an ass, I never spoke to him again, but he won't leave me alone."

I leaned down, brought him to my face, and whispered in his ear. "Bother her again, next time we make a drug deal with your life."

The bouncers arrived and we were escorted out the front door but not before, "Miss Ashton, if you would like to accompany me," I said as I held out my arm to escort her out of the bar.

We gathered the crew and decided the best place to go was, yep to the barracks. Maybe I was the only one that thought it was a good way to end the evening.

"Bossman, this isn't a good idea, I am telling you. We could get sent home."

"Listen if you need a damn cry rag I will give you my shirt, now focus on Betci."

"But I have a girlfriend." Don't forget to mention gay, I thought.

"I save your sorry ass from getting the tar beat out of you and this is the thanks I get?"

"Bossman, Guinea's right," Barbie mentioned.

"Listen, sweet cheeks, I know what I am doing" "let's go" as I was headed in the direction of the car with the hottie in tow.

With knuckles at the wheel, Barbie in the center, and Skip on the outside, Guinea, Betci, Ashton, and I piled into the backseat. We head south on I-95 and entered the West gate of Quantico and breezed through the Marine gate with an 'oorah' and through the academy gate with our contraband in tow. Low and behold the traitors were there drinking beer and doing shots in the parking lot. Intel told us, we had free reign of the place, so I grabbed Ashton and asked her if she believed in God and if she wanted to meet him. The quizzical look on her face was priceless but the expression on her mad face during the fun was extraordinary.

Of course, being woken up but one of the dorm daddies the next day, with the sun blaring in our room told us it was mid-morning. At least it wasn't the neighbor's lawn mower that woke us, especially if it was me, he was mowing around. We were told that we had to go see the Assistant Special Agent in Charge (ASAC) of the Academy. This wasn't on my schedule of planned events for the day, but I guess I should oblige the old man. I put my clothes on, got Ashton's number, and secured her and Betci a ride back to their car in Springfield via Barbie and Skip. I figured she could put in a good word for me when everyone was sober. Damn, maybe I should have thought about that idea for a bit longer. It did work out for a period with Ashton, she and I dated for a year or so before I left for South America.

Opening the dorm room door, there was Guinea who was walking slowly, styling the big head between both paws and I sure one hell of a case cotton mouth.

"Going to see the old Gipper."

"Redskin I told you this wasn't a good idea," acting like his head hurt or something.

We got to the administration building and the office of the ASAC around 11 am on a Sunday and entered the office.

"Trainee Knight and Genovese, good to see both of you gentlemen this morning."

Smiling, "Thank you, Sir, it is a pleasure."

"How about both of you shut the fuck up and listen." Well, ok if you say so. Maybe he was hungover like us but didn't get laid last night and had a case of blue balls, but I really didn't think now was the appropriate time to inquire. Maybe later.

"You both had strict orders to not leave Q-Town and be back here by 01:00. From what I understand either you both are idiots or just didn't give a damn about rules and regulations (which won't be the last time I hear that) so it was either intentional or incompetence, neither of which is acceptable."

Pausing for effect, I am sure of it. "If I take the advice of your father." Well, yee-haw, the Asshat just had to tell pops and I can't wait for the rerun follow on to this conversation with my old man.

"I could kick you both out as suggested by your father or suspend both you and/or have you start over with the next

Basic Agent class or......" may I have door number three, please?

We didn't mind cleaning all the toilets, barracks, and mess hall for the next several days before graduation. As Guinea and I left the office I held up a high five and he glared at me, "I fucking told you." but in the end, gave me that dumbass smirk he always did.

Then, halfway back to the dorm, "We beat the system again." Another successful drug deal was made, and it was just the beginning.

'Yeah, Guinea, we Beat the Man." Guinea was as happy as a puppy with two peckers.

We got 'shat' from the rite of passage in Dec 1990 with Guinea being number 1 in our class and I being number 3. I still attest that he cheated. Our path was already chosen by the Great Spirit; we were headed south.

Chapter 15

BRAGG

Riding down I-95 south on a school bus, "Hey, at least it wasn't a short bus," I mentioned to no one in particular. Loaded with a bunch of experienced field-tested DEA guys, I pulled some strings and made sure Guinea, Rodent, Knuckles, Skip, and Barbie made the cut list from BA Class 113. FNGs, Fucking New Guys, like us didn't get the special slots like this unless, well, you were special, hence the short bus reference.

I glanced at the glowing hands of my battered Timex watch and then out into the darkness of the early morning. I couldn't see much, but I could see and feel that we were slowing and approaching a checkpoint. 'America's Contingency Corps'.

FORT BRAGG
'Home of the Airborne'
And Special Operations Forces

It is commonly referred to as the 'Center of the Military Universe'. Might as well have read ass kickers live, train, and die here. We pulled to a stop in front of a barracks that looked like it housed the japs in WWII.

Up stepped Sargent First Class (E7) Greg James, aka Black 4, our jumpmaster and personal ginormous pain in the ass. Now, Greg is a mountain man. Honest, not much to say, goes straight to work, and likes to hurt people. Married with kids and never looked at another woman in the 30-plus years I have known the man. Always had a mean disposition and one hell of a dry sense of humor. He always had a way to piss off the higher-ups, so we were buddies from the first time he pushed me out of a helicopter, the dick.

Greg was a guy accustomed to pain and would go to extraordinary and sometimes even counterproductive lengths to hide fatigue, injuries, and weakness. Hard as nails.

"God and I have a real good understanding. I don't want to meet him yet." Preached Greg every chance he got. "Most of you, young panty wastes were civilians less than three years ago and spent the last few months busting your ass in training, and now running on fumes. I am going to make sure you can switch over to determination or pride or loyalty, or hell even rely on a giant pair, to keep you going so you don't fucking drop and I don't meet God." Sum Bitch was eloquent even when he told us he was getting ready to piss down our backs and tell us it was raining!

We filed off the bus and into our home for the next 6 to 8 weeks of our lives, Building D 3915.

We spread out and looked for our room and then our names on the bunks. Well, wouldn't you know Guinea the pisser was right above me again. Flashback to Guinea pissing on the bunk passed out from exhaustion and dripping down to you know who.

"Hey bud, I got top this time." I mentioned in passing.

"Bullshit, I was first in class, I get top," Guinea quipped.

"Ah shucks," well why didn't you say so, I thought. "Welcome your highness, all has been prepared for your return, and if you piss on me again, I will bitch slap you right back to Rome or somewhere else on that fucking boot shape country your ancestors call home, Dick head." I give him 'the' salute and he respond in kind.

We unpacked, pissed & pooped, and headed to classroom 103 where the training would begin. We were given the Ranger Handbook which would become our second Bible. Let's start with the man himself, Major Robert Rogers. As any U.S. Army Ranger will tell you, Major Rogers is not only considered one of the founding fathers of America's modern-day Rangers, but he is also the author of the document and standing orders were written in 1759 and still memorized by Rangers today, 'Rogers' Rules'. Its' techniques were developed by American Colonists 'to fight' the French and Indian War and were based on Native Americans; some of the very same techniques I was taught and used back on the Res to fight and conquer the Pale Faces headed by Little Bear and crew.

There are 28 Rules of Ranging and here are a few:

1. Don't forget Nothing

2. Have your musket as clean as a whistle

3. When on the march, act like you are sneaking up on a deer. See the enemy first.

4. Tell the truth

5. Don't ever take a chance you don't have to.

6. When we march, single file, far enough apart so one bullet can't hit 2 men.

7. When we strike, spread out so we are harder to track

8. So on and so on.

The rules also dictated that men take a different route home so they wouldn't get ambushed. They shouldn't cross a river by a regular ford because the enemy watches them. And they shouldn't pass lakes too close to the water or the enemy might trap them. The point is after 200 years it is still as relevant on today's battlefields as back then and steeped in the heritage I was born.

A few other rules but these were taught by my grandfather.

1. Be up before the rooster crows and be ready.

2. Bring the fight to the enemy at first light prior
   to them awakening.

3. Remember the smell of old versus new fires it will
   tell you if someone is awake and tended to the fire.

4. Remember, you can't wash off what the Great Spirit
   made you.

5. Lead from the front and never the rear, you take the first
   arrow for your men and never let them see you hurt.
   There is no fear, there is no pain, you are a warrior.

"Redskin, did your squw of a great, great, granddaddy
write this shit?" Guinea smirked.

"Sure as hell did your highness, with a mixture of your
great, great, granddaddy's blood and his sisters' menstrual sap
for ink, Dickhead." I reminded him. I was always very elegant
in my language, very apropos if I do say so myself.

After getting acclimated with the barracks, the base, our
instructors, and our objective, the first up was Air Assault &
Airbourne School.

Chapter 16

AIR ASSAULT & AIRBOURNE

There are usually two means for getting troops into combat, FRIES, or Fast Rope Insertion/Extraction, where you grab a piece of rope and slide out (repelling) from a hovering helicopter, and just Air Insertion, where the helicopter lands on the ground, hopefully, soft and only for enough time for everyone to bail out and off they go without getting shot up.

We were broken down into 2 groups, only fitting because we were going to learn Air Assault and Airborne. Remember this is not standard Army Ranger Training it is bastardized training for federal civilians. No one receives a contract with the 82nd Airbourne, we are not that badass like those guys.

Air Assault School is a rigorous 10-day course. It starts with the basic Lock-In rappel, followed by what is called a Hollywood rappel. It gets its moniker because it is the one you see in the movies and is basically three controlled brakes to the ground. At the end of the day is shows you how to brake (think air brake) and makes sure you don't crash into the ground. See

I don't mind the fall, it is the abrupt, sudden stop that I don't enjoy. However, it is overseen by a "certified rappel master." If it is done correctly, it's a smooth descent to the ground in an area where the rugged terrain—or in our case most likely into a jungle canopy, and a hurried pace, will not allow for a proper landing. Much like Les Nessman dropping the turkeys for WKRP, no one wants to be the flightless bird. The army has organized rappels from helicopters into three heights: low, below 75 feet; medium, 75 to 150 feet; and high, above 150 feet.

You will graduate to a Combat rappel—a Hollywood rappel when you're loaded with about 30 pounds of gear and a dummy weapon. Perfect for a dummy, not mentioning any names. Before we go up in an aircraft, the training rappels are done from a 34-foot tower. You see, thirty-four feet is where people lose their depth perception. They can gauge who has issues with heights or vertigo from that level.

Standing at the top of the tower and looking down, 34 feet is a hell of a long way down. I figured why not be my normal self!

Breaking the ice, "Hey Guinea, did you hear about the dwarf that escaped by rappelling from Alcatraz?"

"Don't care, but I know you are going to tell us anyway." What's with the negative attitude?

"What?" Knuckles was always one to listen.

"I would tell you, but it's a little condescending."

"Idiot." of course from the prettiest one among us.

After mastering the tower, I was now the Tower Master, it was now onto the real deal. Helicopters.

Helicopter rappelling is conducted in a noisy environment, you have to know the specific commands and their accompanying hand and arm signals. Now, I am sure Barbie's number gesture is really letting me know I am number one in her book and not what you folks think it means. The Rappel Master issues all commands, and we will confirm each command.

First – Get Ready. The rappel master will perform a final check of the hookup, rappel seat, rappel ring, and other equipment. Pull on the rope to double-check the anchor point connection. Second - Throw the rope. The rappel master gives the signal to drop your deployment bag out and away from the helicopter with your guide hand. Ensure the rope does not fall between the side of the chopper and the skid (the legs upon which the chopper lands and not the marks in Guineas pants). The rappel master will ensure the rope is touching the ground and free of tangles and knots.

Third - Sit at the Door. This is where it gets intense. You swing your legs to the outside of the helicopter and get into a sitting position. Now, this isn't sitting on your lazy boy in a comfortable environment, this thing is 'shaking and baking'.

Fourth – Position. Now it's time to brace yourself for the jump. Pivot 180 degrees on the skid so you're facing the inside of the helicopter and the Rappel Master. Your feet are shoulder-width apart, your knees are locked, the balls of your feet are on the skid (and in your throat) and your body is bent at the waist toward the helicopter. Your brake hand is on the small of your back.

Finally, GO. On the 'Go' command, flex your knees and vigorously push away from the skid gear, allowing the rope to pass through your brake hand and your guide hand. The descent should be roughly 8 feet per second, with no jerky stops. You start the braking process slowly when you're about halfway to the ground. Release tension on the rope and move the brake hand out at a 45-degree angle to regulate the rate of descent. When you reach the ground, clear the rappel rope through the rappel ring until the rope is free. Once the rappel master confirms that you are off rappel, he'll drop the rope away from the helicopter—and you're free to take care of business on the ground. Simple, easy peasy.

They totally missed the mark for the name of the Airbourne course at least for civilians. Should have been fall, fall, fall until you are black, and blue, and fall again until you walk with a limp for the rest of your life.

"Pain doesn't hurt, just lets you know you are alive," I told Guinea

"I am not sure which is worse, the 3-foot drop or the 12-foot fall."

Smiling Barbie wanted to show her tits, "You have to be light on your toes, lads."

"Yeah, well you have some Majesty Mammaries to bounce off the ground."

"Fais Do Do." and flipped up the bird." I have a way with women.

"If you read the manual, a parachute landing is a safety technique that allows energy to be displaced, horizontal and survive a high-speed landing." I reminded my folks. "It really means so none of us FNGs break our fucking necks on Sarg's watch," Mr. Lovely explained.

Next up is Parachute Landing Fall (PLF) practice. Always be prepared for a hard landing, remember going splat creates a lot of paperwork for the higher-ups not to mention you will limp the rest of your life if you survive. We were not parachuting but repelling but it could be from a great distance above the canopy and cause a tremendous amount of trauma. I sure as hell didn't need mouth-to-mouth from the Guinea sum bitch because I am sure he would try and slip me tongue. Now, Barbie on the other hand. It is designed to land safely and without injury and is used to displace all the energy over the course of your entire body.

Arms up, feet and knees together, flare, flare, flare PLF. Ideally, you land facing the direction of travel with feet and knees together. Now the first contact made with the ground, the person goes from an upright position absorb the impact by allowing the body to buckle and go toward a horizontal position while rotating toward the side. When executed properly, this technique can allow a parachutist to survive uninjured during landing speeds that would otherwise cause severe injury or even death. The next day we climb onto UH-1 Huey's and practiced what we were taught for 10 days. Only a couple of sprained ankles and a few bumps and bruises but overall, very successful.

Bragg is a unique experience and is one of the Military's top-notch training bases and it was an honor and privilege to learn from some of the best. Next up, even further south, off to Special Operations Command (SOCOM), Tampa, Fl.

Chapter 17

SPECIAL OPERATIONS COMMAND (SOCOM)

United States Army, Special Operations Command
7701 Tampa Point Blvd, Tampa, FL 33621

Finishing at Fort Bragg, we scooted down I95 to the Special Operations Command (SOCOM), MacDill Air Force Base in Doral, Florida. MacDill is an active Air Force installation a stone's throw from downtown Tampa, Florida. Well, a couple of miles. It covers approximately five million square miles of buildings, airstrip, training facilities, and just an overall good time place for torture. It was a host wing, that is the 6th Air Refueling Wing assigned to the Eighteenth Air Force of the Air Mobility Command. It started out as a U.S. Army Air Corps and later U.S. Army Air Forces, installation prior to WWII.

It transitioned to a Strategic Air Command (SAC) installation supporting bombers. Then in the early 1960s, it changed again to a Tactical Air Command (TAC) installation supporting the F-84 Thunderstrike jet fighter before transitioning to the F-4 Phantom II. During the 1960s, 1970s, and early 1980s, it operated F-4 Phantom II fighters under various fighter wings, followed by F-16 Fighting Falcons in the mid-1980s to early 1990s. MacDill became an Air Mobility Command installation in 1996 and then the home to the 6th Air Refueling Wing. Eventually transitioned to Headquarters for two of the U.S. military's unified combatant commands: Headquarters, United States Central Command, and Headquarters, United States Special Operations Command (SOCOM). Both commands are independent of one another, and each is commanded by a respective four-star general or admiral.

A unified combatant command also referred to as combatant command is a joint military command of the United States Department of Defense (DOD). There are 11 unified commands around the world, and they conduct broad and continuing missions and SOCOM training and military exercise are at the forefront.

There, 'the Brady bunch' as we started getting called started jungle training in fire-ant-, gator-, and copperhead-infested South Florida. With practical field exercises planned in Panama later. At SOCOM, I was blessed to reconnect with my childhood friend, David Danielson.

Speaking demographically, Dave's a blonde, barrel-chested, whiskey-drinking Irishman (and, in bar-fight, there was no man better to have standing by). A good ole Southern boy, he's bullish on the U. S. of A. Unlike Greg, Dave's got lady issues— but ones that are 180-degrees-opposite of mine. Dave meets women, loves them, then marries them. Now, the fourth time doing that dance, I'm wagering he might have got it right. I'm just on the outside looking in, but, from here, his Sherrie seems like a great gal.

If at first you don't succeed, Brother Dave, do-over! Number three might be The One. Since Dave and I had chased each other in Virginia's backwoods a decade before, he'd become a Green Beret and would later reach the rank of Lieutenant Colonel. He was conscientiousness, resourceful, and fierce, a terrible combo for foes, and a great set of attributes for the men who made him their leader. This was going to be fun.

"For every adventure, what you sum bitches might call a mission, we follow strict rules of planning, engagement and execution." Lt Danielson stated.

Situation looks at enemy forces (friendlies and bad guys) and what Intelligence we have for placement strength and weaknesses and your basic who, what, when and where with information or lack thereof, we develop a concept of operation. We were taught the information at Bragg but reiterated here because we were going to have live operations.

Most importantly, we learned Survival, Escape, Resistance, and Evasion or SERE. Now official SERE training is done in California, Maine, Texas and other locations. It can take a year plus to get a special forces contract and we were no specials forces, far from it. We were civilians who would mainly have office and field assignments in the badland streets of the good ole USA not fighting a war or disrupting armed conflicts in foreign lands. God bless those sum bitches, they are true warriors placed on this earth with a purpose!! We were being groomed for Operation SnowCap and other clandestine operations in South and Central America on a law enforcement basis, not as a forceful and lethal military machine.

Even after my initiation and all my training, let me make this perfectly clear: SERE Training SUCKS! Did I mention it sucks. It isn't fun and isn't meant to be. However, SERE is critically important for anyone lost, and being chased through foreign land, especially the jungle environment we all knew were going to face. One great factor is that someone knows you are missing, and they are looking for you.

We were taught the Army way, by said buddy Dave in a bastardized format for us civilians specifically focus on their Jungle Training. Since most cocaine is produced in manufactured in the Andean Ridge, Columbia, Bolivia, Ecuador, and Peru, jungle training makes sense. The United States Army first started training troops in the jungles of Panama in 1916, just two years after the opening of the Panama Canal. Now you understand why DEA sent people to SOCOM and eventually training in Panama. It was nicknamed Green Hell by someone who had gone through it and began in earnest in the early 1940s as World War II in the Pacific necessitated the need for soldiers to be well-versed in the tactics of jungle warfare.

The jungle environment is 'wet, and wetter and wettest', just like stink, stank and stunk and yes the grinch is chasing you. Jungle ailments such as trench foot, insect bites, bad food, bad water, parasites, snake bite signaling and rescue. Fortunately, I learned Jungle SERE is the easiest form to teach and to learn; Said who, I have no clue.

The thick, triple canopy and dense foliage in a jungle situation made radios all but useless and reduced visibility to just a few yards. Rain and humidity ensured soldiers were constantly wet and the jungle floor was always slick with mud, which we were going to have walkthrough, maneuver, and even crawl through. But do not worry, there were tree roots and vines on which to trip bust your ass face down looking at a snake, some other plant that offered worse pain. We were instructed and notified, yes notified, that there are over 100 poisonous or injurious varieties of flora. Leaning or brushing against the wrong plant could lead to some rather uncomfortable conditions that make poison ivy look like a pimple on Guinea's backside.

So, if you like plants and I do that didn't bother me, but if the plants weren't bad enough, there was local wildlife to contend with. Poisonous snakes and bugs were at the very top of everyone's list of unwanted encounters. One that stood out was The Fer de Lance. The Fer de Lance, French for spearhead, is the most dangerous snake in all the Panamanian and surrounding country jungles. Snakes waited in the underbrush and in the trees so instead of a pearl neckless, I like giving not receiving, you could get a parting gift of a deadly snake wrapped around your neck courtesy of air mail.

How about enormous spiders that would spin giant webs across narrow jungle paths. I wonder if Barbie thought about something else when the sticky web was plastered to her face. Yeah, probably wishful thinking on my part.

Almost forgot about the venomous and dangerous Bushmaster pit viper. Luckily, the snakes preferred not to contact humans just as much as humans didn't want to contact them, so encounters were rare. Oh. almost forgot about the dangerous reptiles and amphibians in the area and that would be crocodiles that lived in the waterways nearby and that included ones we would have to cross. Last, but not least, the worst encounter for many was the common mosquito.

Looking over my sunglasses, "Barbie, want to know how to say mosquito in Spanish?"

"Idiot." Forgot she was smart and knew it was mosquito. Mosquito is mosquito throughout the world. Guess, I should have asked Knuckles.

The little bastards are ubiquitous in jungle environments and are a terrible nuisance. Although most bites simply leave you itchy, their most dangerous quality is their ability to carry malaria. Fortunately, we all had miliaria shots and miliaria pills which I think probably makes you feel worse that the affliction. In the jungle, a little carelessness can lead to a lot of pain all the way around. For example, failing to properly secure mosquito netting at night could mean waking up covered in mosquito bites. Even with the netting, you weren't entirely safe. Exposed skin, carelessly pressed against the net while sleeping, would be open to bites. We were taught how to survive on our own. But in our case, we would be two member teams. It was considered quicker training at least we were trying to save taxpayer dollars. Of course, I voted for Barbie, but I got, guess who. Yep, Guinea.

"Guinea, good to know that the Army wants to provide a wham bam thank you ma'am training for us NMFT or non-military fucktards."

Laughing, "yep, but at least you know, that your M-16 your holding was purchased from the lowest bidder"

"Barb, what do you think about a little wham bamming in the jungle tonight?" could be sexy I was thinking.

"Idiot." was her response followed by the customary one finger salute. If I didn't know better, I would think I was annoying her. Naw, deep down she thought I was sexy.

Even though we were going in two member teams in the field, in classroom instruction did focus on being alone and understanding and avoiding panic, keep your wits about you, stress and the flight or fight response and the stress cycle and later when the dragons come to roost. We learned which plants are edible and which ones to stay away from back on the Res, we were taught to take a small piece of a plant, if you didn't recognize it and rub it on your gums. Wait ten minutes. No problems or issues you can eat it. However, some of these plants would kill you if you did that.

Also, how to make homemade weapons and equipment should we need it. Like spears, bows and arrows, traps, snares (hare traps), etc. Also, how to make a fire, shelter and basic first aid, how to find and prepare water and food. Yep, Res life taught me a lot of that. In addition, we received a thorough understanding of our future environment and which animals, reptiles and other creepy crawlers are deadly.

"Guinea, want me to teach you how to catch some hair, I know it has been a while." Can't anyone take a joke anymore. Not Hare as in rabbit. Get it?

Once you are separated from your team or partner, try to escape a situation, and run like hell. All the while knowing someone is chasing you and if they catch you, you are not going to grandma's for a home cooked meal. Unless they are serving ball sac soup and said sac would be yours, just in case you were wondering. In my case and Guinea's, wait he doesn't have balls, plain and simple run like hell. More advanced survival training focuses on mental elements such as the will to survive, attitude, and survival thinking to understand your situational awareness just like our field games on the Res. Assess the situation, prioritize the objectives, and execute.

Is it any wonder why military guys make some of the world's greatest leaders?

Chapter 18
2 BY 2

We all boarded the H1-Hueys and were going to be dropped off in different locations and expected to transverse from the eastern to the western side of the base part of which is through couple thousand of wetlands. Growing up on the Res we hunted ducks, geese, and other water laden creatures from the time we could walk. It is hard, slow, and methodical to say the least. Every step in into knee deep muck that is heavy on the legs and lower back especially with an extra 40lbs of gear on. Oh, I did I mention that we would leave at 21:00 and they PT'd us for two days straight with only two hours of sleep per day. Fatigue will make cowards of us all.

Now we would have to cross several areas, at night, and a certain part had coined the term 'gator hole' and just happened to be thrown out there in our permission briefing.

Being born and bred, even if with family members in a big city you are an easy target, "Guinea, have any gators on Staten Island?"

"Fuck no and I don't want to see one either."

Don't worry they said, the water will be darkly stained, like strong tea, there is still visibility due to the white sand bottom in shallow areas, less than 3 feet deep or so. The Gator Hole does have a couple of deep areas say maybe 6 to 8 feet deep and you will find a wide sandbar on the opposite side it can be reached by wading across upstream just above the Gator Hole. Now in the area, the normal gator is under 8ft long. Let's contemplate that for a minute or two. Personally, I consider anything that big, that has sharp teeth, and considers me to be edible, to be very dangerous. Can you swim with them around? Sure but "can" doesn't mean you should. Who wants to wade across a river or stream with something that has the term "death roll" associated with it?

Other problems are the Cypress Trees are the most common type of tree found in Florida swamps, followed by Water Tupelo and Black Gum trees. Cypress and Tupelo trees are usually swollen at the point in which they are submerged in swamp water. These trees have adapted to the Florida swamp by developing pneumatophores, or root appendages that extend upward. Greenbrier and poison ivy are two common vines found in Florida swamps. Greenbrier vines have very long pointed leaves with two rounded ears at the top. These leaves are prickly around the edges, and green with occasional yellow spots. Poison ivy vines grow along the sides of trees in Florida swamps.

Dozens of troops and other assorted personnel have transverse the course many times and no one has been injured by a gator there in the last 30 years or so. Well, shucks if that doesn't give you a warm fuzzy boner after dreaming about Barbie at the O430 wake-up PT call, I don't know what does.

"Last 30 years or so." in my best wee, wee whiney voice.

Guinea looks at me, "I didn't sign up for this shit."

"You sure as hell did, candy ass and just remember I am one hell of a fast swimmer and I only have to out swim your city dwelling ass."

"What the fuck does that mean?"

"Nothing. Nothing at all." Shaking my head, but I figured now wasn't the time for a joke. He was really concerned, and we both should have been.

We were the first team up and dropped at the landing zone. We would be followed every hour by another two-man team until 0400 because they wanted us to travel at night thru a swamp, yeah, they called it wetlands and Godzilla was a lizard, to get real life experience.

At 21:00 we were airborne for a short flight and dropped for our very own gator site seeing tour, minus of course a tour guide. Now, you should be able to walk 1.5 miles under 15 minutes easily. However, this was a swamp, I mean wetlands, and it takes a hell of a lot longer especially when you are try-ing not to splash and attract a new playmate. Knee-deep and even chest-deep water slows your travels immensely. We were dropped at a specified location, squatted, allowed our eyes to get acclimated, and listened for any sign of trouble just like we were taught. Located our position and direction and off we went. It was wet, barely coming up over the sole of our boots that were 8 inches up the lower leg and were waterproof. They were called mud python boots; don't know how or why they got that name but that is what we had.

"Shit this isn't so bad." that was said before Guinea sank up to his knee.

Raising my eyebrows, "You were saying?"

"Fuck off."

This went on for another 25 minutes or so. If you remember we should have been done by now, but since you had to pull your foot out of knee-deep mud and water with each step it was taking time. The earthly soup of muck was dense to say the least. Guinea reminds me of hunting the wetlands back home, so I was used to it but not Guinea. Not to mention the tangle of Junipers and we were already fatigued, and our legs were beginning to feel the burn. Finally, we found the gator hole and decided to move due north to bypass the swimming hole and ford across upriver. Sloshing through the Greenbrier and Poison Ivey was a delight everyone should experience at least once in their lifetime.

Bam, Guinea went face first into the muck and upon getting up it was at least 6 feet deep and the splash that might have been a tidal wave of a dinner bell. And said tidal wave began to course straight towards you know who as fast as greased lightning.

"Guinea get the fuck moving!" I shouted as I was bringing the M16 up. I got off four rounds or so, and should have flicked on the fun switch but I was a little late. Just before the lizard struck, the only recourse I had was to jump straight on top, dropped my weapon, and grabbed my K-bar, as it caught Guinea in full rage driven by a hunger to kill and feed. I drove the K-Bar into the side as hard as I possibly could and it started the death roll. I went with the roll, hoping he would let go of the grip, I couldn't see shit in the tea-colored water but go along for the ride for two rolls before being slung off. I surfaced and swam a few strokes to the shore to get a better look. Up popped Guinea.

"I was getting ready to start praying to Sky Daddy on your behalf."

"Fuck you and help me get out," he gasped. He was hurt.

"Give me your hand." I leaned forward and grabbed him by the flak jacket and under his arm, he screamed, but I got him on the shore. There is a difference between being hurt and being injured and Guinea was injured.

I did a once over for the medical Rapid Trauma Assessment (RTA) we were taught in Basic Agent (BA) school. I am not a Dr and or even an Emergency Medical Technician (EMT), hell I wasn't even a boy scout, but I knew what to look for. A proper RTA can give Emergency Responders critical information when they arrive and consists of a quick inventory of all the body systems to identify injured ones. First, you are supposed to determine responsiveness using what they call an AVPU Scale to describe the level of consciousness.

Is the person Alert, since Guinea already told me fuck off, check. Does the person respond to verbal cues, he did reach out when I told him to, check. Does the person respond to Pain stimulation, Guinea did scream like a bitch when I pulled him out, again check. He wasn't unresponsive, check.

Trying to distract him from thinking about the pain, "Guinea you got a perfect score on the AVPU test."

"God damn, it hurts." He winced out the words through squinted pain filled eyes. He was looking at me for help.

"I know buddy, breathe in through your nose and out through your mouth, and let me look, Ok."

He was turning pale, which I didn't like at all. His airway was clear, he was breathing, and he could move his hand so circulation on the arm was still good, for now. The shoulder on the injured arm was still in the socket but he needed stitches and by the look of it a lot of 'em.

"No one in the last 30 years…."

Opening his eyes with a 'What?"

"Nothing, listen we are going dress the wound, stop the bleeding, get you a few stitches. Nothing is broken, as far as I can tell, and at least you can use your other arm to beat the monkey."

He smirked at that and sorta laughing said, "Thanks, brother."

"I got you, don't worry, now breathe" as I was thinking how the fuck I was going to get both of us out here without getting us both killed.

"He looked at the sky and said "By instinct, I just rolled with him, instead of pulling against the damn thing. I was using my good arm, my right arm to stab my K Bar into his side. Surprisingly, the bitch released me after rolling a couple of times."

"What else Guinea?" trying to have him focus.

"I lost count but then the sum bitch tried to bite me again. I couldn't see him, but I could feel him. This time I drove the knife somewhere at him and I followed the bubbles to the surface, and there you were pulling me out of the water. Thank you, Brother."

"I was worried he might be going into shock. "Relax and sit tight, let me work."

I flashed back to my youth and a conversation with my grandfather, Walking with the Wind.

"2 Crows, for the injustices inflicted on us by the Whiteman, a curse was set upon this river and a death by drowning will occur every year" Walking with the Wind told me. "If you get turned over and over in the heavy current, remember 2 Crows, blow out air and follow the bubbles, because bubbles only travel up to the surface." The current in any river can be extremely strong especially if it rains and the water will turn iced tea dark, I know from experience that bubbles only go up and his wisdom not only saved my life, but his wisdom also saved Guinea's life. I taught this to Guinea the day we became blood brothers. It took several years before I realized that it was our great, great, great, great grandfather that uttered the curse and its subsequent success for over two hundred years. Facts.

The force of the Alligator's bite punctured his forearm, and both ulna and radius had fractures by the looks of it, the M-16 had taken the full force of the bite and it was useless. The punches and knife strikes he was throwing had worked and allowed him to get to the surface.

Shaking his head, "I lost my damn k bar to that bitch."

"Yeah, me too Guinea now let me finish." I took off my shirt wrapped it around his chewed-up arm and fashioned a sling.

"On your feet." as I pulled him upright with a loud grunt. Guinea was wobbly but hard as nails, I can promise you that.

Looking down at the mauled weapon, "Only reason I still have my arm is because it was between my arm and Godzilla's top row of teeth. I had enough time to stick 'em before he started to roll."

"While you were trying to play patty cakes with your newfound friend, I jumped on his back and drove my pig sticker into his side as hard as I possible could right before the three of us went on the merry go round. I can honestly say, I never want to do a threesome with you ever again."

"Roger, roger, let's go." Before we could take a step, the good guys showed up.

"Gentlemen, not playing well with others I see." Captain Dave chimed in. A real trained green beret medic went to work on Guinea while I explained what happened.

"Both of you are lucky to be alive, we weren't close enough to see it, but we can hear it."

I provided an initial sit rep. When the medic said, "Guinea will only need a couple dozen stiches and a cast but Monte that was brave as hell but just as stupid." A strange pattern that was developing and I wish I could say that it wasn't strange and dangerous.

"Copy brother, but what would you have done?"

"Tracking." Things get real, real fast and the time to put what we learned into action would be upon us before we knew it.

No way to get a medivac at our current location so we got up and proceeded in a slightly different path. The easy way out, where an ambulance and the Commanding Officer, among others were waiting. We provided a sitrep and all was over and time to move on and back to exercises. Guinea received 17 stitches, a cast for his fractured arm, broken wrist and put into a sling for the separated shoulder and quite frankly lucky he had an arm at all. He got a first-class medivac lift to medical care and a short trip back to a Tampa Hospital for a day or two. Lucky, no surgery was required to fix the bones.

We all met back at camp and after chow, we were sitting around a fire drinking beer and laughing about dumb stuff as usual.

Staring into the fire, "we were walking along, and Guinea makes a dumbass comment, that this isn't so bad and BAM, face planted and under the water, his ass went. It took five seconds before here comes the fucking party pooper and he was pissed, looked like a small tidal wave coming in.

"Damn."

Barbie leaned back and looked up at the stars, "That's some crazy shit."

"I got off at least 4 rounds."

"Man, you gots to get the fun switch going baby." Rodent bounced around.

"Bossman," Skip looked at me with a question. "Captain Dave said you jumped on that gators' back!"

"Affirmative, only thing I could think of at the time, I could have shot a couple more rounds but I couldn't ID a hard target, so I jumped on."

"Crazy Bastard, I would have emptied the clip and prayed to Sky Daddy for Guinea." Knuckles squawked,

"Sky Daddy, please don't let me nick Guinea, blllll-laaaaaaatttttttzzzzzzz, please." Everyone laughed

It's a memory we still talk about to this day. Both Guinea and I dodged a Raindrop.

Now, it was time to visit Head Quarters and get our marching orders and the team would be slightly dispersed as we learned our deck assignments. Thing is, I knew I had changed, but was it for the better or for the worse?

Chapter 19

ASSIGNMENT HQ
REST FOR LEFTY

The delights of my Basic Agent Training, Fort Bragg, Special Operations Command (SOCOM) and Panama promised a career path stalking savvy cokeheads in some ugly equatorial ecosystem, so it was with no small amount of sangfroid that I began my DEA vocation at a dull desk in DC alongside Guinea, who has seemed to have become my twin. It provided a relaxed atmosphere for Guinea to heal both physically and mentally. The future Shadow Crew was dispersed, Knuckles a short distance went to Huntsville for Explosive Ordnance Disposal Training (EOD), Skip to Miami and was working alongside the Coast Guard, Rodent went to the Washington Division Office (WDO) (District of Colombia) Barbie, Guinea and I were located in the East and West Buildings at HQ performing mundane tasks on the surface but all strategically placed for the game to come. However, I was already working on bringing the band back together. But first things first.

Truth be told, Guinea and I had become blood brothers during our initial break before reporting for our desk duty.

Blood brother refers to two or more men not related by birth who have sworn loyalty to each other. This is in modern times usually done in a ceremony, known as a blood oath, where each person makes a small cut on the palm of your hand the cuts are pressed together and then bound with leather deer skin. The cuts are pressed together, and then bound, the idea being that each person's blood now flows in the other participant's veins and blood is thicker than water. The act has been performed for centuries and on every continent. The process usually provides a participant with a heightened symbolic sense of attachment to the other.

On our first allotted leave, we traveled to the Res and stayed in my grandparents' house. We spent the night out we were alone besides the rambling Pamunkey river, screech owls called, and a chorus of the summer bugs awaking to the coolness and serenaded us all night. The land and night were ours to command and seek the bonding of the Great Spirits approval. We stayed out for three days, bathed in the clear stream that was headed to the Chesapeake Bay but provided clean drinking water. We had natural fruits, summer vegetables, and dried meats from my grandparents' house.

"Monte, after all, I have already seen, this is amazing to have grown up like this."

"It's home Guinea, but never forget in our world, these people we will face want to kill us and we need to want to kill them."

"Gotcha Bossman" as he continued to scan around. "You know, I grew up in a concrete jungle." putting his fingers in the air and quoted concrete jungle, "it is so peaceful here."

"To run with the big dogs, you have to be able to piss on tall trees, Guinea."

Breaking his thoughtful interreflection, "Where the fuck do you come up with this shit? I mean really, piss on tall trees!"

Shrugging, "Karsyn, my baby told me that once."

As dusk fell, we built our fire and laid out our sleeping blankets under a black walnut tree with bounding fruit littering the ground for our cooking enjoyment. We cleansed ourselves with sage and lemon grass like a flame burning off the stains of life as I chanted the cleansing song taught to me by my parents and grandparents. It created a fevered and serene calm in us both at the same time.

Then, we each took a knife and cut the palms of our hands and clasped them together. I wrapped the deer skin around and clasped it tight.

As the blood dripped down our joined hands, "This is a promise of life and a promise of death and forever more we are brothers of the same blood" I put my left hand over top, "my life or death is forever combined with you."

Guinea followed suit and put his left over the top, "As is mine."

Looking up into the starry sky, "Great Spirit, whose voice I hear in the wind, we are small and weak and need your wisdom and strength to guide us on our travels and protect us. When the time arrives, as the sun is sure to set, let us die as warriors and come before you without shame and sit at the Tribal Council with our ancestors."

Then we broke out the Fire Water my grandparents and all the elders warned me about. This is what the younger generation called Devil Spit or moonshine, straight from a mason jar. Let the fire dance begin. We spent the night talking about our lives up to this point, our families, and how we were so different, yet the same.

"Guinea let me tell you a story."

This story is told in some variation among numerous Tribes whether the Cherokee, Navajo, Lumbee, Seneca, or all Algonquin-speaking people like mine.

In the beginning, the Great Spirit above gave to the animals and birds wisdom and knowledge and the power to talk to men. He sent these creatures to tell man that he showed himself through them. They would teach a chosen man sacred songs and dance, as well as much ritual and lore.

The creature most loved by the Great Spirit was the eagle, for he tells the story of life.

The Eagle, as you know, has only two legs, and all living things in the world are divided into two. Here is man and woman, male and female and this is true with animals, birds, trees, flowers, and so on. All things have children of two kinds so that life may continue.

Man has two eyes, two hands, two feet, and he has a body and soul, substance, and shadow. Through his eyes, he sees pleasant and unpleasant scenes, through his nostrils he smells good and bad odors, with his ears he hears joyful news and words that make him sad. His mind is divided between good and evil. His right hand may often use for evil, such as war or striking a person in anger. But his left hand, which is near his heart, is always full of kindness. His right foot may lead him in the wrong path, but his left foot always leads him the right way, and so it goes; he has daylight and darkness, summer and winter, peace and war, and life and death.

To remember this lesson of life, look to the great eagle, the favorite bird of the Great Spirit. The eagle feather is divided into two parts, part light, and part dark. This represents daylight and darkness, summer and winter, peace and war, and life and death. So that you may remember what I have told you, look well on the eagle, for his feathers, too, tell the story of life. Look at the feathers I wear upon my hand, the one on the right is large and perfect and is decorated; this represents man.

The one on my left is small and plain; this represents woman. The eagle feather is divided into two parts, dark and white. This represents daylight and darkness, summer, and winter. The white tells of summer when all is bright, and the dark represents the dark days of winter.

My children, remember what I tell you, for it is YOU who will choose the path in life you will follow — the good way, or the wrong way.

In my case, a little of both.

Chapter 20

BACK TO REALITY

Back at Headquarters, we weren't too distant from the watchful eye of my dad. I thought it was cool to be a DEA guy and have three thriving pot plants in my back bathroom at the time. I didn't smoke, but my girlfriend did—and so did the balance of my friends. We had our normal Bama Party and it fell on a Saturday as usual. Everyone in my family was stalking through the house—only Dad was conspicuously absent.

9-2 'Bama was on TV at 1900 and ended up smoking Florida at the Georgia Dome for the SEC championship, 34-7. It was gleeful chaos all night long at the Knight house. Cornhole, horseshoes and late-night drunk basketball. We had childhood friends, the Lees that was made up of seven boys and one girl, that lived close to the Res and would come play on our stamped-down dirt court at the elementary school, but we thought everyone played on dirt courts unless you were in middle school. The Lee brothers called their game Lee Ball, which meant no blood, no foul. You drive the lane expect a close line.

Getting boxed out meant an elbow to the ribs. Now, it wasn't just one-sided, as much as they dished out, they more than received the same thing in return. Over the years, not one fight among us. They were as much Native as we were Rednecks.

On a hot mid-August summer, I was midway through my 17th year on Mother Earth, Little Bear, Warner, Carter, and I went up to the school and the four of us came upon a group of 12 or so guys playing on the court. I knew most of the guys because they were all my age or older and I played sports against them for years. Now we didn't care, so we went up and asked if we could get downs after the game but needed one of them to play with us. Mickey Buckwalter was a star athlete, but we called him Buckwheat and he hated it. He was the group's supposed leader, I knew Buckwheat from a rival high school, and 3 sport athlete, football, basketball, and baseball. Mickey liked to think he was tough, but I trucked his ass every time we met in the hole in football, a violent collision that left him looking up and counting stars speaking in tongues to his Sky Daddy.

Walking up, "Buckwheat, what's up, we got downs but need one of your punk ass pale faces to make it five."

Turning to look at us, "Fuck off Knight, you and the slack jaw faggots couldn't beat us with 20 more heathens, but you can have Marty."

"Buckwheat, Marty? Really? How about Big Butt Mak!" Then, glancing over at Marty.

"Buck, where is your little sister, I will take her, after a long pause, again." Well, that started the pushing and shoving and name calling. Truth be told, I only hit a triple on her cute little ass, but Buckwheat thought I was Elvis the Pelvis and gave her a hunk of my burning love. It was only a triple, but I still scored, and everyone knew it. Plus, it bothered the hell out of Buckwheat.

We split into teams and started playing. It only took two trips up and down the court before it became obvious, we were in much better shape and could shoot the ball and just a better overall team.

In Algonquin, "these guys are dicks," Little Bear mentioned, and everyone confirmed that assumption.

Mickey got in Little Bears face, "What the fuck did you say?" Little Bear just looked at him.

"Buckwheat chill out, it wasn't anything."

He looked at me and said, "you stay out of this." Guess the bitch was tough outnumbering us three to one.

"Fuck all you Reskins especially Little Pickle here." poking his finger into Little Bear's chest.

"Mickey we are here to play basketball not fight, man."

Turning to me "Knight have you been a pussy all your life?"

"Buckwheat, since I know you are on your premenstrual cycle, I won't drop your ass like I did all last fall." With that his boys moved to surround us, and I knew this wasn't going to end well. For them. Mickey pushed Little Bear and I stepped in front.

"Ladies, Ladies." I heard to left of me, "it seems as though we might have a situation here. See some of you fuckers are on our court without permission, ain't that right Buckwheat?" Said, Jethro Lee, accompanied by his six brothers. Now, good ole Jethro was about 26 and had spent a little time in the slammer for well, being Jethro.

"Jethro, we don't have a problem with you, it's with these "Skins, here." See, no one ever had a problem with the seven Lee brothers because everyone knew, you fight one, you fight them all and they all loved to fight and would fight for no reason whatsoever. Hell, even the youngest, a sister named Kim would fight like she was the third monkey on the ramp of Noah's ark, and brother, it was starting to rain. Big butt Mak told me that once, that's why I was looking for her earlier.

"Hey, Mickey, Little Bear asked me if your dad was still fucking that Russian Prostitute over in Richmond." he said smiling.

Little Bear took his chance for a verbal shot, "Jethro, I said his mom was a Russian Prostitute." Well, that did it. Before even a few punches were thrown, Mickey got knocked out by Little Bear. The rest decided they wanted no part of the Lees and us combined.

Mickey was slowly waking up, "Hey Custer, get the fuck out of here and take the rest of your bitches with you." Little Bear resounded standing over the indigent prick.

As they were leaving, "Hey Buckwheat, tell Cora, her real Daddy is back in town and would like to take her to meet god again." He flipped me off, but they were done. We continued our game with the Lees. One thing about the Lees and basketball. No blood, no foul. We grew up that way, so we were used to it.

'Bama QB, Tyler Watt, was tearing the Gators up left and right, and the homestead's front privies were filled with beer-knackered piss-champs from my own A-team when my Ma petitioned for a seat. Dumb Monte: I recklessly steered her to the back john. I forgot it was also my grow room. Though she favored me like she did, seeing a trio of happy marijuana stalks around her while she laid a stream was a bummer. She quick-slapped me with complaints once her bladder was drained. ("You've got kids!"). The next day she squawked at Dad. Oh Boy.

It was a blunt, sunny Monday two days later, and I was busy with the usual half-legal skullduggery at my North Building desk, doing my darnedest to save the world from dope's dark shadow, when, at 10 a.m., my dad's girl Friday, Blanca, rung me up.

"Oh, honey, you better get your sweet ass up here—and with your tail 'tween your legs."

"What?"

"Daddy needs a talk, Sweetness—and I promise it ain't to plot out your Christmas wish list." As she rang off.

Ah, Dad.

With a skip in my step, I caught the lift to his Global HQ on the 8th floor. I quick hopped through lockdown security, then arrived at Blanca's desk. She wagged a head and index-finger at me, then smirked, and jabbed her thumb at Dad's office.

I flashed her a coyote grin, and kept it stuck on my face as I walked through the Global Security Chief's dark double doors. He had a big-ass corner berth with a generous view of the Pentagons' south point. There was a formidable ash conference table at one end, and a smattering of Mies Van Der Rohe office chairs stuck around it.

I strode boldly in, entranced by the sunny penthouse view beyond his hulking shoulders, a plane was taking off from National Airport right behind him. As he spun around in his chair, I could see the mists of wariness and tolerance moved over his meaty face, but he was steaming.

With consummate cool, he said, "Sit down." We waited patiently till I made myself comfortable, then he started in.

"Your mom had some interesting news to tell me about the party for this weekend," he said sarcastically, then he boomed, "YOU HAVE SOME INTERESTING PLANTS growing in your FUCKING BATHROOM, Boy! You realize you can GO TO JAIL for that?"

I smiled. "Those plants are for an experiment to distinguish male from female plants." I used this as an excuse because there is a difference. To determine the sex you have examine the nodes. At these junctures between the main stem and branches, you should see early signs of a male or female plant. Male plants will grow ball-shaped pollen sacs, yep a cock and balls, but females will have wispy white hairs. These thin hairs are called "pistils," and they're designed to catch pollen from male plants. Why would you care you ask. Male plants are hemp and won't get you high. Females on the other hand contain large amounts of THC, the substance that does get you high.

"I live way out in the country as you know, I'm gonna see any posse coming from a mile off, Dad, don't you worry."

"OK, smart ass. Just GET IT OFF YOUR PROPERTY! TO-day!"

"Bonfire with weed!" I said crazily. "Done!" And I snapped to attention with a salute.

We both knew I wasn't about to do a damn thing about it. And we both knew he was partly assuaging his conscience—getting an opinion out, then getting on with it. I respected that he wanted me to escape a dire fate, but he was also sweating his own rep. "DEA World Security Chief's Son Jailed for Pot Crop" wasn't a headline he wanted to see not to mention his grand babies.

A few weeks later, I chopped it all down, sun-dried it, and slipped it to my friends. I fought for the law but was no stickler for it. I wasn't completely my Daddy's son.

When my pops was dying after his first heart attack at 71, he ducked into a coma for a few days, then, when he woke up, they wheeled him out of the ICU to a crowd of well-wishers biding time in the visitor's lounge. After we delivered our varied messages of cooing and encouragement, he called me over, stabbed his finger across the room, and whispered conspiratorially in my ear.

"Go to that soda machine and grab me a diet Coke."

I stood up, stepped away, and said, "No way, Pop. Doctor says it's against protocol!"

Gentle reader, knowing he and I so intimately now, you might think I said this just to needle the man, but I didn't. I sincerely feared he'd puke up a fizzy drink and asphyxiate. It was a fear the Docs had conveyed to all of us.

"OH!" he shouts in a hoarse voice barely audible. "I'M AT DEATH'S DOOR and the one fucking time my outlaw son, who has broken every fucking rule known to man," not quite but I still had a to do list.

"Come on pop, I am listening to the Doctors." I pleaded.

"Decides today is the day, he is going to do a 180 and adhere to PLAY BY THE RULES now that dear old dad is bedridden and just wants a GOD-DAMNED DIET COKE!" He loved his diet coke not sure why.

I stayed with him night and day. After a week at his bedside, needed to get some rest, shower, and hoped he was getting better. The next day around 0100, there was a knock on the door, and I knew. The cops were there to tell me he'd gone. Officer Giles was standing at the door and just looked me in eye. No words were exchanged. I nodded and he put his hand on my shoulder, nodded, turned, and walked back into the shadow of the dark night. The Great Spirit had called him home to sit in his place at the Tribal Counsel.

They say sometimes your relatives need private time to do their dyin'. In hindsight, that was probably Dad's plan, he needed me to leave to take the next path.

Maybe I should've given him that diet Coke, but I didn't and I have regretted that decision every day since. Mom put one in his casket when everyone was gone but I saw it as they closed the lid. The gesture was meant for both of us.

With this, you'll better understand the spider web of ideologies, operations, and political players surrounding me when I joined the work-clan of my dad. We all know illegal drug use soared in the sixties, but, at first, nobody did much about it. The DEA was created by a special directive of President Richard Nixon in 1973. We won't go into that man's 'checkered' history here, but one thing he was doing was trying to attack the heroin use that had spread to America after our grunts had adopted its' use in Vietnam and brought the scourge home.

The DEA was created by a special directive of Richard Nixon in 1973. We won't go into that man's checkered history here, but one thing he was doing was trying to attack the heroin use that had spread to America after our grunts had adopted its use in Vietnam and brought the scourge home. President Nixon had a cocker spaniel named, yes the name was Checkers, no pun intended, and had nothing with him mentioning the dog during a televised speech denying any alleged misuse of campaign funds.

At one point and time the idea of the Clinton Admin was to take down the black family unit by bringing in illegal drugs to their side of town, having blacks serve time and provide prison labor such as prisons are the main source of firefighters in Cali and also prepare chopped and cleaned veggies for places like Central Market, also making license tags for the state.

While Blacks are reduced to slave wages the Prison Industry which elites' profit from make billions. Clinton's

"Three Strikes You're Out Laws" insured they would screw up and be returned to prison plus the fact they were not allowed to live with family collecting housing assistance. Which many fatherless families qualified for the assistance however if you associated with criminals, left parolees vulnerable to repeating the cycle of selling drugs or resorting to theft. All the while pretending to support blacks, the Clinton Administration instead undermined the Black's ability to build a family unit, buy a home and thrive. My mentioning this is that it seems to rush to failure and just made my job harder.

Clinton huddled with his AG, John Mitchell, as early as 1969 and together with John Dean and some other Watergate alumni, they shaped the 1970 Comprehensive Drug Abuse Prevention and Control Act, which created the famed 'schedule' of bad, badder, and baddest drugs—among other intervention strategies—some of which were rehabilitative, you might be shocked to know. With an attack strategy formulated, Tricky Dick declared our first 'War on Drugs' the following year—labeling narcotics 'public enemy number one'.

Decades later, Nixon's aide, and Watergate figure, John Ehrlichman, would confess that Nixon launched his "Drug War" plans partly to get pretenses to raid political gatherings of Blacks and Hippies—both of whom opposed the president's policies—and who were thick with heroin and weed-users, respectively.

After re-election in '72, he put his pen on Executive Order 11599. This made the Special Action Office for Drug Abuse Prevention appear in 1971, and positioned clinical professor,

Jerome Jaffe, at its head. Nixon morphed this into the DEA after two years, nesting it under the Department of Justice.

Chapter 21

SHADOWS & DAGGER

This is why, in my work at 800 Army Navy Drive, I often ducked over to 950 Pennsylvania Avenue and hunkered down with the proles sweating it under Attorney General William Barr. Yep, same guy. I blinked when he returned in 2019. He was both the 77th and 85th AG.

If you look at his weird behavior under The Donald, it's a near point-by-point re-enactment of what he did under Bush I. No exaggeration—interfering with special prosecutors, calls for his resignation over tampering, coverups—the whole kit 'n kaboodle. Barr was rotgut—but he was my other Capo dei capi; my boss's highest boss.

The later 70's saw a handful of states decriminalizing marijuana possession for small amounts, but Ronnie Reagan wasn't down with that. Shortly after taking office in '81, he said, "We're taking down the surrender flag that has flown over so many drug efforts; we're running up a battle flag." In '82, he assented to vice-president Bush's idea to stick the CIA in the fight. Reagan's wife, Nancy, started cooing "Just Say No" to drugs in the run-up to the '84 elections. To her credit, the lady had a point—even though her hubby was part of the problem.

Shooting deaths had up ticked in every major city due to criminal maneuvering for market-share of an ass load of cheap Latin American coke coming into the country—partly 'cause Ronnie's Nicaraguan Contras were assisted by the CIA to ship it to the U.S. (more on this, below) and partly because the Contra's shipped it to Ricky Donnell Ross or "Highway Rick". He was the dude who set up California's network for formulation and distribution of crack—which birthed an addiction epidemic that ruined lives in inner cities everywhere.

In the 90s, I'd see similar sorts of underhandedness at the DEA. Despite the enlarging drama, most took the nation's new storm of drug use and street violence in stride, but on June 19, 1986, a coke overdose killed 22-year-old Len Bias the day after Boston picked him #2 in the NBA draft, and eight days later, coke deep-sixed Cleveland's 23-year-old Don Rogers, who was Rookie of the Year and picked 18th in the NFL draft two years before. The deaths of these promising young men stirred us. Legislators were quick to respond. Congress passed the omnibus Anti-Drug Abuse Act of 1986 in four months flat, and Ronnie Reagan signed it gleefully. It inaugurated the first money-laundering laws, enhanced sentencing, and channeled more money to my father's firm. The Gipper got his own War on Drugs.

With new resources flowing in, the DEA needed bigger digs, so, in 1989, my future base of operations—the skyscraper at 800 Army-Navy Drive—was created. Reagan had set up his Vice Prez, Bush, to head the South Florida Task Force, charged with increasing drug interdiction there, at the same time that GB was running Black Eagle, a program that lent Fairchild C-123's to Panama's chief of military intelligence and later president, General Manuel Noriega, to fly 'blow' to the U.S.—after these same planes had flown guns and ammo to the stinking Contras from his Panamanian bases. The shit hit the fan when longtime CIA contractor, Eugene Hasenfus, got shot down a month after the passing of the Anti-Drug Abuse Act.

Though he believed in the work, he confessed everything to the Sandinista government and any U.S. reporter who flew to Managua to gab with him. Nevertheless, Bush and his Teflon boss just denied it all. Documents on the bodies of the plane's dead crewmembers linked them to Ollie North, and the Iran-Contra affair exploded the following month, but, again, after the crapfest passed through the intestine of public conversation, Bush and Reagan came out smelling like roses.

Bush laughed last after he followed the Gipper to 1600 Pennsylvania and threw 24,000 soldiers into Panama 10 months later. Noriega was dragged from the Vatican's diplomatic mission in Panama City and tossed in a state-side penitentiary. After more prison time in France, he was extradited to trial in Panama. Jailed again, he was diagnosed with a brain tumor, and his life ended in 2017 while still serving a Panamanian sentence. Bushie appointed Rob Bonner as the fifth Director of the DEA in 1990. RB was a Kansas boy and Navy vet who'd earned his narcotics-smashing stars by riding prosecutorial shotgun on two high profile money laundering schemes in the late 80s—called Operations Pisces and Polar Cap. He was an Los Angeles DA then and had the additional distinction of jailing three of the Mexican nationals involved in the famed torture and killing of DEA Special Agent Enrique "Kiki" Camarena Salazar in 1985. Polar Cap cut into the cash stream of Pablo Escobar, and, on Bonner's watch at the DEA, the Policía Nacional de Colombia would kill Pablo, and I got the opportunity to be in on the hunt.

Though he was flummoxed by tax problems and fumbled the ball there, losing the love of his Republican buddies and the '92 election, where coke was concerned, Bush could unloose all his well-sharpened CIA skills, and he always came out on top. I'm sure he loved the drug wars. And, frankly, I did, too. H.W. set the tone that sent me to Colombia, gave me M-16's and Glocks, and got me trading fire with traffickers in tropical jungles—a life I loved, and one I miss to this day. A former CIA Director under Ford, Bush knew what was what, but also knew enough to stay out of the loop when my rogue buddies and me bought weapons and gave out illicit cash in the early 90s.

These days, the DEA maintains 23 domestic divisions, 222 field offices, and 92 foreign offices in 70 nations. It gets $3 billion per annum and employs 10,000 people, of which 5000 are Special Agents and 800 Intelligence Analysts. As you'll see, I wore both those hats.

Reagan had decided we needed to kill the coke-makers in their jungle hideouts, so an eight-year defense deployment known as Operation Snowcap was born in '87. Both Clinton and Bush kept to it till '94, allowing the DEA to spend $80 million per year sending soldiers to nine South American nations where coca was grown. Snowcap organized DEA battle-teams of 12 to 15 men for 90-day temporary duty tours—though you could sign up for more, if you were sweet on chaos. Together with host-country soldiers, we shot down planes, bombed drug labs, and sent squads to rainforests for facility and personnel attacks.

I was assigned to the Office of Intelligence, Special Operations Division, Special Projects. Imagine my shock and surprise when so was my blood brother. Trained to shoot, repel, drive, and kickass, they reserved a grey cubicle for me doing voodoo accounting on Army Navy Drive in Arlington after I first hit town.

Chapter 22

SNOWCAP

Coca bushes are unique to one place in the world and that is the Andean spine of South America. Colombia, Ecuador, Peru and Bolivia are the original source countries for all the world's supply of cocaine products. We call it the Andean Ridge Initiative or code name, Snowcap.

It was a counter-narcotics operation conducted by the Drug Enforcement Administration (DEA), U.S. Border Patrol Tactical Unit (BORTAC) and military/police forces in nine Latin American countries. At an annual cost to the DEA of $80 million, and involving approximately 140 agents at its onset, Snowcap was the largest counter-narcotics operation that had been launched in Latin America.

The U.S. Department of Defense "leased" a bunch of UH-1 Huey helicopters, yep the same ones used in Vietnam and were originally designed to meet the Army's requirements for medical evacuation and a reliable utility helicopter for small personnel transportation, and it first flew in 1956.

Always makes you feel good when you are flying around in a ride that potentially was constructed in 1956, shot to pieces in Vietnam, put back together will duct tape and super glue and now you are counting on it to get you in and out safely. Hell, who was I kidding, I was most likely getting shot anyway and really wouldn't remember anyway.

The Bell Helicopter, the UH-1 Iroquois, nicked named the Huey, is a utility military helicopter powered by a single turboshaft engine, with two-bladed main and tail rotors and it was the first turbine-powered helicopter and my first ride on a helicopter. It was named after the Iroquois or Haudenosaunee which is an indigenous confederacy in the northeast United States. I am part of the Powhatan Confederacy. During the colonial years, the French referred to them at the Iroquois League, and later as the Iroquois Confederacy. The English called them the Five Nations. The five nations were the Mohawk, Oneida, Onondaga, Cayuga, and Seneca much like my own Powhatan Confederacy.

In addition to the birds, we provided flight training to allied South American allies, especially Bolivia, air force pilots and Special Forces training for Unidad Móvil Policial para Áreas Rurales (UMOPAR) and DEA agents. The UMOPAR was created in 1987 as a subsidiary of the Special Anti-narcotics Force of the Bolivian National Police. It is a Bolivian counter-narcotics and counter-insurgency force that was founded by, and is funded, advised, equipped, and trained by the United States government as part of its "War on Drugs". Good ole Uncle Sammy providing worldwide support. Technically,

UMOPAR is headed by the Defensa Social, a branch of the Bolivian Interior Ministry but they are controlled by DEA and the United States military officials based at the U.S. Embassy in La Paz.

La Paz, Bolivia, is a lovely place unless you don't like to breathe and don't mind headaches. It is one of the largest cities in Bolivia and is the highest capital city in the world at 12000 feet above sea level. The extreme altitude affects almost all visitors to some extent. The air is much thinner at high altitudes, so the body absorbs less oxygen which leads to symptoms such as breathlessness, nausea, headaches, fatigue, a lack of appetite, and insomnia. Think about exercising and training and not being able to breathe and your head feeling like a pumpkin on Halloween with a bunch of drunk teenagers with baseball bats hitting it like a piñata.

Coca is known throughout the world for its psychoactive alkaloid, cocaine. However, the leaves have very low alkaloid content, and they are used as a mild stimulant — unlike the high produced by the chemical cocaine. Importing the leaves into the United States is prohibited — the Coca-Cola company has an exemption, because they remove the cocaine traces, I have often wondered where the traces end up, from the plant during its manufacturing process. However, in the Andes the leaves have been chewed and brewed as a mild stimulant for centuries. We were not allowed to partake in such remedies. La Paz is officially known as Nuestra Senora de La Paz or Our Lady of Peace. It is set in a big canyon, surrounded by high mountains and the triple-peaked Illimani that are always

snow-covered. It is a little disconcerting the first time you circle the toilet bowl several times, banking extremely hard, and
you're thinking, damn, are we going down, just to get out of the
bowl and into the airspace.

While the United States planned its operations, provided intelligence, and lead the drug raids, UMOPAR was
used mainly as a "strike force" for U.S. operations. Operation
Snowcap recruited U.S. Army infantry officers attending the
Army Infantry Officer's advanced course in the late 1980s.
Senior lieutenants and captains attending the course were given
classified briefings attempting to recruit them from the Army to
participate in operations in Bolivia and Peru. You had 10 DEA
folks and 4 special operators that combined a mix of explosive
ordnance disposal (EOD) specialists, medics, and communications specialists, but, first and foremost, these campaneros
were shooters. The asymmetric warfare brutes were aboard to
provide their special sauce of lethality, of course. Regardless,
DOD just likes funneling these folks through the Agency's
South American scrums to provide live-fire hours—to let their
brutes taste blood and then to the real fight in armed conflicts
in other countries around the world. Scrums is a framework
that helps teams work together. Much like a rugby team, where
it gets its name, training for a game, scrums encourage teams
to learn through experiences, self-organize while working on
a problem, and reflect on their wins and losses to continuously
improve.

Snowcap was established under Bush and revamped
under Clinton. Operating under different names but had the

same mission. While working on a problem and reflecting on the wins and losses continuously work on improving. In a few years, I was lucky enough to hand-pick the men filtering through Bogota who was nearest and dearest to me into Shadow Strike. We were young and crude hooligans and proud to call ourselves "sum bitches" and "knuckle-draggers."

We had a very dedicated team of DEA, United States Coast Guard (USCG), United States Customs and Border (USBO), and various United States armed services members who supported our Latin American neighbors during operation Snowcap, our Drug War.

Although a lot of top brass, whom I loved to piss off every chance I got, insert Peterman here, bemoaned the program for several reasons, we minions thoroughly enjoyed participating in helping our counterpart brethren heathens in Latin America take the fight to the source. When you look at it from the outside we seized and destroyed thousands of kilos of cocaine, coke laboratories were demolished, hundreds if not thousands of traffickers were arrested, and their transportation airplanes were taken or destroyed, and we blistered their entire infrastructure in their own backyard.

Chapter 23

PANAMA

The US invasion of Panama ended its twenty years of backing the drug-trafficking dictator Manuel Noriega. Yes, he was considered a friend to the US and Pablo Escobar too. However, all the coca produced and manufactured in the Andean Ridge Countries made its way through Panama.

First, thing you think of when the word Panama comes up is the Panama Canal. Panama has been traditionally controlled by its tiny European elite. All that changed in 1968, when Omar Torrijos, a populist general, led a coup that allowed the black and mestizo [mixed-race] poor to obtain at least a share of the power under his military dictatorship.

Unfortunately, or intentional accident supported by the Christians in Action (CIA), they are doing the lords work we just don't know what that is, in 1981, Torrijos was killed in a plane crash. By 1983, the effective ruler was Manuel Noriega, a criminal who had been a cohort of Torrijos and US intelligence.

Yep, someone in Intel Community (IC) might have known what was going on. Where is that business card again?

The US government knew that Noriega was involved in drug trafficking since at least 1972, when the Nixon administration considered assassinating him. But, yep insert big a big BUT here, Noriega stayed on the CIA payroll. As mentioned, the rise of the Medellin cartel, the influx of cocaine into the U.S., and the violence associated, mainly due to crack, with drug trafficking and drug use complicated all law enforcement at all levels, CIA, IC, FBI, DEA, etc. So much so, in 1980 DEA developed a Miami Based money laundering task force called Operation Swordfish.

In 1983, a US Senate committee concluded that Panama was a major center for the laundering of drug funds and drug trafficking. Bet you didn't think you were going to get a history lesson on a central American country now did you? The US government continued to value Noriega's services. In May 1986, the Director of the Drug Enforcement Administration (DEA), John Lawn, praised Noriega for his "vigorous anti-drug trafficking policy."

A year later, the Director 'welcomed our close association' with Noriega, while Attorney-General Edwin Meese stopped a US Justice Department investigation of Noriega's criminal activities. I met Mr. Meese on several occasions and consider him a true gentleman. We were at a super bowl party at Senator Laxalt's house, my girlfriend at the time, Brook, was Laxalt's brother's administrative assistant.

Brook introduced me to everyone George Schultz, Casper Weinberger, you name it. I was standing alone watching the game and a gentleman walked up and extended a hand, "Ed Meese."

I extended my hand and said, "Wayne Gretzky." As you can imagine it took Ed a step or two back but being a politician, he went with the flow and followed it up with "Big Fan". Later, Brook forced me to tell him the truth. Years later, I was in Fredericksburg, VA at the Kenmore Inn. I was standing talking with Brook, beer in my hand, and got a tap on my shoulder, as I turned, there was Ed and he looked at his wife and said, Ursula, I would like to introduce you to Wayne Gretzky. I can't make this shit up. We all got a good laugh out of that.

In August 1987, a Senate resolution condemning Noriega was opposed by Elliott Abrams, the State Department official in charge of US policy in Central America and Panama. And yet, when Noriega was finally indicted in Miami in 1988, all the charges except one were related to activities that took place before 1984 - back when he was our boy, helping with the US war against Nicaragua, stealing elections with US approval and generally serving US interests satisfactorily. It had nothing to do with suddenly discovering that he was a gangster and a drug-peddler - that was known all along. His independence threatened our interests in the Panama Canal. Everything always leads to a money trail.

On January 1, 1990, most of the administration of the Canal was due to go over to Panama - in the year 2000, it was to go completely to them. We had to make sure that Panama was in the hands of people we could control before that date. Since we could no longer trust Noriega to do our bidding, he had to go. Washington imposed economic sanctions that virtually destroyed the economy, the main burden falling on the poor non-white majority. They too came to hate Noriega, not least because he was responsible for the economic warfare (which was illegal, if anyone cares) that was causing their children to starve.

Next a military coup was tried but failed. Then, in December 1989, the US celebrated the fall of the Berlin wall and the end of the Cold War by invading Panama outright, killing hundreds or perhaps thousands of civilians (no one knows, and few North of the Rio Grande cared enough to inquire). This restored power to the rich white elite that had been displaced by the Torrijos coup - just in time to ensure a compliant government for the administrative changeover of the Canal on January 1, 1990. Throughout this process, the US press followed Washington's lead, selecting villains in terms of current needs.

But Noriega hadn't yet become outright disobedient. He was our man in Panama, and the Arias party was considered to have dangerous elements of "ultranationalism." The Reagan Administration, therefore, applauded the violence and fraud and sent Secretary of State George Shultz down to legitimatize the stolen election. The Washington media alliance and the major journals refrained from criticizing the fraudulent elections but dismissed as utterly worthless the Sandinistas' far more free and honest election in the same year - because it could not be controlled.

In May 1989, Noriega again stole an election, this time from a representative of the business opposition, Guillermo Endara. Noriega used less violence than in 1984. But the Reagan administration had given the signal that it had turned against Noriega. Following the predictable script, the press expressed outrage over his failure to meet our lofty democratic standards.

Then we get to Honduras and although it's not a murderous terrorist state like El Salvador or Guatemala human rights abuses were probably worse there than in Panama. In fact, there's one CIA-trained battalion in Honduras that all by itself had carried out more atrocities than Noriega did. Human rights abuse along with child trafficking has been and is an atrocity that continues to this day.

In fact, at exactly the moment it invaded Panama because of its outrage over Noriega's abuses of human rights, the Bush administration announced new high-technology sales to China, noting that $300 million in business for US firms was at stake and that contacts had secretly resumed a few weeks after the Tiananmen Square massacre. On the same day - the day Panama was invaded - the White House also announced plans (and implemented them shortly afterward) to lift a ban on loans to Iraq. The State Department explained with a straight face that this was to achieve the "goal of increasing US exports and put us in a better position to deal with Iraq regarding its human rights record...." Just more talking heads looking out for us.

The Department continued with the pose as Bush rebuffed the Iraqi democratic opposition (bankers, professionals, etc.)

and blocked congressional efforts to condemn the atrocious crimes of his old friend Saddam Hussein. Compared to Bush's buddies in Baghdad and Beijing, Noriega looked like Mother Teresa.. After the invasion, Bush announced a billion dollars in aid to Panama. Of this, $400 million consisted of incentives for US business to export products to Panama, $150 million was to pay off bank loans and $65 million went to private sector loans and guarantees to US investors. In other words, about half the aid was a gift from the American taxpayer to American businesses. We see this pattern even today.

The US put the bankers back in power after the invasion. Noriega's involvement in drug trafficking had been trivial compared to theirs. Drug trafficking there has always been conducted primarily by the banks - the banking system is virtually unregulated, so it's a natural outlet for criminal money. This has been the basis for Panama's highly artificial economy and remains so - possibly at a higher level - after the invasion. The Panamanian Defense Forces have also been reconstructed with basically the same officers.

In general, everything's pretty much the same, only now more reliable servants are in charge. As is with most invasions. There is a standard pattern I just wonder why the average person doesn't recognize it.

Chapter 24

OFFICE WORK CONTINUES

The true job and the cover for my cover story. My current real-life gig involved moving goods and services around, maybe I should have been a cruise director, I paid lots of visits to an obscure 45,000 sq. ft warehouse in Lorton, Virginia, 9 miles and another dilapidated building lying about 100 yards east; warehouse #13. It was my second office that no one knew about except Rodent, Guinea and I and of course the higher ups. Barbie, Skip and Knuckles were working in different locations and working on their own vocations. I made sure to endear myself to the lady that managed the warehouse, shit who am I kidding, she ruled the warehouse with an iron fist. Ms. Brenda Hightower. The lady knew her job forwards and backward, nothing entered or left the warehouse that she didn't know about. I spoke to Brenda on the phone and as soon as she spoke, I knew she was a coon ass. Now good ole First Sergeant Sparks had edumacated me on the speaking of the art of coon ass.

"Ms. Brenda you know the Fais Do Do?"

"Ole Lordy, lordy, miSTA Knights, lordy." Brenda retorted.

"Ma'am you call me Mr. Knight and I look for my daddy."

"Yes sirs, yo daddy is a goods man, lordy yes." Now, that is coon ass speak, she speaks the King's English and writes it better than I do so don't let it fool you. It is the same thing for me, as soon as I hit the Res, my accent is back!! Love that woman.

I needed a friend in Ms. Brenda because I was going to be shipping a lot of $5000 dollar hammers and $10,000 toilet seats, a little exaggeration but you get the point, all over hell's creation and did not need or want any prying eyes. Where is that business card again?

Enter the Diplomatic Pouch or "bag" is any properly identified and sealed package, pouch, envelope, bag, or other container that is used to transport official correspondence, documents, and other articles intended for official use, between: Embassies, legations, consular posts, and the foreign office of any government. That my friends is the Official United States Government description. I considered it my own personal United States Postal Service. Not that I used it to send fresh coffee from Colombia to my office via the warehouse and then distribute it amongst family and friends. I don't drink coffee so, nope wasn't me.

My fourth-floor boss, Niceley, let me run there at any hour, but she had to know (after I'd pleaded off this job and that job, passing work assignments to others 'cause I 'didn't know a thing] that Monte was sweating at his desk and shuttling to the 8th floor for conspiratorial reasons. I don't doubt other desk jockeys were whacking their word processors for other

2 CROWS *in the* SHADOWS

padrones there, as well. I kept my head low, and eventually, my desk mates left me to my wiles.

We all knew how to play Sergeant Shultz at the DEA, I know nothing and as my youngest, Elise, use to say, Dad, you have to remember not to pet the barking squirrels....you know the black ones with the white stripe down its back....smells really bad.

At warehouse #13, there were secret rooms and code keys and fancy computer screens—still very new then. It was all James Bondy and soon I was setting up some shipment of crates that said "office equipment" for a flight to El Paso's Biggs Field, an old army airbase that used to host B-52s. The DEA Intelligence Center (EPIC) lay just outside its concertina wire. EPIC was established in 1974, to provide tactical intelligence to federal, state, and local law enforcement agencies on a national scale. Owned, operated, and staffed by DEA and some representatives of the DEA and the INS, EPIC has since expanded into a center comprised of 21 participating agencies that share a common quest: identify threats to the Nation, with an emphasis on the Southwest border.

Today, EPIC is an all-threats center with a focus on the Western Hemisphere, and a particular emphasis on the Southwest border, that leverages the authorities and expertise of its partners to deliver informed intelligence.

EPIC offers tactical, operational, and strategic intelligence support to Federal, State, Local, Tribal, and International Law Enforcement Organizations. The center provides access to Law Enforcement (LE) systems with the opportunity to collaborate daily through exchanges with LE analysts and operators, as well as routine engagement with our sister organizations. Its eyes and ears were our backbone and provided major intel for boots on the ground. The key to EPIC's success is a culture that transcends parochialism it is a team approach. Collectively, they deter threats and protect our nation.

Bigg told me there'd be some extra "stuff" in some of the plywood boxes, but he didn't let on to what, and I sure didn't ask.

"Knight, you and your daddy's other son, along with the rest of the rag-tag Brady Bunch you associate with, are headed to Bogota and you should be prepared to stay for a while. All of you will be assigned to strike teams to continue your education" he casually mentioned, as I was dismissed.

This would be our first opportunity to engage the source of our mission. "Knight, try to remember, Colombia is run by Pablo Escobar, and he is no a joke."

"Roger." Fucker hadn't had the pleasure of meeting me yet.

Shock soon turned to excitement, and I could have been the boy fumbling with my girlfriend's bra in the backseat of my old man's car trying not to make a stain on the front of my pants.

As soon as I walked out, I called my brother. "Guinea, guess what?"

"I just heard, we are headed really, really south, and hell yeah."

"Guess who else is coming along?"

"Yeah, we are finally putting the band back together for our Brady Bunch reunion tour."

How in the hell did he hear first? Pops. Thought I was the favorite. Ass kisser.

Chapter 25

INTERSECTION OF
THE CROSSROADS

Our future shadow team, Guinea, Rodent, Knuckles, Skip, Barbie and I were headed further south for an execute what you have learned. We were being groomed to takeover, what we later learned, was the New War on Drugs. Once Pablo Emilio Escobar Gaviria, yeah, just plain Pablo to all of us and the world, was a Colombian drug lord and Narco terrorist who was the founder and sole leader of the Medellín Cartel. Dubbed "the King of Cocaine", Escobar is the wealthiest criminal in history, having amassed an estimated net worth of US $30 billion. Pablo was shot in killed on a rooftop in his hometown on Dec 2, 1993. He might have been running but the bastard was shooting back when he went down. Now, you won't be able to see the pictures but there we a lot was taken down, with the dead Pablo and each person pointing a gun at his head and with a smile on their face. The Search Bloc was given all the credit, and no one is actually sure who delivered the kill shot.

How do I know all this, well I might have been the FNG, fucking new guy but I was there. Who shot him, ask Jon or Frank. That's a different story already told. The New War on drugs was created every time a new administration came to power and decided to rename, rebadge, re-smoke screen, whatever you want to call it. The practice was the same, the training was the same, the execution was the same, well you get the picture.

Welcome to Panama and Howard Air Force Base (AFB) our games would begin in a little place in Cecapal on the southern part near the coast would be the starting point. The United States Army first started training troops in the jungles of Panama in 1916, just two years after the opening of the Panama Canal. Now you understand why DEA sent people to SOCOM and eventually trained in Panama. It was nicknamed 'Green Hell' by someone who had gone through it and began in earnest in the early 1940s as World War II in the Pacific necessitated the need for soldiers to be well-versed in the tactics of jungle warfare.

Howard Air Force Base was a former United States Air Force base located in Panama. It discontinued military operations on 1 November 1999 as a result of the Torrijos-Carter Treaties, which specified that US military facilities in the former Panama Canal Zone be closed and the facilities are turned over to the Panamanian government.

The airport is located six miles southwest of Balboa, at the southern (Pacific) end of the Panama Canal. Most of the area around it was uninhabited and formed part of the Panama Canal Zone watershed, although Panama City could

2 CROWS *in the* SHADOWS

be reached by crossing the nearby Bridge of the Americas. It was the perfect starting and returning point for us to get real life experience of being dropped into a Jungle area, locating a target, and exfiltrating or exfil out without getting caught. Yes, these would be known and potentially unknown drug traffic routes. We had gotten a taste, via hors d'oeuvres – you know the one or two bite items before a meal, but the main course was getting ready to happen.

On a bright and sunny morning outside a town called Cecapal Forward Operation Base in south Panama, we filed into the briefing tent and settled in.

"Hey, Guinea, you ready to swim again and really lose the pink wet spot between your legs?" I casually mentioned.

Amazing that I was greeted with a fuck off. I assume is still a little pissed about Godzilla.

Truth be told, it was all our virgin mission where we would get to put into practice everything we had learned and maybe just maybe run into some nasties that wanted a firefight, at least we all hoped that would be the case. We had flown on other controlled missions where we flew around repelled down attacked a specified control target and exfiled just like a live fire mission, but this was going out by yourself, and the training wheels are going to fly off. Everyone was a little on edge and a little nervous but excited.

Lt. Col Kenneth Rand, United States Army Green Beret, entered and started the brief. The Col explained, again, and provided the mission concept of operations, timeline and we had been trained and briefed as to the objective. "It is KISS, Keep It

Simple Stupid, and elementary enough that even Special Agent Knight can understand it."

Rodent leaned in, "well, well, never thought he would know your Pops and obviously they are close personal friends."

"Same as your mother, Rodent."

We have two strike teams, Alpha and Bravo, 14 operators on each bird, we would set out with common objectives of capturing anything we find in the way of illegal drugs while being backed up, you guessed it, real Special Operations warriors hell bent on making sure the Fucking New Guy (FNG) civilians understood the SERE training we had received and executed as instructed. Nice guys in all and I still get Christmas cards from a few of them, of course, it is addressed to fucktard or dickhead, but I know they really miss me.

"Gentlemen, we will fly a short flight from Howard to Cecapal and execute your mission in three days. Remember this is and can be hostile territory and most likely your comms are not going to work 100% in a thick canopy. A Special Forces Captain, an Army Sargent First Class, and two more special forces experts will be on each bird to assist if necessary and then you 10 DEA fucks. Remember, they will be under your command and will only step in if you run into the bad guys or one of you wants to do something stupid and I will have to put a toe tag on you and send your dumbass back to wherever you call home. Clear?"

"Roger!" was a resounding affirmation.

Lt. Col Rand continued, "This will emulate the advisory missions in support of the host countries in South and Central

America and has been known as SNOWCAP, so welcome aboard the crazy train."

"As you know, your mission is to land short and fast and secure the landing zone and proceed to your objective of the Crossroads. Designated on the map is the crossroads that leads from Colombia North and the other road connects both of the coasts. At least we have live combat tested Green Berets providing support. We need to take the crossroads and stop a Conoy traveling with a major shipment of narcotics and all the while being alert for potential child trafficking."

"Wow, you know Barbie, I think he likes you, or maybe just your tits."

Looking over, "Idiot." she still loves me.

As an afterthought, the Col reminded us, "Oh, try not to get shot or killed, hell of lot of paperwork for me."

"Tender sum bitch if I ever met one." I told Knuckles.

"You think?" Knuckles shrugged.

"Stay safe and when I retire, I am opening a critter control business so when you get state side you all will have a job." Rand joke. He did open a critter control business too.

"Gentlemen, let's go make a drug deal."

"Roger, Roger."

We broke the meeting, grabbed our gear, made sure we were locked and loaded as we headed to the birds. Alpha Team and Captain Dave loaded up on Rubber Duck and we, the good guys, boarded Big Bird. Everyone remembers Smoky and the Bandit and who could forget Sesame Street and these two would be instrumental in futures excursions. We climbed on board, got the headsets and were ready to roll.

"Pig Pen", Alpha one, seven, niner on standby ready."

"Alpha one, seven, niner clear for takeoff."

"See you on the flip side, Pig Pen."

"Roger, Roger Duck, you boys have fun."

"Copy, over."

Engines were roaring now, and we lifted off in a deliberate manner. These boys had done this a time or two. I looked down the opposite row and Skip, Rodent and Knuckles were calm and didn't say a word. Barbie was cool as the back side of a pillow on a hot evening after horizontal loving courtesy of some MTL. Yep, Monte Turbo Loving or just plain MTL for the uninformed or who have never had the greatest time this side of heaven. Of course, Barbie worked the streets of Miami as cop, not a street walker, and no fear in her.

As were started leveling off, Black 4, flicked on the great Jimmy Buffet's song 'Let's get drunk and screw' in our headsets. One of the many traditions, I learned and carried on with me and my teams. Smart move, the look on everyone's faces was calm, all except the special operator guys, those sum bitches were asleep. It was also, a fond memory I have carried with me my entire life.

"Hey Barbie," I gave her the wink, smiled, and tapped the ear set and again greeted with a one finger salute and a smile. That is twice in 10 minutes, new record for me.

As we got height, it was and is one of the most intensely liberating feelings, and my thoughts rushed back to the Res remembering my namesake perched atop the tallest trees within eyesight looking down on the land below. When they fly, I often wondered what it was like and what they were thinking, I knew they were catching the first warmth of the sun while we are standing on the ground looking up, still watching our breath on cool mornings, earthbound while we watched freedom in their wings.

It seemed that we had just taken off before we soon received the signal for radio silent and get ready. We came in low, fast and then put on the Air brakes for Ground Insertion and Black 4 was giving the hand signal for Go, Go, Go. We hopped off both sides of the bird got 15 yards and squatted. No one was shooting at us, at least as far as we could tell. The birds pull off while only touching down long enough to drop us like a deuce first thing in the morning.

"Hey mom, dropping the kids off at the pool."

Time to focus and remember what we were taught. Alpha Team headed off as we gathered, and I gave the hand singled to move forward in a single formation. Dense vegetation will limit our lines of sight and arcs of fire but can provide ample opportunity for camouflage which we did brush ourselves and plenty of material with which to build fortifications, but that was not our mission this time. This was cat and mouse, and I wanted a kill. Jungle terrain, often without any roads much less good roads, can be inaccessible to vehicles and so makes logistical supply and transport difficult, which in turn places a premium on air mobility but we already knew that. Assessing the situation, this environment was also inherently unhealthy, with various tropical diseases that have to be prevented or treated by medical services which were very limited, but it was supposed to be a short trip. Supposed to be, right?

Likewise, the terrain can make it difficult to deploy armored forces, or any other kind of forces on any large scale. Successful jungle fighting emphasizes effective small unit tactics and leadership. That's why we were here, and they had me for leadership. Cocky much, yep often.

Based on satellite photos we had only to proceed less than five miles before we should encounter the "crossroads" an intersection of two dirt paths, call them roads if you want to, where drugs are transported and changed hands from one Cartel to a mule company hired by the Cartels. See they knew the lay of the land better and knew who to pay off, most likely family members, and it was precision work. Everyone made a lot of money and would do anything to protect it.

We picked and moved out in our standard formation. As I mentioned before, we keep to formations, so one bullet can't take out more than one person, it allows leaders to keep track of everyone and what they are always doing. We needed to hack our way through dense undergrowth, and it was slow work. As we slowly worked our way to the coordinates, I notice a breeze cutting through the stale air. If you have ever been under a triple canopy, you know there isn't a breeze. Then the sound carried on the wind, a Harpie Eagle, Panama's national bird, was screeching in the distance and I froze. I gave the signal for everyone to stop and squat. Barbie was looking straight at me and gave me the what the fuck look, I shook my head with a slight movement of no. She squatted down. Knuckles, who was closest, mouthed what is it.

"Listen." I whispered, touching my ear.

"Bossman, I don't hear shit."

"Precisely, no birds, no insects no nothing." I continued thinking to myself, you may have eyes pale face but yet you still cannot see.

But there was something alright, a trap.

Black 4 on point was signaling now. Enemy, 30 yards straight and spread for assault on both left and right flank. Alpha is high alert.

"Guinea, take seven, you pick'em and go back 20 yards and swing wide left to cover our flank, you have 20 mins, sync."

"Roger." and he went to work and slowly started moving back where we had come from.

Black 4 was signaling Alpha to do the same. "We have 20 mins, remember once it starts, kill every man, woman, dog, cat, and bird, if it breathes shoot it and let God sort out the good ones, got it."

"Roger, Roger."

The Great Spirit whispered in my ear in the dense jungle, it wasn't a crow, but it was a bird and clear enough. How did these guys know we were here. They couldn't. So, if they weren't expecting us, who were they expecting? I said to only myself.

If they weren't expecting us, who............Ba BOOM!!!

What the fuck was that? Followed by another, and another and another in rapid succession. Now when I say boom, I mean earth shaking boom. The ground underneath our feet shook for a second or two and I thought I was on Soul Train for a hot minute with the moves I was displaying.

Black 4 came charging back at a full sprint and was signaling fall back, double quick. Screaming, "Artillery, artillery, incoming, get down, get down."

No need to sneak around now. Remember, Black 4 was an E7 special operator and if he said it was artillery, time to get down. We were stuck on the move, so we have to opt for cover and any type of concealment. The jungle was out best protection, we didn't have fox holes, because trees drastically increase your chances of survival since most shrapnel won't go through a tree but watch out for falling branches. Artillery is kind of a big, thundering fireworks shows that looks awesome in movies, but this wasn't the movies and I sure as hell am not Rambo.

Obviously, only one thing could shoot like that in this region and that had to be the United States Navy some distance offshore. But why and what was the target? More importantly, why were we so close to artillery. The Navy was trying to hit with as many rounds as possible in the first blast (was there going to be a second or third?) using a method called "time on target" so all the shells rain down at the same time. Maximizes the amount of destruction before poor sum bitches like us can rush for cover or hop into a ditch.

"Pig Pen, Black 4 over."

"Go ahead, Black 4."

"Pig Pen, we have artillery danger close, over."

"Copy Black 4, we have ceased all artillery.........drop red smoke, Big Bird and Rubber Duck are in bound, over."

Does it seem to anyone else, that someone in the Pig Pen knew artillery was coming!

"Copy Pig Pen."

"Black 4, we are inbound Hot coming hard." Duck dropped into the convo.

"Keep fire north to the smoke, look for black bellowing and dump on perimeter over."

Within seconds both birds came screaming over and shortly a blaaaaaaaaatzzzzzzzzz sound resonated for 20 seconds each and then banking. Came in again and sprayed the area over.

"Everything quiet now."

"Bird, we are moving in, Black 4 over."

"Copy Black 4, we are circling."

We reengaged with the plan, spread into formation, and moved cautiously towards the objective. As we approached, the blast became evident. We had to cut through the trees that were blown to shreds and created an enclosure around the blast craters. There were multiple large craters and what looked like three or maybe four large military vehicles blown to pieces and burning. Lots of bodies strewn around, and if anyone or anything survived, you wouldn't know it. No signs of life. There was no Intel to gather whatsoever just burning ruble. We spent about 10 minutes looking around, turned and went back the same way we came. They didn't know we were coming but they were prepared. Prepared for who is the question in my mind.

I looked at Black 4, "what the fuck is going on Sargent?"

"Hell, if I know Bossman but we will find out soon enough, I am sure." I never liked being a pawn in someone else's game, especially when it almost got all of us killed.

Later I learned that the United States Army had misplaced 101 Laws' Rockets. The M72 LAW (Light Anti-Armor Weapon) a 66mm one-shot rocket fitted with a high explosive ant-tank (HEAT) warhead. Everything is an acronym. It was first used in the Vietnam war but like the Huey is still in active service today. It's lightweight and compact design means the LAW is well suited to fighting against insurgents who lack such support vehicles, like heavy armor, but may fight from pickup trucks or from inside bunkers, buildings, and other fixed positions like in South America.

Yes, I said misplaced. Our training was supposed to get us to the crossroads and intercept the trucks carrying the cargo. Nice if someone had briefed us on the specifics of the mission instead of intercepting the cargo. How did the powers that be know the LAWS were headed to the crossroads? Someone had intel, via satellite photos, that showed consecutive explosions on the road moving north from Colombia to Panama and a destination unknown. The Narcos was trying to learn how to use the LAWs. Fucking great.

Turns out a former west pointer, turned DEA agent, had given the call that said our teams were not danger close and approved the inbound artillery. His name Winston Wigginton Pendergast, V. More about this Asshat later.

We were all debriefed and it was classified as Top Secret and so nothing else was mentioned until we were back at headquarters and even then, it was brief and forgotten. Dodged another raindrop but didn't get to personally make a drug deal though the result was the same, bunch of dead tangos.

Going back to HQ, since play time was over.

Chapter 26

REASSIGNED
BOGOTA, COLOMBIA

After a year plus of office work, and ferrying 'stuff around' via paper, phone or fax, I'd get to put on camo, strap on a weapon and join a team to learn firsthand what the war on drugs all about. In the future, I would get my chance to lead one of those teams called 'Shadow'.

On a bright sunny morning, the Brady Bunch boarded a commercial flight to Miami, and we would join other DEA folks we had been working with and trained with at Bragg and SOCOM.

Boarding the plane "They let anyone on these flights." Rodent greeted Dave with a handshake and a salute to his seat mate, Black 4.

"Rodent since you are third world ugly, you should feel right at home." Black 4 interjected.

"Your momma let you out the house dressed liked that?" he countered.

"This sure as hell must be the last train to Clarksville." as I greeted both these knuckle draggers.

We hit Miami for the layover, made our way to the next gate and plopped down at the bar. Round of Jack for everyone except me, 'never drink the white man's fire water' my grandmother would be proud.

It was a hop, skip and a jump before we got to Bogota. Yes, it was a third world country by the United States standards, but most countries can't compare, and we should never forget we live in the greatest country in the world. However, it eerily felt like coming home to me, even though I had never been here before.

Bogotá is the capital and largest city of Colombia. It is situated in the center of the country and a perfect location for our center of operations, and it was also the center location for all DEA operations in South America. It was at an elevation of 8,660 feet and has a population of nearly 10 million people. Prior to us departing were briefed that despite its proximity to the equator, Bogotá enjoys a year-round moderate temperature, although days and nights can be quite fresh due to its altitude. We packed accordingly as to have layers that you can take off and put on as needed, just like an onion.

We stepped off the plane, onto the tarmac to a warm, humid day that spoke of a potential thunderstorm in the distance. We would soon learn that it rained almost every day at exactly 1600 for 30 minutes and then it was done. Much like Miami in the summertime. The sky was bluer than blue, and I thought of the Res in the spring. We got the first whiff of the smell of the country and city, a combination of fresh, yet a stained wind blowing saturated with problems, that gave me a sense of paradise in trouble. Natives learned that air could tell you everything about where you are all at once.

I looked around and noted at the far end of the airport there was a section that had a fence with concertina wire all along the edge of a doubled fence line; interesting. There were armed guards on both sides of the fence. Several hueys whomp whomping while hovering over on the other side. Dave walking beside me stated, 'Private side," and kept walking as Black 4 passed with a follow-up, "you will get that tour later."

As the fragrance of some of the world's best Colombian coffee aroused our senses when we were greeted by Special Agent Lumb, a fantastic percussionist, and an avid KISS fan, he might have it tattooed on his ass for all I know, guess I need to ask Ms. Terry or Guinea about that. Captain Dave and Black 4 were met by several green berets and threw us the finger and see ya at the barracks," parting ways.

"Gentlemen and Ladies, I am Special Agent Lumb, and I will be your interface and liaison while you are in country alongside Intel Analyst Officer Misty "Gummy" Williams." I should write a book about people's names. Misty was an interesting lady, a registered nurse turned Intel Spy. Sexy as hell and a wonderful personality. Yes, of course, we would be eventually coach bouncing but hey, I am sexy, and she knew it and loved me a long time.

"Welcome to the great country of Colombia with lots of nice people and a few deadly scumbags." Lumb stated spreading his arms. All the gear was Dip Pouched, along with camos and civilian clothes, plus the clothes on our backs, book bags slung over our shoulders and of course the side arms. We would get long weapons when the time was appropriate.

As we climbed into our Culitivos, armored and bullet proof black Suburbans, Agent Lumb reminded us there were spies planted throughout Colombia, especially at the airport, and on a drug lords' payroll to identify us. It started as soon as you landed at the airport and continued and off for the duration of your stay. It was part of Pablo Escobar's method of operations to identify anyone entering or leaving Colombia that was a gringo or associated with the gringos. Pictures were taken, distributed and sometimes, if you were lucky enough a bounty was placed on your head, that's when you knew you had made it to the Big Leagues.

Unfortunately for the Cocaine Cowboy, the United States had an Aviation Division, and its mission is to provide aviation support to operational and intelligence elements within DEA and the law enforcement community to detect, locate, identify, and assess illicit narcotics-related trafficking activities. It is critical to DEA's strategic mission of disrupting and dismantling drug trafficking organizations that have a significant impact on America's illegal drug availability. To accomplish its mission, the Aviation Division employs a fleet of airplanes and helicopters flown by specially trained Special Agent/Pilots.

The aviation program started with a single aircraft in 1971 as part of DEA's predecessor, the Bureau of Narcotics and Dangerous Drugs. By 1973, when DEA was created, the program had grown to 24 aircraft and 41 Special Agent/Pilots overseen by a Chief Pilot. In 1994 it was granted field division status and the Chief Pilot position was converted to a Special Agent-in-Charge. Today, the Aviation Division consists of approximately 135 Special Agent/Pilots and 100 aircraft.

Ms. Gummy and Lumb escorted us to the United States Embassy Colombia in vehicles driven by Foreign Services Nationals (FSNs). All Embassies and Consulates employ FSNs to assist with all sorts of support from mundane maintenance to Confidential Informants (CI) and quite frankly we couldn't do the job without them. We were taken to our new home for the duration alongside the current inhabitants, Marine Corps Embassy Security Group. As we walked in, the two Marines at a desk watching TV, jumped up and snapped to attention.

Lumb quickly announced, "It's just us and not a general, Sargent."

"Speak for yourself Lumb," I countered.

Introductions were made and more Marines filtered in and welcomed us. Uncle Sammies misguided children are some hard sum bitches and it was nice to meet some of the good ole country boys.

"Hey any of you jar heads know a coon ass named Sparks. Well, that set the Marines off like Chesty Puller himself had walked into the room and chants of 'Fais Do Do' and 'Majestic Mammeries' followed. Mardi Gras in the barracks.

"Sir, who doesn't know Gunny Sparks?" more a comment than a question.

.

"Yeah, he was our PT instructor at the academy for all of us DEA boys."

"Yes, Sir, everyone knows Gunny Sparks, yes sir."

"Man, listen, you call me Sir and I look for my Dad, its Agent or Monte, got it." I mean shit, we were closed to the same age if not the same age.

"Yes si......Monte, gotcha." I am Nathan Javaras." He said extending his hand.

"Javaras? I know a guy from back home in Virginia named Danny Javaras, marine, one hell of a drummer and fast as hell."

"Yes, si...ahh, Monte, that's my dad but I am the better drummer and a lot faster too." No doubt in my mind, brother.

We made nice, nice with everyone and little did I know at the time, that later, Nathan help defend our team and make the ultimate sacrifice in doing so. Mad respect for Nathan. Agent Lumb checked us into our new confines.

"See y'all at 0730 to meet the Country Attaché' and Department of State, Regional Security Officer (RSO) to get a standard security and intel brief for Bogota and other host countries in the region," Lumb mentioned as he said goodbye.

Wouldn't you know it, bunk beds...It's a damn curse or conspiracy and neither one is acceptable. This time, I got top. "Piss boy, you got bottom."

"Fuck off!"

Captain Dave, Black 4 were already there, sitting at a table consuming some tasty beverages, gave us a nod and continued whatever the discussion was going on prior to us interrupting. A Captain Harlin Stutton, III, entered the building, yep another name with a fucking number behind it, but everyone called him George. Not sure why, I think his wife use the name as a cover story. George spotted Dave and greeted him right away. They played rugby together and were classmates at West Point.

"Brother, how you are doing, man?"

"Brother Dave, great to see you, I was told you would be in my LZ, to watch over you so I knew that meant I was assigned latrine duty – to keep your ass smelling good and straight."

"Good luck with that, Skip chimed in." George scowled in Skips direction.

"He's a Skipper, George."

"Ah, makes sense, shit for brains boat driver."

"Ahoy, you got it." Skip giving a salute, "at your service."

George provided an overview of what we already knew but this was new Intel from boots on the ground and prior to our meeting with the Country Attaché, Big Poppy D. Keith Wilson and the Regional Security Officer (RSO) Matt Joblonski, a nice Long Island fellow who loved the Mets and Giants. Only good quality when it came to sports, he hated the Yankees and New Yorkers for that matter.

It was late so we got dinner and sacked out for the night. 0430 the Marines were up, and I figured we should join them as a team for PT.

"Sargent Javaras, care if we tag along?"

"The more the merrier, Sir." Again, this this Sir crap.

We needed to learn the layout of the Embassy Grounds, the do's and don't of the place. Gunny Sparks would have been proud, these Jar Heads weren't just exercising because they wanted to, they loved it and it showed on how they went about PT'ing – 'ooorah' the entire time.

After a shower and quick breakfast, I was checking my watch when I heard, "Ready?" at the doorway. Agent Lumb showed up right on time and walked us to the rear entrance of the Embassy. We were met by two Marines, flashed badges, even though the guys had met us less than 24 hours prior, they still held strong to protocol. We went in through a bullet and blast-proof glass door that had to have weighed 400lbs. Then we side stepped the standard metal detector, mainly used for Americans working for the government or Foreign Service Nationals (FSN) that provide various support to the Embassy and were there on a daily basis. Embassy life would be a lot harder without these dedicated people trying to make a better life for their families and Uncle Sammy gave them a fantastic opportunity to do so.

Any vehicle trying to enter the Embassy was allowed entry after passing into a sally port. A two gated system enclosure where you were allowed to enter the port and immediately face a second gate. The first gate was closed behind you. It prevents direct enemy fire from a distance while the vehicle is inspected by running mirrors underneath to inspect for explosives. It also prevented the vehicle from taking off into the Embassy compound with a load of bad guns and or explosives.

We all went to the elevator and stopped at the third floor and followed Agent Lumb toward our goal, a large conference room.

On the way, we ran head on into an absolutely stunning Brunette, no ring, great body and don't tell me I can't do quick surveillance, accompanied by two other professionally attired gentlemen on each flank, who I didn't even notice until I ran smack dab into one. Everyone stopped, could be a Mexican standoff. Now, this would be an awkward moment for most, but for me, not so much.

"Excuse me." as I muttered and still staring at the hottie.

"Hey, you should take a picture it would last longer." To which I heard a giggle from Barbie and the hottie.

"Sorry buddy, I was just hoping the lady, looking straight into her beautiful puppy dog eyes, might want to join our group, it's called Jews for Jesus, maybe you have heard of us?"

The escorted lady smirked at me, turned and with a warm, bubble voice "Let's go."

"You never cease to amaze me," Barbie chided.

"What?" She was beautiful so of course I looked and Barb, it usually takes me about 5 minutes before someone realizes they can't stand me.

"Where is your shirt?" I am guessing that was in reference to the shirt stating I never want to get laid.

We all filed into the conference room, I grabbed a water and the others jumped on the coffee and donuts. I never drank coffee, and everyone thought it was strange but I was a little strange we already knew that. We had just planted our backsides into a seat when we sprung up when Big Poppy made a grand entrance. At 6'5" he was a large man originally from Northern Virginia, could drive just about anything because he was a volunteer fire fighter in his youth and drove the largest fire truck they had. Plus, an excellent mechanic and could fix just about anything, especially with a hammer, WD40, and duct tape. He was flanked by his second in command, Jacob Wilson, no relation though it could have been a father son or older and little brother lookalike contest, the Assistant Special Agent in Charge (ASAC).

"Gentlemen and ladies," even Big Poppy knew Guinea was a bitch. "I am Country Attaché Wilson, but you can address me as Keith when we aren't around other non-DEA folks. We will be working long intense hours and sometimes dangerous ones at that, and I like to keep it informal when we are together, roger."

"Roger." all around.

"This is my right-hand man, Special Agent Jacob Wilson, no relations but like a brother to me."

I had to slap Guinea, "Younger, annoying brother."

"Agent Knight, do you have something you would like to share with the class?" Great, he recognized my authority right away, I was moving up in the world.

"No Sir, just excited to be here."

"Your jacket says, and I quote, good, sometimes great at operational effectiveness, natural leader, does not like authority and has a propensity to blow smoke up people's asses." Before I could even say a word in my defense, it went around the table.

"Yep."

"True!"

"Nail on the head."

"Yes, Sir, true."

"Exactly."

"Arrogant fuck." Now, I wonder which sum bitch made that comment.

Even Agent Lumb piled on, "I have known him less than 24 hours and I would say that is an accurate assessment, Sir." What the fuck Lumb, did I mess around with your girlfriend or something.

After an ice breaking round of laughs, we settled down for the task at hand. I must admit, Big Poppy was smooth and knew exactly what he was doing. Putting the team at ease in a very beautiful, but just as dangerous, paradise.

Jake chimed in and said Keith is known as Big Poppy then looking straight at me, "Damn, I just realized your Harmon's boy."

"Yes Sir."

"I was told you were a window licker half breed."

"Sir, correct on the half breed just add heathen and, and to clarify the matter, I drove the short bus for Agent Genovese, and the rest of The Brady Bunch but Guinea was the window licker, Sir."

Everyone laughed and we settle down for business. "How is the old man, Knight?"

"Still a gi-normous pain in my ass Sir."

"Funny your mom says it's the other way around." At least he knows mom too and doesn't get a one-sided story lined with make believe and half-truths when it comes to me.

"A true southern Lady with style and grace and as feisty as a banty rooster but I fear she may have her facts misconstrued."

"Ahh, yeah, ok lets get started."

Big Poppy went into an hour-long detailed explanation of what we could expect, what we could and could not do and that as of today we were guests of the host country and temporally assigned to his command and at the discretion of the Chief of Mission (CM), the United States Ambassador to Colombia. In other words, we could be sent stateside for any and all reasons without questions.

Even though this was a short trip, The Brady Bunch proved and endeared ourselves to the staff and crew of the Embassy, both inside DEA, and outside with the other Agencies at the post. I was fast and quick friends with Big Poppy, Jake, and others especially the FSNs whom I became friends with, and they looked out for me.

Next up, Regional Security Officer (RSO) Matt Joblonski. We stayed put and Matt came to us and provided the standard Security Briefing. Since we were not leaving the Embassy other than by escort and specifically for a one-time mission a lot didn't apply to us this time. We knew about the FARQ and host of other radicals, the car bombs, gangs roaming outside the La Zona Rosa, occasional snipe shot, kidnappings that plagued the city and child trafficking. Nice place to visit in the Springtime.

However, it was information that we could expect if any of us were lucky enough to get an overseas duty station. We would get morning briefings about events in the host country, other Embassies around the world, daily events in the US and other countries, basically a classified version of USA Today.

Matt is a super nice guy and knew his job forward and backward. We are still good friends to this day and he is a true believer in his faith, God and Jesus Christ. Matt has tried to convert my heathen backside on more than one occasion, but it hasn't stuck. Not yet anyway, but I give him credit, never quits on me. I am a believer, but my terms are a little different than his. One my hardest times I ever experience, Matt stood beside me, pushed me, and even carried me and I cannot thank him enough. Thank you, Brother Matt. Thank you.

With the meetings finished, we gathered for lunch in the cafeteria. The food is comprised of good old USA standard meat, potatoes, salads, and a flare of local and host nation cuisine.

"Is this seat taken?" as I glanced a Guinea and Barbie.

"Why no, please sit down, with that mountain of food on your plate."

Guinea gave me the not here look so I stood down and didn't snort any food.

"How is everyone doing?" Misty asked.

"Great, but when do we get the real tour," Rodent followed up.

"After lunch, we will tour the Embassy and Compound, go to the secret side of the airfield to start the briefing of what to expect."

We took the tour, saw Marines and .50Cals on the walls, all the entries and exits, all the counter measures.

"Agent Lumb, it is a little strange to have some of the larger buildings so close to the walls."

"Yeah, when the location was selected the US Government was not anticipating a drug war with RPGs and car bombs, however we have made adjustments and are fully prepared." Good to know. We had already been provided intelligence briefs on car bombs back at HQ.

Car bombs were not uncommon during the decades-long conflict between the Colombian government and left-wing rebels of the Revolutionary Armed Forces of Colombia (Farc). But came to the forefront with the war on drugs and specifically the Cartels. A car bomb, bus bomb, or truck bomb is commonly referred to as a vehicle-borne improvised explosive device (VBIED). It is an improvised explosive device designed to be detonated in an automobile to inflict as much physical and mental damage as possible. Think about being worried about family members going to the grocery store because someone is mad at the police and wants to blow up the police station. Well, welcome to Bogota.

The bombs can be roughly divided into two main categories: those used primarily to kill the occupants of the vehicle, often as an assassination, used when the drive-by shootings weren't enough to make an impacting impression of who was really in charge and those used as a means to kill, injure or damage people and buildings outside the vehicle. The latter type may be parked the vehicle disguising the bomb and allowing the bomber to get away, or the vehicle might be used to deliver the bomb often as part of a suicide bombing.

It is commonly used as a weapon of terrorism or guerrilla warfare to kill people near the blast site or to damage buildings or other property. Car bombs act as their own delivery mechanisms and can carry a relatively large amount of explosives without attracting suspicion. In larger vehicles and trucks, weights of around 7,000 pounds (3,200 kg) or more have been used, for example, in the Oklahoma City bombing which we will get into later.

The bombs are activated in a variety of ways, including opening the vehicle's doors, starting the engine, remote detonation, depressing the accelerator or brake pedals, or simply lighting a fuse or setting a timing device. The gasoline in the vehicle's fuel tank may make the explosion of the bomb more powerful by dispersing and igniting the fuel. Welcome to the daily strain of civilian life in Colombia, courtesy of terrorists.

We received our Intel and Planning brief at the airport later that day. We learned that tomorrow was live action so get a good night's sleep.

Chapter 27

TRAINING PUT TO USE

O630 our first day of reckoning. A gray drizzle descended from the silvery clouds creating a surreal atmosphere as we boarded three birds: Pink Panther, Big Bird and Rubber Duck, yep same birds and crew from Panama. As I mentioned, the birds were Huey's from the Vietnam Era and retrofitted for DEA's purpose.

As I boarded, loaded up with everything a growing war fighter needs, all that was familiar, everything that anchored me to my past seemed to be receding.

Captain Dave (Alpha Team) on Big Bird, Captain George and The Brady Bunch (Bravo Team) on Rubber Duck, and Black 4 (Charlie Team) on Pink Panther the Shadow Team. Pig Pen was the command-and-control center. Our now vital mission had been hammered out as a team while becoming acquainted and reacquainted these past several days at the Embassy. Specific goals and how they could be accomplished were clear. The unknowns were many so what was not clear at all was how unidentified hurdles would be surmounted.

We were all aware with so much at stake our enemy would be in a dire struggle for survival, most likely stirring hellacious firefights.

As much one prepares for events that could turn your life on a dime, it is often what you were not expecting that first comes to mind when ruminating on the past. My first time in a fire fight has remained forever etched into my memory in milli or microseconds, just as much as my first time with Tracy Johnson in my grandfather's barn. Both became photographic memories as clear as can be in Kodak living color. Playing in my brain, those memories held in a clear orb I can seemingly pick up in my hands, turning over and over examining every detail, from every angle and even recalling all the five senses alerted by that experience. Tracy's large breasted torso leaning against my chest as she locks her wrists lightly around my neck, the scent of Daisy cologne from her throat and Johnson's Baby Powder from her cotton underwear stirring my early awareness of manhood. The same green pungent scent of the damp jungle underbrush wafting through a thick, humid jungle air as my boots bear down lightly. Faint rustling sounds of team members following stealthily behind. The sweet, sickly odor of sweat rolling down oily faces and unbathed bodies when fear is ever present amplified by the pulsating, quickened, loud beating of my heart and temples I am sure this unseen enemy can hear.

Based on intel, some flights we would be dropped into a targeted zone as a drop and go. Sometimes we were merely scouting to seek or report intel or waiting while intel upline or downline was reported back to us. Some assignments action was encountered because a defensive position or sortie was stirred. Other days could be long stretches of boredom punctuated by life-threatening flashes of action…some days could be both. In other words, no matter what, stay alert because you never knew what to expect.

"Pig Pen, Alpha one, seven, niner standby ready for launch."

"Alpha one, seven, niner cleared for takeoff."

"See you on the flip side Pig Pen."

"Roger, Roger, Duck safe flight."

"Panther, brakes off."

"Big Bird, Brakes off."

This lift off was a feeling of being yanked up by some invisible rubber band, then the tail tilting to an extreme angle and collectively applied then went swooping away. Quickly reaching an altitude of 3,000 feet and leveling off at that point as a cruising altitude. Morning was a mixture of a lot of things and prop wash to one side or the other intensified everything to the point there was no guessing the weather, you were thrust right in the middle. Some mornings the cold chill of low temperatures was apparent, or the occasional rains would dampen our spirits by a good soaking. Other times in the early dawn stillness it was beautiful and reminded me of spring and the mist rising off the river to greet the warming sun back home. Cold days brought the wop, wop bounce as the prop was in dense air, much more so than in dry conditions. Late nights were few and far between, but we did have a few. At night there was an absence of ground-based lights as many places, especially parts of the jungle areas didn't have electricity and only had small fires or lanterns and were often extinguished at the sound of our coming presence. The stars were so bright in the night sky they seemed to be your one familiar sight that you could cling to when the cold was all around you.

I was in my standard uniform, camouflage, combat boots, carrying my Smith & Wesson 1076 10mm in my thigh holster along with 11 clips of ammo that had 9+1 rounds and elongated 15 round magazines with a total of a 135 rounds of hydro shock that would blow a man's head clear off. My M16 rifle and later a MP-5/10, was pulled tight to my chest with a few hundred rounds of .556 M193 ammo. The M193 cartridge is a center-fire cartridge with a 55-grain, gilded metal-jacketed, lead alloy core bullet.

In the upper right-hand pocket of my combat vest was a SATCOM, satellite transceiver, and in my left pocket a picture of my mom.

On the Res we played a type of dodgeball game that used lacrosse balls. You learned to be mobile, agile, and hostile or you were black, blue and ball busted. The best time to play was mid-August when the mist and fog from the river drifted low in a crosswind across the Res and provided perfect cover for sneak attacks. Elders said these foggy kinds of days correlated directly to how many snowstorms there would be in the upcoming Winter.

As usual, at the courtesy of Black 4, we had Jimmy Buffets 'Let's get drunk and screw', among other songs, playing in our headsets for the hour plus ride to our destination.

As we started to descend over the jungle tops, inching closer and closer to the target in the hot, humid air the music was cut and were getting low fast. It was already decided the Bravo would flank Charlie to the right, set a perimeter quickly followed by Alpha. Bravo would break into 10 team members leaving Black 4, Guinea, me and a special operator in the middle. Alpha flanked us right with 10 team members and sent another special operator, Barbie, Knuckles and Rodent to us to form the middle contingency supporting Charlie.

We flew in low and slowed to a crawl, as go, go, go, was heard loud and clear and we were on terra firma again. We spread out and knelt until the birds flew off taking with it all sounds of our breaking the silence of the land. Hand singles were exchanged, and all three teams moved forward into the abyss.

Barbie was not the first female agent to work under the guise of Operation Snowcap. As the Washington Post Reported. "All five Drug Enforcement Administration (DEA) agents aboard a twin-engine plane that crashed in the Peruvian jungle Saturday were killed, federal officials said yesterday."

Peruvian and DEA rescue teams, who had been hampered by dense vegetation, rain and fog, reached the site yesterday afternoon and discovered the bodies of two pilots and three agents amid the mangled remains of a Casa twin-engine aircraft.

"That's a heavy price to pay," DEA Administrator Thomas A. Constantine said in a telephone interview.

While the cause of the crash is not yet known, officials said there was no indication the plane was forced down. DEA aviation experts were on the scene and other federal aviation officials were expected to analyze the wreckage, officials said yesterday. The area of the crash is known for air turbulence, Constantine said. I received my first DEA award from Tom Constantine. Mr. Constantine was always very stern in photographs but actually had a smirk on his face when taking a picture with me. Yeah, there is a reason for that, but you need to read on.

The five agents who died in Peru were conducting a routine patrol mission, which began at the Santa Lucia base camp, when the plane lost contact with air traffic control and disappeared about 15 miles away in a heavily forested area of the Huallaga Valley where most of the world's cocaine originates. The agents were part of 'Operation Snowcap', a training and assistance program in which the DEA works in concert with Peruvian officials to stem cocaine production and smuggling from South America.

The agents were identified as Frank Fernandez Jr., 38, stationed at DEA headquarters here; Jay W. Seale, 31, stationed in Los Angeles; Meredith Thompson, 33, based in Miami; Frank S. Wallace Jr., 37, based in Houston; and Juan C. Vars, 32, who worked out of DEA offices in San Antonio. I met Frank Fernandez in Oklahoma City. He survived the Oklahoma City Bombing only to lose his life 6 months later in Peru. Another example of True American Heroes one and all!

One by one we descended from the safety of our ride and into the shadows and spread out with Black 4 taking point and the rest following suit. We spread quickly as the second bird was inbound and our heads were on a swivel for any sight of the enemy. We were on time based on the clock in my head. The smell of rotting leaves on the jungle floor along with flowers, fresh and stagnant water greeted us. As the second bird lifted and moved off in the distance, a symphony of sounds cascading through the air caught all of our attention, or at the least the attention of the FNGs. Black 4 signaled to get into formation and lead Charlie Team into the jungle as I saw Captain Dave doing for Alpha and Captain George was with Bravo team a short distance away.

One major problem with southern Colombia is that it was controlled by the Revolutionary Armed Forces of Colombia (FARC). Nice group of fellas known for kidnapping, child trafficking, and mass production of cocaine all to support their ideology. I could not give 3 buckets of monkey shit, to know what that was, I was here to destroy the lab and take down as many of them with the lab as I could. Black 4 made the stand ready sign to Alpha Team and to our left and then to Bravo Team on our right and inched forward. Black 4 went forward for a sneak, and peek to get a count on the bad guys, how many innocents, check the perimeter for sensors, or sentries, or my personal favorite, C4. These pencil neck terrorists loved Ak-47s and C4 and they had an endless supply of both.

We moved slow and deliberate for the first 30 minutes or so, getting our bearings and marking the makeshift coca producing lab. I knelt and listened to the amazing sounds of insects, birds and whatever else was that was coming to life again after the helos were out of sight and making no more wop, wop, sound. I felt calm and nothing gave me an uneasy feeling, but I was coiled tight ready to spring. My mind wandered for a split second to great times on the Res with Little Bear...AND had he killed all my plants and flowers after all. Dave, George and Black 4 went forward for a snoop and poop to get intel.

Black 4 returned and provided a SITREP or situational Report. Open hand then closed fist - the enemy. 25 plus tangos, no electronic sensors, no sentries, no C4 - if they felt safe this was going to be a fatal mistake for them. Three different buildings with camouflage netting to process cocaine in different phases and Jack Pot, a twin prop Merlin loaded and ready to depart in within a day or two went to the front of Alpha's wish list.

"Listen" Black 4 whispered, "Y'all are going with me right up the tail pipe." referring to Guinea, Rodent and I. Black 4 gave hand signals to both teams and we moved out and crept into the shadows. Each team knew their jobs; take out tangos, rig each building with explosives and gather any friendlies and Intel. Each team has a communication, medical and EOD specialist. Of course, the big prize the Merlin.

Suddenly, automatic weapon fire erupted to our right. Charlie Team rushed forward as automatic weapon fire could be heard coming from the left and exactly where the Merlin and Alpha Team were. The friendlies hit the dirt. Bravo and the two of us lit up the building on the right and middle. Bravo was already to the building and started taking friendlies and rigging the 'Coke' building. It came across that somewhere along the line Alpha was missing or had a malfunction with the charges or rigs not exactly sure, but Knuckles took off in that general direction and I followed suit providing some cover as I ran. As we sprinted to the left, we were immediately encountered by a tango and before he could react, I hit him with half a dozen rounds and punched him back against a tree as the crimson blood surged from his chest. My left arm flew up and I took several ricochets to my flak jacket, but I pressed forward and followed Knuckles as we sprinted from tree to tree until I located Alpha. Our movement had drawn the attention of everyone in the compound and the tangos were letting loose with whole mags at once in our direction. The spray and pray method. Fire as many rounds as possible and pray that you hit something. I think these guys hated trees because I took a couple of splinters to the face and neck. I found it perversely enjoyable.

Linked up with Captain Dave and Knuckles worked with their EOD guy and BAM, no pun intended, they were in business. Knuckles felt like good ole Saint Nic handing out his bag of goodies like it was Christmas eve. We turned and sprinted towards the Charlie Team, who had pressed forward when we drew a lot of the fire in our direction. Hauling ass, we were showered with AK-47 rounds and more splinters, without the use of soap or shampoo. There was a quick succession of explosions from the direction of Bravo. Light, camera action. Time to put the women and children to bed and give the rest of these tangos a dirt nap or jungle nap in this case.

As soon as I got close to Guinea, "Oh shit I have been hit," Guinea squeaked as he bounced backward but still stood.

"Get down, get down dumbass, get down." I was yelling as I was running at him. I as I closed in, I can see he is bleeding profusely, a vast improvement to his face if you were to ask me. Sargent Javaras was standing on this other side and unloading in the direction of the tracer rounds. I lowered my shoulder and dropped his ass like Dick Butkus with a form fit textbook tackle straight to the jungle floor. Did I have to hit him that hard? Well, maybe, maybe not. I did a quick assessment, still breathing, still ugly, he was starting to realize the 'by the book' first in class will get you killed.

"Great hit." Sargent Javaras screamed over the roar of gunfire.

It was only a superficial wound, a ricochet to be exact, but his face was only a couple of feet from mine. I could see the tracer rounds rolling between the two of us. Lucky as hell or just plain good. Yeah, but I can dodge rain drops.

"Ok, puss nuts how about getting up off your ass and start shooting back."

Black 4 and the others had pressed forward and straight into the firefight, and I wasn't going to be left out. As all three groups press the action, the bad guys thought it was a good idea to run like hell. The group let off full clips just to make sure they understood the fire power against them. Most were hired merks and didn't have skin in the game, so they were not going to risk thier life for an above average payday.

Black 4 turned, "Time to go, call the Birds." I drifted back to the Res and remember how I could call the crows to come to me when I needed them. I could also send the crows to the sick. At night, right before I go to sleep, I would pray to the Great Spirit and ask for his guidance and to send the crows to heal the sick.

"Bossman, call for the birds." Black 4 yelled.

I pulled the SATCOM and requested transport. "Alpha one, seven, niner." paused "Alpha one, seven, niner, Kitty Cat, over."

"Gotcha Kitty Cat,"

"Exfil, over."

"Copy, inbound for the cat box in 10, Kitty Cat."

The Spec Op Captains did what they were trained to do and as efficient as ever we were headed back the way we had come. We had gone into about three minutes of a cascading symphony of explosions and provided the enemy with a loss of over a thousand kilos and potentially a couple million dollars of coca going up in smoke in just a few seconds like a group of sailors pulling into a foreign port dropping three months of salary on hookers and alcohol. The big prize, one tricked out Merlin that provided a treasure trove of information and two dead pilots.

We were escorting 15 friendlies, and subsequent families, headed for the United States of America, courtesy of Uncle Sammy and your tax dollars, however we did take out 17 tangos that wouldn't be helping cast the Grim Reaper onto our streets back home especially to reservations.

Bob Barker provided my parting gift of 10 plus stitches to the face and neck, eight stiches to my right forearm, new camo outfit for my shredded Swiss cheese attire. Guinea and two others needed stitches and a few sprains, bruises but overall, no one was severely injured or killed so no paperwork for Lt. Colonel Happy Pants. Gunny sparks, always said the mores you sweats in training, the less you bleed in combat. Luckily, we had that guy on our side.

Since the broom welding neighbor from downstairs was banging the ceiling for us to be quiet, it was time to exfil.

We climbed onto the bird and started our ascent, Black 4 turned on Sweet Home Alabama and I was looking forward to several cold ones and introducing some young thing to MTL. It is my sparkling personality that draws them. We had three days to get checked out, fill out reports, down time and then back state stateside

Back to civilization and HQ for me and the Brady Bunch.

Chapter 28

MEETING THE MAN

Three months after my first time in Colombia, I was snatched from that dim cave by Martin Sullivan, Chief of Special Projects. Who was dear old Sullivan? Like Bushy-Bush, he emerged from the Lone Star State, though he was a purer son of The South. As soon as we set eyes on each other, we recognized a brother. Indian that I was, I even overlooked that Lone-Ranger-Esque white Stetson he wore. Martin was something out of a movie, but then, so was I. We were true-blue dudes, willing to stir shit up to get a job done.

In no time at all, I'd be up to my neck in it, but let's start at the beginning.

One bright sunny morning in June, Martin rang me up. He told me to high tail up to the DEA's den of all mysteries, the 12th floor, where I was to meet someone. Happy to leave my word processor (remember, this was 1991, sports fans), I went straight to the stairs and bypassed the elevator and flashed up twelve stories. Yes, I always took the stairs, I wanted to stay in shape. Ok, ok, I took the stairs so I could drink beer and stay in shape. I scanned my card, inputted the correct code, and was granted access to the glass ceiling. I endured the usual prepping and primping to wind through security, then I was at Sullivan's desk, in front of Mr. Bigg's big digs.

He stood, smiling, and held out a hand. We looked through one another coolly and I didn't say anything, but I like most people first off, and I wagged his firm hand with a grin. He added, earnestly,

"Good to see you."

"Thank you, Sir."

"How is your family?" as he turned to corner his desk and take a seat in his high back chair.

"Good, Sir."

"Harmon seems to be happy you are here and doing a good job. I guess he is providing you some guidance on weaving through the perils of work."

"Sir, as usual a gi-normous pain in the ass."

Laughing, "I heard it was the other way around, but I did see you and your playmates have received a few trophies for your actions down range."

"Flesh wound, I just rubbed some dirt on it." As he motioned me to take a seat.

"Your future boss, Mr. Bigg, is behind those doors. He's got something for you." Then he turned back to work, "Knight, good job son."

"Thank you, Sir." and I stepped lightly over the threshold toward six years of freak-showing the DEA way. And we'd freak it with the NSA, CIA, and the Policía Nacional de Colombia, too.

Sullivan had a pretty view of the tarmac and planes buzzing Washington National Airport (soon to be renamed for just-retired Great Father, Ronnie Reagan). If you looked down, you could see the greens below the DEA's south side, too. The acreage of his chambers nearly matched that of my dad's. In the coming months, I'd get used to the view.

There are Texas characters of all types, from J.R. Ewing to almost every cowpoke John Wayne ever played, but the best template for Wildman Mr. Big was Bo Darville from *Smokey and the Bandit*. Like Bo, Martin was warm, reckless, and loyal as any backyard brother from my BB-gun days. He was wearing jeans, cowboy boots, dress shirt with a leather woven bolo tie and his jacket and cowboy hat hanging close by.

After a hearty hello, he said, "I can tell you're Harmon's boy. We are going to do right by you."

"Yes Sir, I will do my duty." Boy, did he do right.

You'll never uncover it on a website search, but Bigg was in the early stages of setting up Project Mercury (which had not a thing to do with John Glenn going around Earth in a rocket). The initiative would take advantage of my clerical skills as well as my familial inclusion in The Administration's inner circle. I was the son of a duly-feared *capo*, after all—and believe me, it was some mafia-style shit, me, Bigg, and other *capos* sent in by Great Father Bush, were about to institute. Was it an accident that Guinea was assigned to Special Projects in Lorton, VA as well?

Once back at my desk in the dungeon of the fourth floor under the watchful but unknowing eye of my ostensible boss, Sara Nicely, I began acclimating to the work. But Bigg had given me a 10,000-foot view of what I'd be doing, and I was invited to "read on" to the project. They were going to create an intelligence division at the Administration, and I'd eventually get an overseas post of duty. I was going to pretend that I was an IT guy while I laundered money for Mercury to ship 'things' to various places, and use my field training to hunt drug lords and their labs. Which I just finished a training exercise in Bogota and realized it was a test. A test that I passed with flying colors as did The Brady Bunch. Eventually, I'd meet with the Bushie's political appointees, and we'd dance around the words we needed to use to communicate just exactly how we were steering government resources around in ways that were Illegal. But there was integrity to the game. As we pow-wowed with other agencies about attacking drug activity on a global scale, we worked faithfully to pull resources together— both the legitimate sort and their opposite—for a well-ordered war that would bring real results.

After Bigg sketched it all out, I was a true believer.

"You in, Agent?" he asked.

The whole thing sounded like a good romp to me, so "Hell, yeah, I am in Sir!"

Once you get into that spook stuff, you don't share it with anyone—not even your wife. At the same time, you have to rest in the trust that none of your colleagues are gonna rat your ass out as well.

2 CROWS in the SHADOWS

Bigg said that, if I got caught, I was only allowed to say, "I want my attorney," and he tossed me the card of the litigator I should call.

Fantastic fucking backup plan because I was thinking it had Fucked Up Beyond All Recognition (FUBAR) written all over it. That's right folks, bases loaded, bottom on the ninth, 2 outs and a SWIIIINNNNGGG and a miss, welcome to 15 years in a federal penitentiary.

By chance, I met the lady once at a conference at the DOJ after Eric Holder took over as Clinton's Deputy AG in '97. She was this Jewish girl, Nina, and mean as shit in the courtroom. At first, I just did some secretarial sleight-of-hand. I cooked the books that recorded the fate of 'hammers', 'staplers' and 'lamp stands' ordered for DEA offices all over South and Central America.

As you might know, they first started investigating the fantasy pricing of such items in the 1980s, and I've read lots of explanations of how toilet seats could cost as much as $10,000 in the government's various wings, but I can only bear witness to the machinations we were working in Mercury. A 'hammer' was an AK-47. A 'stapler' was a grenade launcher. 'A toilet seat' was 50,000 rounds of ammo so on and so on. I was stockpiling weapons for, technically it was for training and advisory purposes, transfer to Colombia—and these bore their actual military price tags—even if they flew beneath a more benign flag.

I'm probably as good-looking as Oliver North, but my bone structure never won film time before a Congressional Committee like him, thank God. Though, it could have.

I started doing my Ollie-North-style dance for the department heads. I was the foot-soldier set up to be the fall guy if an expose' happened. I worried a bit about that, but once I figured out what's what, who's who, and the widgets in the wheelhouse they'd assigned me to, I became cocky about the advantages of my sticky widget, too.

I came to realize, they needed my skills, knowledge, and chutzpah just as much as they needed their handsome mugs to be hidden. 2 Crows naturally juggles the high and the low, the dark and the light, and, in time, I learned just how to make myself both free and indispensable in a way I'm sure few other faceless bureaucrats ever were.

I remember feeling so empowered much of the time, with so many high government officials guarding my back, that I saw myself pulling out a G-Ride (government-supplied vehicle) into traffic on DC's Army Navy Drive and shooting up and or running over as many pedestrians as I had a mind to—and remained certain nothing would happen to me. Arrogance, well maybe.

Chapter 29
TAKING MY TURN

It was late June, and we flitted out around 13:30 from DC's Bolling Air Force Base. Near 17:30, we got near the Texas-Mexico border where red mountains ringed a utilitarian airfield in eyeshot of El Paso International—just on the other side of the Liberty Expressway was thick with the evening commute. We jockeyed our C-130 around the tarmac once we landed, steering toward a dusty depot at the field's edge. As we slowed, a small pack of M520 cargo trucks came laboring up, and our back door ramped open to welcome them and the extreme heat of west Texas.

The Shadow Strike Team Bunch strolled out the door to find a sortie of Army personnel without nametags happily unrolling forklifts and snagging more blond crates to stock up our fat turboprop.

"Hey Skip, see any toe tags on these sum bitches?"

"Hell, won't be that easy."

Let's open one and check the inventory." Rodent chided

"Naw." not yet, the time wasn't right I said in my mind's eye.

I knew it contained weapons, munitions, and mostly American greenbacks. I immediately thought of Ollie North, Iran Contra and where was that attorney's business card!!

Knuckles turn and with a shrug, "let's go make a drug deal."

"Amen."

No one asked any questions, everything went smoothly, and soon we were flying south again. Stuck in a crappy old jump seat in that cold-ass hold, some of these C-130s were 35 years old by then, and those thrones had seen plenty of grunt's butts over the years. The rest of the Brady Bunch were even more less informed than Guinea and I because of our high-level briefing. For all appearances, everyone on the flight seemed to be even less informed about what the heck we were up to than I was.

"Bossman, what gives?" Skip asked.

"Yeah, what gives?" Barbie seconded.

"Listen and trust me, when the time is right."

"Roger, Roger." all around.

This is the flight where I met a piss-poor West Pointer, turned DEA agent, who none other than Winston Wigginton Pendergast, IV. Remember this fucking guy, Mister Artillery danger close himself. Where did this guy's parents come up with this shit? West Point is known for developing some of the brightest badass sum bitches the world has ever seen. Well, Peterman, yeah, I had to rename this asshole, slipped thru the cracks and of course, someone must graduate last in every

2 CROWS *in the* SHADOWS

class. Enter former West Pointer and Special Agent, notice I said SPECIAL, Peterman.

"Cold as hell." I muttered and looked at Barbie, "You got THOs?"

"Fuck off Idiot." For those of you ill-informed patriots out there it stands for Titty Hard On (THO)

"Your first flight in one of these?" Peterman smiled.

"Yep."

"You?" referring to Guinea.

Guinea nodded.

"You?" To Barbie. Now is this duck, duck, goose.

"Yes, Sir."

Looking at me, "All these people with you?"

"Yea, the three of us are triplets and the other three are our brothers, Jim, Jimmy, and James."

The fucktard looked at me, then Guinea, then Barbie and then back at me. Then looked at our supposed brothers and shrugged. WTF, I am sure was going thru his feeble brain. Got skull fucked and didn't even know it.

"You're native?" Referring to me.

"Yea I am Jeronimo, he's Sitting Bull and she's Pocahontas, and the J brothers over there are Tom, Dick and Harry. The boys were all smiles. Nice to meet you slur, as opposed to Sir, but numb nuts didn't catch it.

"No need to be disrespectful to a superior…ah, hum Agent." Peterman fumbled for a rank even if this wasn't the Army.

"Sir, I get it but we aren't in the Army and my Redskin ass doesn't report to you." I quipped.

"We will see about that, half of these items are mine.... Agent" again stumbling for a rank geez this idiot. I wonder if he needed instructions on how to wipe his dirty ole rosebud.

"It is obvious you don't know what you are doing"

"Ding, Ding, Ding!" I guess the sum bitch wanted a cookie.

"Much better if you keep it that way and your disrespectful comments to yourself" Really, God damn genius, I wish we had thought of that, and Guinea read my mind with that annoying fuck smirk I dealt with all through the academy. Barbie just cast her eyebrows skyward and rolled her eyes like a teenager.

"Listen, General......." Guinea chimed in. Well, that scorched his ass.

"You listen, Agent, I am a former United States Army Captain and just like you, now a Special Agent and also your superior. Peterman gasped and he enunciated every word. UNITED, STATES ARMY blah, blah blah. "I have heard all about the younger generation of supposed DEA Cowboys". Dude, I just told you we were Native.

"Do you think we are trying to initiate another wounded knee, sir?' Again, kinda like slurrr.

"What, both my knees are fine" again searching for a rank, I wonder if idiot was clearly stated, bolded, and highlighted, in yellow, on his resume.

Two seconds and "Agent, stick to your job and execute the plan and don't screw it up and I will make sure I delivery my report on your actions to the Country Attaché Wilson."

"Tell Big Poppy, Jeronimo said what's up?"

"What, wait, what?" I had enough of this idiot.

"Sir, I have more important things to do, saaayyy, like play with my balls."

"You are going on report."

Great, I am caring around a bunch of Whatamycallit, to deliver to Mr. Nobody, and I better not screw it up and I have to ride with this Asshat. Sure report whatever you need, but Big Poppy D. Keith Wilson and I were kinda friends. More like father and disrespectful son, oh yeah just like my current relationship with my ole man. Pop knew what I could do and loved it and so did Big Poppy so report away cat turd.

Another a few hours and we were landing in the beautiful city of Bogota, Colombia. We had been downrange to Colombia a couple of times before (and Peterman had not), once for observation and once for a live fire exercise that got me and the Brady Bunch recognition and a chance to start our careers in a blaze of glory. It was the a start of my life path that would change me forever in both a good and a shadow way. I am sure Guinea's panties were already soaked.

After touchdown at El Dorado International Airport on the Private Side of the Airport, which didn't exist, I did my clerk duties in that strangely cold air, steering crates into a special holding space close to where a few other C-130s idled outside the night lights—all painted up with Fuerza Aérea Colombiana

(Colombian Air Force FAC) colors. These were American gifts to the FAC to fight the drug war.

We were greeted by Agent Daniel Lumb, Sargent Javaras, and several other gentlemen in suits and sunglasses, and three in camos and carrying fully automatic weapons.

"Lumb, what's up Brother?" and "Nathan" with a bow and gave each a high five.

"Agent Knight, I believe you have some cargo for us." Oh, so said suit man, in dark sunglasses mind you, knew my name. My sterling reputation and way with people had proceeded me.

"I am not so sure, do you have a paid invoice or receipt I can review?" I retorted.

"Half this cargo belongs to me, Agent Peterhead just had to chime in and let everyone know who was in charge. Of what, the blue space between his butt cheeks.

"Ok smartass, move out of the way and let us take what is ours."

"How do I know what yours is and what is mine?"

Lumb, "Bossman, let them look."

"Hold on Hold on, I am Special Agent Pendergast, the ranking agent and some of this is mine."

The three camo guys locked and loaded on us, which means these sum bitches just chambered rounds. Well, you fucktards want a Mexican standoff, ok, lets order take out and watch this movie unfold. I hand signaled and The Brady Bunch immediately spread to formation so one bullet can't take out two people and all drew and chambered rounds.

Peterman, "wait, wait, wait, everyone stand down. Again, with the "I am the Senior Agent in charge of the cargo, we just need to make sure what is yours and what is ours."

It took a second, "Oh I get it, you are the Christians in Action." I mentioned. I knew this because 'they' funded a portion of my project.

"What the fuck are you talking about, Knight?" Suit man countered.

"You are doing the Lord's work but the rest of us don't know what that means."

"Fuck you, Knight, move out of the way."

"Say the magic word."

The camo guys smirked and lowered their weapons, one of which, Mikey V, would become a lifelong friend and ran all the counter terrorist activity worldwide for the Agency before retiring. You see the Christians in Action are the CIA, they are doing the Lord's work all over the world making sure the United States is protected.

"Knight get the fuck out of the way before I remove you"

"I stepped in the sum bitches face with my 6'3" frame and with his nose to my chest, "Magic word, pale face mother fucker if you want to keep your hair line where it's at." I casually mentioned as I had my hand on my Kbar.

It took a second but hearing his guard dogs giggle, he relented." "Ok, please cocksucker."

"Thank you, you may enter." "By the way, cock sucker would be Guinea and Barbie." Got the one-finger salute from both Guinea and Barbie, a fist bump from Mikey and Nathan, and a round of laughs from the rest.

"Do you have to piss off everyone, everywhere you go, Bossman.? Barbie mentioned as she walked by.

"It's just my remarkable people skills."

Peterman, "I am added this to the report."

"Swell, sllluuuurrrr. Just swell."

We loaded up and were shuttled to the Embassy thank God Peterman was in the second vehicle alongside Guinea, what, I did not do it intentionally. I needed to speak to our brothers in the State Department but first a visit to the head and then to Big Poppy Wilson's office. We got to the Embassy and I had to race like a piss horse.

Standing at the pisser, "thanks for sticking me with Asshat."

"Guinea I just needed you to get some Intel."

"Oh, don't worry that Asshat hates you, wants you to get reprimanded and sent home."

"Good, at least I made a lasting impression, can't wait for him to meet Black 4."

"By the way, Christians what was that all about?"

Fucking wop, "they didn't teach you shit on Staten Island did they, **Christians In Action**."

"I know that's what you said."

"Ok, Peterman, C I A." I didn't let on that I didn't come up with that, it was a term I heard my father use but hey he didn't need to know that.

"Oh, oh....Ok, I knew that, wasn't sure what you were trying to go with that."

Turns out Asshat beat me to Big Poppy's office, and we had to wait half an hour before said Asshat came out of the office and smirked at me.

"Well, well, well, three amigos or is it triplets, hope you have some ass left."

"Why is your mom hungry!" Fucktard.

We entered and immediately encountered a rather upset Big Poppy.

"Sir,...."

"How about the six of you sit down, have a coke and a smile, and shut the fuck up." or that works too.

"Roger." all the way around.

"I know what you and your merry band of misfits have accomplished in a very short time, but do you have to talk shit to a superior and make fun of him?" "Never mind, I don't want to listen to your 'made up' story.

Ok, fair enough. "Listen this guy has the resume and the connection within DEA and on the Hill so he can cause problems. I don't need problems."

"Roger, Roger" All around.

"Now, you already know Agent Lumb and Gummy and they will get you to settle into your quarters. Get settled for tomorrow and I will see all of you at 0730 Thursday."

"Roger, Roger."

"Knight, try to stay out of a Colombian jail for at least 24 hours?" Who me?

Chapter 30

EMBAJADA DE ESTADOS UNIDOS EN BOGOTA

Welcome to the United States Embassy, Bogota. In diplomatic usage, there are two ways to call the main dude who runs the show at each Embassy. First is the Head of Mission (HOM) and the second is the Chief of Mission (COM). Everyone I know called him or her, the Chief of Mission (COM). It came from the French "chef de mission diplomatique" (CMD) our oldest ally, so it makes sense. If you remember Benjamin Franklin was the head of a diplomatic representation to France during the American Revolution. While they are primarily referred to by the other titles mentioned above, it is common for the diplomatic corps of several countries to use CMD and Deputy Head of Mission (DCM) as the primary title for the second in command of a diplomatic mission.

Missions and foreign services ambassadors are political appointees rather than career diplomats, the deputy chief of mission may be a senior career foreign service professional and is generally understood to be more than a "deputy." This was good and bad. Career politicians are there for a reason and sometimes it is to advance their own future and career and don't always make a decision that is in the best interest of the boots on the ground. Bogota had a fantastic Ambassador and a smoking hot DCM, also great at her job.

Yeah, the lady I almost tripped over myself when I first saw her was the DCM. Later, I met her twin, who was from Italy via Costa Rica, in Santa Cruz Bolivia. Beautiful lady named Ale.

Agent Lumb had initially put us in the barracks that were inside the gates of the Embassy. This time were going to the Dog Pound which was a guard and gated community specifically built for United States citizens performing overseas assignments or Temporary Duty (TDY) assignments. They also allowed Agents to acclimate living abroad while waiting for family members to join them with senior level personnel were allowed to rent apartments in the La Zona Rosa district. The Dog Pound was only a couple of miles from the Embassy. It was like any other gated community back home except for a dual wall one with broken glass bottles laid with concrete on top of a cement wall, parallel to the outer wall. The glass was a cheap form or razor wire. Most of the time, employees don't actually live at the embassy with the exception of Marines and other emergency personnel. In most countries, the embassy is just like a normal office building, but with more security. Most people would go there in the morning, then go home at quitting time. The Brady Bunch and other essential personnel would be in and out at all hours of the day and night.

In most countries Diplomats lived in large homes or apartments that are individually rented/leased by the government that employs them, or in compounds, like walled apartments or housing complexes and in my case the Dog Pound, that belonged to the U S government. Rarely, are individuals expected to find their own housing, which must conform to security and cost requirements, and the government either rents those quarters or reimburses the occupants. However, this was Bogota and for all intent and purposes it was a war zone.

For us, we all lived in the Dog Pound. We doubled up with two people in a house, in what looked like a normal subdivision except we had our own security. Some individual houses occupied by the highest ranking, most visible, employees who do a lot of essential social entertaining had specific security details. Others rented or owned quarters are visited a few times a night and once or twice a day by a roving patrol of hired and trained local guards, who look at the place from the street and confirm that all seems okay. Of course, a lot of the drug lords knew who we were and only tracked us and didn't interfere.

Your neighbors were your work colleagues, there was a shop where a lot of familiar foods and duty-free alcohol was available. You could live and work there with little outside contact, depending on your role, if you so choose to do so.

I had regular contact with my local Colombian counterparts, and I was interfacing with several locals, and no not just the ladies, who spoke the language so had a better window on the society and normal everyday Colombian life than most. I imagine that this life is somewhat analogous to living in a tiny tight-knit village in past times because there is a hierarchy, there is expectation of shared values and duty, there is caution regarding outsiders and of course there is always knowing each other's business. It can be comforting or a little annoying and invasive. I don't need 'Aunt Bea' in my business.

Chapter 31

THE DOG POUND

The dog pound for me was very peaceful and quiet with lots of trees and various plants. Any town USA if you didn't know that you were in a third world country. A gated community with children playing in the streets, bar b ques, play dates, the normal stuff you would find on any given Saturday back home.

Guinea and I shared a house, on a cul-de-sac with three other houses in our circular world. They all had inground pools and of course we installed a hot tub for relaxing with the ladies.

Some reason our house became known as the whore house.

"Bossman, I just got off the phone with Loretta and she had all kinds of questions."

"Dude, I have been telling you to come out of the closet for months now."

"Look Asshole, all jokes aside."

"Ok, what?"

"She somehow found out that our house, or should I say your house, is called THE whore house of the Dog Pound."

Finally, some recognition for all the hard work I had been putting in.

"Really, does that surprise you, you know she made friends with Gummy, right?"

"Yeah, well, they are like besties and in fact they are talking about wedding plans."

"Wait. Wait, please tell me you didn't give her a ring, when we were home?"

"What if I did?"

"Then congratulations, you are hereby sentenced to life in prison with no chance of parole." I calmed him down, called Loretta and told her it wasn't as bad as it was made out to be, 'wink, wink' and it was me and not Guinea because he was a choir boy, so not to worry.

We had a gardener to keep the landscape looking good and the biggest convenience is the full-time foreign service national (FSN) maid, named Pamela. FSNs are a huge part of Embassy life, it makes our lives easier, and they get paid five to 10 times what they would make anywhere else. They were happy, very loyal, and we always treated them with the utmost respect, because they earned it.

Pamela was your grandmother type and tried to keep us out of trouble, well mainly me. She would always have our breakfast and lunch made prior to us leaving in the morning. Anytime we were at the Embassy she would call and ask what time we would be home for dinner and on the dot, when we walked in, it was on the stove, table was set and ready. She was a fabulous cook and kept the place immaculate too boot and she didn't kill any of my plants which was a big plus.

1800 Guinea and I entered the house, on the table was the traditional Bandeja paisa which is fantastic and one of our favorite meals. It includes beans, white rice, chicharron, carne en polvo, chorizo, fried egg, ripe plantain, avocado and arepa. With Pamela around and feeding us, I had to exercise to keep the sleek turbo machine in prime condition. We settled in just like if we had an apartment in Crystal City Virginia and walked to headquarters every day. It was a typical, normal daily life: Get up, go to work, work out, more work and home. Normal everyday life.

The war on Drugs had changed since the death of Pablo, it created a power vacuum, and a lot of scumbags were trying to fill the void. Our intelligence told us that coca production had increased in areas all over the Andean Ridge and we were tasked with disrupting and destroying the pipeline. 0900 on a bright and sunny Monday morning, we entered the briefing room, Big Poppy, Matt, couple of embassy types, Army Colonel, the usual planning a mission suspects and of course Asshat. We all exchanged nice, nice greetings.

Big Poppy looks at me, smiling, here we fucking go. "Knight you remember Agent Prendergast." Fuck you, Big.

"Yeah, its Winny Willy the 12th, right?'

"No, you know its Agent Winston Wigginton Pendergast, IV, thank you, Agent Knight."

"Great, but for now, I will be the one asking the questions around here, Peterman." Peterman looked for help from Big Poppy but didn't receive quarter. The bitch.

"Knight, Jesus, can we get on with the meeting?" Big said with a smirk, he fucking loved me.

Matt was watching and lowered his head laughing. I sat down next to him. "What?"

"Knight, you never cease to amaze me." Matt said smiling.

"Oh, you want to join my Jews for Jesus Club too?" Matt just shook his head again, but he likes me for some reason. Remember, Matt is very religious and, like everyone, if I like you, I have to prod you, just a little, and I loved Matt.

"Team", Big Poppy Keith started off. "We have planned a double attack on the same day in southern Colombia". See a double attack was something we had never done and quite frankly, I was wondering who thought about this and said great plan. It had FUBAR written all over it and if you forget the acronym, Fucked Up Beyond All Repair. Of course, it only took a few seconds before we found out 'danger close' Peterman was involved with the planning. Go figure, you are having a wet dream and are startled awake by his ugly creepy ass before the release. Yep, same feeling you get knowing Asshat planned this. He worked with the Army Col Roels stationed in Bogota to devise the plan that we were going to execute. Said full bird has a relationship with Peterman's father, a retired General.

"Operation Double Tap, gentlemen." Col Roels started off, "is the name for our planned mission." as he turned to focus on the map projecting on the screen. "This, as you know is camp

Bear" pointing at the compound on the map and referencing the Satellite Communications (SATCOM) photos from a few days prior. "This is Tap One and this is Tap two." again pointing at the locations and the SATCOM photos. "As you know, the dense vegetation can limit lines of sight and arcs of fire, but it will also provide ample opportunity for camouflage and keeping communications at a minimum". Jungle environments can also be inherently unhealthy, with various tropical diseases that must be prevented or treated by the spec op medical professional that were on board. "Your training was specific to jungle fighting with emphasis on effective small unit tactics and leadership" he continued." "We know the location, size of the force, everything, even what time the guards take a piss".

Glancing at Matt, I gave the Peterman is a turd look as I leaned in, "You know every classroom had a kid that ate the paste and I guarantee you the planner of this op is that guy." Matt, again shook his and head smirked.

Remember the War on Drugs was heating up, at least for face value, and DEA makes no bones about it, this was a push all the chips in by the United States government and it was multi-agency/military all the way around. Ever feel like a pawn on a chess board, yeah me neither, only when Peterman was around.

It seems the Christians In Action, the Army and Navy had decided to build, in less than a week a Forward Operating Base (FOB) for training purposes only. The Seabees showed up one day in the Chaparre Region in Bolivia, out in the middle of nowhere and in the blink of an eye a square mile of the jungle was cleared and a base established.

Yeah, you heard it, training purposes with live ammo, live fire and live training. Of course, they did. Remember the Vietnam war, yeah just like that. That is one thing that amazed me, you have dense jungle for 200 miles around with no roads, barely trails and one day you have a FOB. I will provide some details, so you get the picture. A FOB is any secured forward operational level military position, commonly a military base, that is used to support strategic goals and tactical objectives. Now remember the United States Government is only in South American for an advisory role to help instruct the Foreign governments on tactics, skills, leadership development, blah, blah blah. Now a FOB may or may not contain an airfield, hospital, machine shop, or other logistical facilities. The base may be used for an extended period of time and traditionally supported by a main operating base that are required to provide backup support. It also vastly improves reaction time to local areas as opposed to having all troops on the main operating base. The Seabees are incredible at what they do. A personal lifelong friend Kevin Haverford was a Seabee on the adventure. A great guy that had no sense when it came to selecting a university for his education but a great man and father. Later in life when he was retired and gotten his last child out of the house and off to join, you guessed it, the Navy, his wife announced they were having twins. So much for the new boat.

Chapter 32

SEARCH & DESTROY X 2

The Brady Bunch and the original team that had trained and functioned together, first as an instructional phase, then as a real fire exercise were sent to Forward Operating Base (FOB) in Bolivia. Welcome to Camp Bear, after the legendary Bear Bryant, Roll Damn Tide. DEA was just 'leasing space' primarily for surveillance aircraft but occasionally to act upon the Intelligence we gained from reconnaissance. Camp Bear was operating as a primary base for locating, identifying, and destroying clandestine drug labs and any enterprises supporting those efforts.

Bear would be our home for several days as we were going to carry out two strikes as fast as we could so one covert coca base could not be relayed to the other clandestine manufacturing facility and have the product and supplies moved to another remote location unbeknownst to the good guys.

One question I did have? Why was Uncle Sammie investing so much time, resources, and fat stacks of cash in the middle of nowhere for a sole purpose of drug interdiction? Don't think I will need that business card way out here.

After a final briefing on the latest Intel at Camp Bear, we lifted off in the early morning and the flew into the darkness. We were flying low and leveled off at 2000 feet or so as the first crack of sunlight started to break the darkness. We flew for about 40 minutes and started descending quickly to about 40 feet above the beautiful green, lush canopy, and the country below. As the sun began to rise, a beautiful rainbow sprang from the mist announcing our arrival but also displaying the humidity rising from the earth and the night that produced it. The pungent smell of leaves rotting on the jungle floor were already engulfing our ride. Colorful parrots were springing from the trees below trying to get out of our path.

As I looked across an occasional open area but mostly jungle, I could not help but wonder if a better place to live was right down below me. A calm, soothing place away from traffic, loud noises, violence, and crime.

I drifted to the past which I often did to seek my peace. I walked down the path to the river, I knew the geese would be up and flying announcing their flight with the same 'wa, wonk', 'wa wonk' that I heard for years. They were declaring the oncoming of fall as they were searching for a place to settle down for the evening. The flock, with bellies full of the alpha fields we had planted for our and their consumption were coming in low.

A storm was approaching from the south, I could smell the rain. I heard the thunder in the distance announcing the storms' location. Lightning flashed across the sky in its inter-mittent rhythm and spectacular form all the while heightening my senses of something lost. Not my ancestors but something of my own undoing. When night shatters the daylight into the brilliance of stars they fall on a broken heart, my heart. I bowed my head, asking forgiveness that can never be accepted for what I have done. I will always have a place in my heart locked away for my lightning in the bottle that I dropped and shattered into infinite. Fake friends are like Shadows, they follow you in the sun but leave you in when darkness settles in.

I was quickly brought backed to Black 4's loud, mini-boombox, blasting the usual playtime lounge lizard music, when it was abruptly turned off. Lights and music out.

These days, GPS can get you to within 11 inches of something with a cellphone. developed in the 70s to guide cruise-missiles to Russia's tundra silos before they could wipe out America, the U.S. had the only viable, full-planet system in the in the early 90s. Conveniently, it saved us the trouble of having to make "aerial bombing maps" of every centimeter of the Earth's surface—as we had before. In 1991, GPS promised to get us within 70 meters of our target, but we also had satellite photos and other means to steer by.

With satellites as guides, we flashed through the jungle via "Nape-of-the-Earth" flying, shunting down low between hills and under the jungle canopy when rivers were available—avoiding gunfire from our guards, or alerts from village look-outs on the cartel dole.

Flying low also kept the sound our rotors from traveling too far. Equatorial jungles are thick, as everyone knows, and the air gets more humid the closer you get to all that writhing plant life. Staying near the humidity and the canopy helped keep our rotor-burp from propagating very far. Our LZ was deep in the rainforests of the Reserva Nacional Natural Nukak Tunahi, not far from the subcity of Tomachipan, 425 miles south-southeast of Bogota and in Bolivia.

Alpha, Bravo and Charlie teams were galloping in on the three birds that were just as much on our team and guardians in the sky all under the protection of the Great Spirit. The Hueys weren't the same choppers that crashed in the Iranian desert and inspired my dreams of chasing baddies back in 1980 but these machines and the pilots that flew them were my kind of sum bitches, hardworking and reliable.

Not that this mission would resemble Operation Eagle Claw much because failure was not an option. These were damp jungles (not dry deserts), and our final target wasn't an embassy, but a tarp-covered coca factory in the bush. Also, The Great Spirit would be on the American side this time, and he had given us nice, clear weather, at least. The Huey's rose up over the last ridge and hummed low into a small clearing we'd targeted. The Intel was spot on, now I knew Peterman could not have been involved in planning this. The quick up and down put a pleasant feeling in the gut like an over quick elevator stop.

On the res we'd played a type of dodge ball that used lacrosse sticks and balls. The balls are hard, really hard when thrown at you 70 plus miles per hour and of course they hurt plenty if they hit you. The game taught you to be mobile, agile, as well as more hostile than the other guy. Otherwise, you ended up black, blue, and maybe even ball busted. The best time to play was mid-August when the mist and fog from the Pamunkey River cascaded across everything and provided terrific cover for ambushes. The elders told us the number of these fog days directly correlated with the number of snowstorms we had during the coming winter, but we had our doubts. Thinking back, I should have checked the Farmer's Almanac.

Just like in the BB-gun days, we sported no face gear. The sphere used in lacrosse is hard as a baseball, and flies from a stick just as fast. We fired them low, 'cause we knew thigh-shots hurt like hell and slowed adversaries down. Once, I got one in my hammy and fell instantly to the ground—it felt like my leg was broken—and it took me 6 months to before the fist-sized bruised healed. The impact-point looked like a comet. broken blood vessels trailed behind a tumescent, black-and-blue wound.

Sometimes, you'd think about pain as you headed toward a firefight. You think about friends, family, loss and the future. But like our initiation, those dodge-ball events endured me to pain, something that'd serve me well in the encounter to come.

Unseen missiles marking up my body were still dancing in my mind's eye as we hear, "Three minutes," comes over the radio.

Black 4 repeats "Three minutes." as we all make sure we are locked and loaded.

"One minute."

"Touching down."

"Touch base, two-foot, one foot, go, go, go!" the Huey's wheels touched down on target as lightly as Tinkerbell.

We were on the other side of a ridge from our objective. We had a good mile and half to tromp through before initiating encirclement and recon. In route, we passed over another open area. We'd call back to our Huey's to settle there after we cleared out the hostile groundcrew near that landing area. Also, a great place for "Dust-off Inbound" helicopter code for what the military called a medivac helicopter if anyone was wounded. Think back to Gator Boy and his amazing 'death roll'.

As we walked, the jungle smells along with that of rotting plant life, and stagnant water again envelops us but much more because we were enshrouded in our environment. Yes, humidity dampens sound, and most people don't know this, it increases odor; though they may have experienced that fact in a humid, stinky town, like New York. With heat and high humidity, there's more water molecules in the air to bind and carry odor particles to our noses.

We immediately split into groups, head on a swivel until everyone was accounted for. One-by-one, we descended into the shadows of the jungle. We spread out with Black 4 taking point for Charlie. I followed Black, then Guinea, Knuckles, Spec Op 1, Rodent, Barbie and Spec Op 2. Distanced about five yards from each other so as you know, one bullet can't take out two people. We saw a worn path but Black 4 moved to the right. Now why was there a path leading into the jungle, Intel said the target had it's own crude runway like most remote labs to use small planes to get in and out. Intel also said there was a small village that the laborers stayed at with their families at certain times and usually only seven to 10 people. It seemed odd but we didn't want to take a chance of running into anyone, so Black 4 cut our own path. Now progress was measured in feet and not yards, it was slow going. Black 4 was alert for trip wires, traps and like the Grinch in Whoville we wanted to avoid Noise, Noise, Noise. After a good thirty minutes we heard it. Is that music as Black 4 gave the hand signal, we squatted and waited. He moved to the left and disappeared into the jungle. If I didn't mention it, I love this guy and we are still friends to this day.

He came back and signaled to follow him, and we worked our way to the path we had seen before. It was a nice break, the air was cleaner, not as heavy and the grayness was a distant memory. We inched our way forward and could see an opening with a large berm directly in front of us. We moved forward and spread across the berm and waited. After 10 mins or so, Alpha company broke free and spread to our left followed shortly but Bravo on our right. See they didn't have a path, but they were all highly trained spec ops guys and well, you get it.

We crawled up the berm and peered into what looked like a church celebration which made sense, it was Sunday, but Intel was a tad bit off. Everyone was nicely dress, at least for being in the middle of nowhere and in the jungle. People were sitting on makeshift picnic tables while a couple guys with a guitar and horns played festive music. Large round pots were sitting on fire pits boiling and steaming food. Black 4 sent Skip, he was fluent in Spanish and Guinea up to see what they could learn. Good idea sending Guinea to get a SITREP. The rest started setting up a perimeter and shortly they were waving us up,

"Great, you assholes give away our position!," I whispered.

Black 4, "I thought the same thing." he signaled for four us to get up and follow with the others would cover and watch our six. Alpha and Bravo followed suite but only left one behind for each flank and four others spread out wide as the main group moved forward for the meet and greet.

I got up, went forward, and learned it was a Catholic Celebration and they invited us to join them. Well, ah shucks making friends again. As we approached, I was watching the dishwasher scrape food off the plate, dip the plate into another bowl of soapy water, and finally rinse it in another bowl of dark river water that reminded me of the Gator Hole.

"Hey Guinea, like some of the dark iced tea they are washing the dishes in, they said it's called Gator Juice." Got the finger and the smirk.

Here's your nice clean plate. I like my small intestines exactly where they are, so I told the everyone to watch me. I loaded up the plate with corn, two inches thick, and didn't put anything else directly in contact with the plate. The corn is called elote and is bigger than the normal kernel but has a great taste.

Looking at the team, since I was first in line, "Remember, do not eat the big white mint you probably found in the urinals during a night of drinking." I casually mentioned.

To a man, "roger that!" the food was great and like most local people, they were afraid of the Cartels and were forced to work to protect their families. They made a ton of money by Bolivian standards, but it was forced labor to a degree.

Reminds me of stories told by the campfires back home. The whites came and our way of life changed forever. Our traditions and even language was changed or subverted, and they introduced disease, which we had no defense and of course Alcohol. I remember being told, "You don't look native." How about I get drunk on fire water, kick your ass and then scalp you, would I look native enough then.

We kept a perimeter but learned that it was a traditional holiday, and the cartels were celebrating in their camp a few thousand yards ahead beyond a small stream and were most likely drunk. Plus, it was a day of rest and more drinking and hopefully they would get a few new breathing holes courtesy of The Brady Bunch.

Small stream? "Hey Guinea, they say there is a small Gator Hole up ahead."

"Fuck that and fuck you if you think I am dipping a toe in that bitch."

"It should be fresh water so only caiman and they are smaller and less aggressive than your ole friend Godzilla." the brains and beauty of the group mentioned.

Fortunately, no one lost their stomachs enjoying the meal, the people provide valuable intel, so we paid them, told them we would return but to gather everyone and be ready to evacuate.

"Pigpen, Black 4 over."

"Go ahead."

"We have 15 plus friendly's that need exfil at original location, proceeding to target."

"Copy Black 4, Panther inbound location."

We instructed then to head back the direction that we came and wait for a helicopter, they were getting out of here. Then we start off in the direction of the target and to Guinea's potentially new swimming hole.

After 30 minutes of drudging through the jungle at a snail's space we encounter the Gator Hole. We continued and before you knew it, we were chest deep with M16s above our heads and we slowed way down. To make matters worse it started to rain and there was mud and silt and everything else clogging down everything and eventual we were worn out and the weapons got pushed into the river water. One by one we climbed to the far back and clambered out, after 10 minutes the rained slowed to a drizzle and steam rolled off our overheated bodies and it was a relief. Nathan pointed up and through the trees you could see smoke lifting in the distance, and he also pointed to a makeshift bridge to our right with Bravo company waving at us. Villagers failed to mention that.

We stripped our clothes and squeezed the excess water and other shit out of our pockets, boots and butt holes, then, took apart the M16s, rinsed the springs, followers and magazines clean. All the while Bravo set the perimeter and laughed at us for not seeing the bridge.

I did, however, manage a glimpse at Barbie's assets. "Hey, Barbie, you sure you aren't Cinderella, 'cause I sure as hell can see that dress disappearing at midnight." Of course, you know how that conversation ended.

After half an hour we pressed forward. Black 4 gave the signal and Dave and George moved forward for a sneak and peek. They came back and provided a SITREP to each group independently. Around 30 cartel members all celebrating and no one guarding anything. If we hit them hard and fast, it would be a total surprise and we can cut all communications immediately for our next attack without anyone even knowing we were here.

Alpha team on our left and Bravo team to the right, us in the center. We pressed forward at slow, cautious pace. We moved about 15 yards when the roar of the fully automatic weapon fire broke our silence. Well, the residents of WhoVille knew we were there with all that Noise, Noise, Noise. We took off double time and let loose in double tap fashion looking for fresh targets on the move. This was again a true fire fight which Intel advised that they would 'spray and pray'. As fast as it started, it was over. The bad guys had taken their drunken and/or hung-over asses further back into the jungle to escape didn't leave much of a trail unless it was some of the empty Jack Daniels bottles strewn here and there. Yep, these guys liked JD.

We set a perimeter and looked for anything that could provide intel for future operations. Out of nowhere, "Gentlemen, drop Red on your location." Came Duck over the airwaves.

"Roger."

Duck buzzed in a drive by fashion 20 feet above us that would have made the Bloods and Crips proud. We did as we were instructed and not 10 seconds later Big Bird was just above blasting the nose cannon exactly where the bad guys had retreated.

"Beautiful, beautiful."

"How's that Black 4?"

"Roger that, looks like you wiped them out."

"Roger that, banking, for one more flyover."

"Beautiful, you hit right on those mother fuckers."

Once the birds were done with the crop dusting, we moved in. We found flight charts, large amounts of cocaine to be transported from the site and had an approximate idea of when and where it was intended. We relayed the information to Pig Pen. We set the charges on everything and made sure to destroy all communications equipment and fortunately for us it appears that all radios were in one place. Dumbasses. Radios weren't going to work in the jungle to alert anyone more than several hundred yards away.

Fire-in-the-hole and we moved out and after 20 seconds there was a loud explosion that shook the ground we were standing on and left a large black smoke trail spiraling skyward. If they didn't know we were here by now the smoke could be seen for miles, I am sure.

In all, 13 tangos were face down for a jungle nap and by the looks of some of the trails laced with maroon streaks several wounded and potentially fatally wounded lie in the distance. The boys and Barbie only had some minor scrapes, bruises and maybe waterlogged toes. Well, Guinea did have diaper rash and skid marks in his britches.

We got back to the Church Celebration, and only a few people were left, the Army had come in and scooped almost everyone up and departed in true military fashion, precision as its finest. We gathered the remaining men and got them ready for the first step in a very long journey to the greatest country in the world in a matter of weeks for resettlement state side.

Flash to young me sitting in front of an Elder and him explaining that we are judged by the fierceness of our enemies. You will face trials and tribulations and you must learn when to kill and when to spare a life. The greatest warriors are defined by the fierceness of his enemies and how he treats his defeated enemies.

We were getting good at what we were doing, and I liked it. I liked the violence. Maybe too much. But time for the next show.

Chapter 33

PHASE II

After 20 minutes, we were all on the Birds headed for the next target. We all got food, MREs and lots of water and closed our eyes for the 40-minute flight going fast and low. We hung on tight because the pedal was to the medal. We knew the target was a major transportation port, by jungle standards, and if we hit it today, there was a good chance we could put a major dent in the Cartels Airforce, transportation, distribution, and supply network.

We flew in hot but again it as soft as falling on a pillow top bed. We did the drop and hop, scrambled, spread out before all hell hit the fan. Not sure if they were warned or they just got lucky, but we were spotted or maybe heard. Rubber Duck didn't hesitate one second and the door gunner was blazing the edge of the jungle. One thing that jumped out to me was when a tango was hit, it stunned him and I could actually see the bullet go out the back of him in a crimson mist along with bone and flesh. I couldn't see it go in his front but I sure as hell could see the bullet go out the back. That's up close and personal, you can't see that shit from higher up.

Big Bird was banking hard to the left in the direction of the coca camp, and we could hear the nose cannon going off as it disappeared out or site. Alpha, Bravo and Charlie were spraying the tree line and started moving when the noticeable fire had reduced to single pop shots. Reminded me of mom making Jiffy Pop for Saturday night movie nights. Kernels popping like crazy, then slowing to only a pop every now and again.

Out of nowhere here comes a slow and low flying twin prop trying to get altitude. A bird rolled in from behind with the nose cannon lightning his back side up. The plane was so low, and being blazed, we all dropped to the ground as dark, heavy, smoke began trailing as the plane lowered to earth and crashed into the jungle couple hundred yards away before another copter was on it with another full spray from the nose. It must have burst into flames because within seconds the gas tank exploded. No bayonetting the wounded today.

We turned our focus to the jungle and double timed it, well as fast as we could. Coming right back at us were obviously the tangos that had been cutoff when the birds hit the landing strip. Unbeknownst to us, Big Bird spotted the plane just coming up over the canopy and lit his ass up and radioed Rubber Duck to drop the hammer effectively strafing the runway and cutting off any chance of escape to anywhere but back towards us. Like herding cats' boys.

Dusk was now settling in and the sunset was waning and soon complete darkness would envelop the landscape.

2 CROWS *in the* SHADOWS

Although the burning plane behind us would provide light, it would also create silhouettes like paper cut out targets for our foes. Black 4 gave the signals left and right and we pressed the advance forward. I was snagged and flung to my left, spinning before I hit the ground but was up fast and returning fire. Damn, that felt like when I got kicked by a horse when I was a teenager. When we entered the jungle, we could make out figures moving back the way they had come but the Birds were hovering around the airfield.

We continued to press forward until I could squint into the darkness and just make out the thick row of white gas-cans and tent-poles reflected in our target by a few cans that were on fire and two planes on the ground that were engulfed as well. The cans would be holding kerosene or acetone, used in the refining process of coca and were highly flammable. We'd be happy to make that cache go boom.

But I saw moving figures there, too, sprinting across the airfield to the other side while the door gunners were letting the guns eat.

We were here to inflict as much damage as we could and destroy their lab and take as many of them down with it as we could in the process. Suddenly, I was face to face with a bad guy. Where the fuck did he come from. He was just as shocked to see me, and stood straighter, his eyes wide, and tried to lift his muzzle, but before it got straight, I clicked off six rounds, punching him back against a tree and, in the dim light, watched a swell of black liquid oozed across his chest. I didn't need to worry about him.

However, a lot more tangos were breaking free to get the hell. More fire scattered my way. I had exposed myself with muzzle-blasts. Then my left arm flew wildly up from reflex, stinging pain shot through my triceps as bamboo shrapnel pricked it and popped against my flak jacket and the side of my neck and face. All at once, the tangos began throwing whole mags at us, just spraying and praying in all directions, exactly as we had be warned.

I think these guys hated trees, because the poor plants, shrubs and trees were fragmenting everywhere like a giant weed wacker had ascended from the sky. Probably because of the lacrosse games back on the Res (and so much else in my life), the pain was perversely enjoyable. As I said before, I'm not normal. I don't even have any empathy for myself so think how I felt about someone shooting at me. My campmates knew this by now.

We kept moving and linked up with Black 4, then began firing like hell at our tangos, now in full throttle with their AK's. I distributed oodles of goodies back at them like Santa gone mad, flinging candy canes at the Christmas Parade. And as Dave and Alpha Team held their ground, I turned and sprinted back towards Black 4 to get round their flank and help close the little pincer move we'd orchestrated.

Again, AK bursts struck all around me, more wood chips flew, and bam my ass went backwards, stunned for a second, I was awakened when I heard explosions from the direction of Bravo. What we didn't know was that there was another group of tangos that had just arrived for a changing of the guard.

2 CROWS *in the* SHADOWS

Bravo's timed fireworks display was rocking the night. The processing areas spasmed into flame, I retreated into the darker brush back from the assault's front line, beyond our tango's immediate scope of attention, and the enemy's fire tapered off.

Didn't say anything but I thinking I broke my rib, pain don't hurt, just lets you know you are still alive. Looked down and saw the trail of blood right below my flak jacket. It really pissed me off and hoped I got the sum bitch that shot me. It was a ricochet and not a full on shot from a AK-47. If it had been full on, I wouldn't be here today. That's twice if anyone is counting.

Sound of the fire fight was diminished very quickly, again dwindling down to only sporadic fire. This time, they were really running but there's no white flag so keep shooting just to be sure. As I learned, Cartels, whether good or bad, seemed born to revel in death, bullets, and blood. In the Bolivar wars, the cry 'no prisoners' was like an echo chamber!

With constant assassinations of both the high-born and low-born in Bogota and everywhere else in the region, it seemed like nothing would ever change. The Andean Ridge wars were not gentlemanly affairs the gloves were off, hell, they didn't have gloves to start with. Like that Maryland set, this was a tribe of piss-poor shooters. They did little, if any, targeting practice, I'm sure, and they used AK-47s—a ubiquitous, cheap and reliable machine-gun—but most of our guys used M4's—with less recoil, more range, and better accuracy. Plus, we trained with our tools—and we trained on how to advance as a team.

We set up a perimeter and looked for additional intel, but it was dark, and we were staying put.

"Kitty Cat, Pig Pen over."

"Go ahead Pig Pen."

"Birds are headed home, stay low and wait for exfil at first light."

"Roger, Pig Pen."

We all knew we had been in a real fire fight and no way I was going to sleep. I was now in hyper vigilant mode. It was something that haunted me for many years, along with Post Traumatic Stress Disorder (PTSD) but I never told anyone or even spoke about it. They say the dragons will come to roost. We got something to eat and even heated it up because no way those mother fuckers were coming back. Some slept, mostly spec op guys because, well they are spec op guys, as we traded off picket duty.

I saw Barbie sitting by herself looking up at the bright moon. "Beautiful, isn't it?" as I approached. She quickly turned her head, but not before I saw the tear running down her cheek. "Are you ok?

"I'm fine." As she faked a smile.

I sat down beside her. "What's going on Lucretia?" Yeah, I used her real name, I have a heart sometimes.

"You know 2 Crows, when my parents were killed in the car accident, I was sent to the other side of the Res to live with my uncle. He was supposed to raise me. Well, he raised me alright. From the time I was 7 until I knew better and put a stop to it."

"Holy shit, I am so sorry." As I put my arm around her.

"No need. You know Res life. Women and children go missing all the time and it is kept quiet. It's not reported, and people don't talk about. Well, I was not going to be quiet."

"Yeah, I know, and things are kept close."

"You mean hidden." I could only nod.

"My uncle was an alcoholic and got drunk a lot, especially at night, and he liked to smoke in bed."

"I'm listening."

"Well, one night the house caught fire and burned down. It must have been a lit cigarette that caught the sheets on fire when he passed out. I guess we will never know, now will we." She said with a smile.

"No, I guess no one will ever know." I said giving her a smile and a kiss on the forehead.

Indigenous women are more likely to go missing or be murdered than any other ethnicity. Because the population of Indigenous people is small (making up 2% of the population), it is not reported on a lot and kept 'hidden'. However, more than four out of five American Indian and Alaska Native women have experienced violence in their lifetime.

As I got up and started walking away, "Hey Bossman, this doesn't mean we are going to be swapping spit in the shower later."

My turn, I gave her the one finger salute and a smile. "I gotcha, Barbie."

We were up 30 minutes prior to daybreak, remember our rules? We collected anything useful and destroyed everything else and boarded the birds for home. One of our special operators trained medics spotted the dried blood and asked to see the wound.

"Bossman, congrats, looks like you have been a shot."

"I am good."

Reaching into his medical bag, "You are looking a little pale. Reached over, pushed my eyelid up, examining my pupils. Looks like you might be in shock. Let me give you a drip and a little something to relax."

"I am good, Brother."

Black 4 looked at me, shook his headed and said, "Please, cock sucker." See Black 4 wasn't asking me, he was ordering me. I just nodded. Thanks grandpa. You know, one thing I do know, I never heard Superman ask for help.

I did as ordered, relaxed a little and got on the happy train.

We were flying fast and out pacing the other birds which seemed a little strange. As we approached, I could see it. A gurney was being brought out. Ok, Really.

I looked at "Black4, I fucking walked on this bird, and I am fucking walking off."

"Copy Bossman, but you know the rules." Pushy bastard. So, I want to walk, Black 4 said I need a ride, who am I going to make happy, right. Maybe blame my poor upbringing.

I thought to myself, "Way to ruin my day or week or month."

Luckily, Bear had a surgical center, again I was wondering why but they did. I had a surgical procedure to remove a small piece of shrapnel, received a few stitches and a couple weeks of Rest and Relaxation (R&R) and some time to meet some lovelies back in Bogota. It wouldn't be long before once again I would be lurking in the shadows looking for the next raindrop to dodge and making sure the crows were watching over me.

I had been scathed and done a lot of damage to a lot of people. In reality, my sword was double edged and the walking wounded survived.

Chapter 34

RECOVERY

All and all it two successful missions and a first for two raids executed in one day, a true interagency mission. For the DEA folks and a few others, we received the United States Attorney General's Award. The highest award within the Department of Justice (DOJ). The team and I returned to Bogota where I was assigned to rest and stay away from the Embassy followed by a month of light duty which meant boring.

"Guinea, what are we doing tonight, it's Friday and let's go."

"Boss, your wounded ass needs to sit your ass down, chill. Watch some TV, drink a beer, get in the hot tub." Now, if there was a hot brunette involved, that would be a great plan, but I didn't consider Guinea hot nor sexy.

"Senior Knight, que hora la cina?"

"Cinco por favor, Pamela"

As usual all you have to do was give Pamela an estimated time of arrival (ETA) and something fresh and delicious would be on the table at exactly that time. If you were late, it never phased. She didn't have a big family and she looked at me as her grandson. Loved that lady.

"Senior Knight, why don't you put a revolving door out front?"

"Why is that?" I asked.

"For all the women that come here."

Well now, "I have a lot of friends." I quickly countered.

"Oh, yes, I understand, Guinea and your boys....and a different woman every few nights." stated firmly why hands on her hips. "Why don't you try and settle down with a nice woman, a nice Colombian woman."

"I don't need a nice woman, I have you," I said with a wink.

"Your tricks don't work on me, and I am married."

"Yes, but you love me in spite of my small, singular fault."

I tried to make the place feel like a home by decorating with some of the artifacts I had brought with me. I large dream catcher with a black fox head in the middle. It was my grandfathers, Walking with the Wind prior to being handing down to my father and subsequently me. Pops thought it was a good idea that I brought with me on my travels. Maybe he knew that in the future some dreams might haunt me. Pease pipe and everything to do my cleansing that included shell, wooden matches, sage and sweet grass. Had my poster of Daisy from the Dukes of Hazzard on my closet door. Yeah, I kept that and Farrah for old times sake.

I also had plants and fresh flowers, especially if Guinea was coming over, sweet cheeks liked roses. Most people do not know that Colombia is the second largest exporter of flowers. I keep my house and yard covered in shrubs, plants and flowers year-round Chrysanthemums, Roses, lilies and the like.

The hot tub was large and a nice way to relax and frolic. One rule, no clothes in the hot tub, it will ruin the filters. Unless you are a dude, and no such rule applies and of course it is never mentioned. My bedroom was adorned with as afore-mentioned, Roses and Lilies and this always made me think of the Res; honey suckle in the early summer, blackberry picking, sun flowers in the fall and gentle snow covering the home. Fall is my favorite time of year on the Res, when the leaves of the live oaks and hickories cascaded down to the forest floor. The forest has the earth smell and a sense of peace.

Colombia is known for its music and there was no short-age of clubs for us to go hunting. I got to meet a little-known singer at the time and hung out with her on a couple occasions, Shakira. She was only famous in Colombia and came from a town called Barranquilla on the Caribbean Sea which is the largest city and third largest port in the northern Caribbean Coast region I was dating, if you call it that, Catalina, her sister Rosa and Shakira were besties as they went to private school together. See Catalina and Rosa's parents were both dentists and well to do. However, kidnapping was huge in the 80s and 90s, so they always had to be careful and had body guards until recently.

We attended one of Shakira's rarely performances in an arena in the countryside with about 2500 people. Yep, 2500 out in the middle of nowhere Colombia. After the concert we all gathered under a makeshift veranda on picnic tables and drank a lot of cerveza, snacking on nuts, shredded meat, beans, rice and cheese. When it was time to go, all seven of us climbed into a cab, yep, and little Miss Shakira got the privilege of sitting on my lap. Didn't know until years later that the little hottie sitting on my lap would become famous and an international Super Star. Her loss. Claim to fame for some, I guess. But I had bigger fish to fry.

On a nice warm summer night with the smell of flowers, and food trucks covering the area like a welcoming invite, we entered the Disco District. Two or three roads that dead end with bars, and a ton of beautiful women. The joke was that one guy had to populate the entire country, because the other guys were too short and ugly.

We went to the Gato Negro (Black Cat); a beautiful indoor/outdoor dining and dancing club, where in fact I met Catalina and Rosa. Hey if you are successful, why change that up. After dinner, remember it is customary to have dinner at 2000, 2100 or so. It is also customary that as the evening got later, the lights got dimmer and the music got louder. People would be dancing on the dance floor and eventually as the tables were cleared on the tables. Now these were sturdy old school tables and a 350lb could get up there and be fine. Now, I don't want to see that, but Guinea might. He liked going hogging. Fortunately, all the women here were in shape and sexy. After a while the bar would become saturated with people on top of tables. You just tapped a leg, they stopped and you got your drink. Never work here in the states but it sure as hell worked there. The place was full of beautiful young ladies in sun dresses and not to mention every woman in the country wears high heels. The music was South America traditional and famous Hispanics living in the United States, Ricky Martin, Shakira, etc.

"Damn if this isn't a target rich environment." Guinea said with a familiar twinkle in his eyes.

"Yeah, talk to all the boys you want."

"Knuckles and Skip hit the two in the left corner, leave the guys for Guinea."

"Roger."

"Roger."

"Why are you such an asshole?"

"Born free and just plain lucky would be my first assumption." I asserted. "Plus, don't you have a betrothed back in Staten Island?"

We have a rule, no one goes alone and always designated driver so to speak. It did not take 5 minutes before the target was lit up and one of the most attractive women, I have ever seen made a beeline towards yours truly. It would appear as though my painted target had other ideas about being a target and distinctly though that I was the target – and my first impression was, there is a God, and he loves me!

Alessia introduced herself and her friend Margarite to Guinea and I and asked if we worked at the Embassy. Both spoke excellent English and that told me they had money, and lots of it by the way they were dressed, and most likely received their high school or college education in the good ole U S of A.

"Yes, I am Manuel Noriega and my twin brother, Guinea, he is gay and just got out of prison." Of course, they both laughed and then called me a liar.

"Yes, we both do computer work at the Embassy." Guinea chimed in flashing that damn ugly smirk. Was he trying to FUBAR this before it started.

"You will have to forgive my ignorant friend, prison life was hard on him" Again laughter, a way to a woman's heart and her thighs is laughter unless you are Guinea then a roofie works just as well.

"No, no, you two are either Drug Enforcement or CIA." Wow, now everyone in country thought anyone who worked at the embassy was DEA or CIA. They didn't understand, yeah there were a lot of us but there were computer personnel, electricians, HVAC, plumbers all kinds of career paths.

"Let's dance."

"Absolutely."

I took Salsa dancing prior to leaving the states. Language and dance classes as Gunny Sparks would always say, be prepared and know your adversary so I planned to dance my way into the sheets so to speak.

When I got the opportunity to add the pulsating move of Michael Jackson's hips into the crotch of Alessia, Dios Mio was the first thing out of her mouth. Yep, could have pointed to the outfield wall like Sultan of Swat, Babe Ruth, because this was a homerun and all I had to do was round the bases and slide into home plate. But......A big but, something was not right and my high and tight stood on end. The Great Spirit was speaking to me. We talked, we danced but I could not shake the feeling. I made a hasty retreat and of course, the ribbing I received about my manhood would follow.

"See you tease me about men, now we see the truth." Guinea stated with that annoying smirk.

"Bossman, what gives, she was smoking hot."

"Yeah Boss, what gives, maybe a sheep or goat would suit you better." Knuckles chuckled as the last of the Peanut gallery chimed in.

"Let's go, I need to go to the Embassy."

"It's 4 O'clock in the morning, can't this wait?" Skip asked.

"You guys hit the sack, I have to check something out."

I left empty handed but not in my mind. I enter the Embassy and head to the SCIF. I am looking for classified information and any Intel on Code Name: Super Model X – Yes, I came home empty handed and no I did not get Super Model X mud for my turtle but there was something else.

A few weeks later and the same thing happened. Alessia was there and of course beelined straight to me and she had a purpose and was intent on satisfying the itch in between her thighs. See, sometimes girls just want to be bent over a couch and banged like a screen door in a hurricane.

"You never called me and never returned any of my messages"

"I was really busy." I countered kinda caught off guard by her persistence.

"Pamela was so nice." The bitch was at my house?

Off we grinded, kissed and basically fucked on the dance floor but something just wasn't right. My 'spidy' senses are never wrong.

This lady would not give up and I had zero Intel and that made me nervous. It was like she didn't exist. I called the Country Attaché Big Poppy and let him know that I was going to hire a Confidential Information (CI) to get the Intel on a person I had no evidence was doing anything wrong but I wasn't satisfied. Maybe I should have called his cell and not his land line at 0200.

Yep, still empty handed, no mud for my turtle and nothing on what I really wanted; who is she?

A few weeks later, still resting and relaxing, we went out and about hunting again and eventually went to the Gato Negro and low and behold, Super Model X. Unfortunately, this time I was drinking, and I didn't go home empty handed, and I did get mud for the turtle and a lot more than I expected. About the time, Miss, or should I say Mrs. Super Model X walked her very satisfied sexy ass out my front door and was heading home to wherever that was, the phone rang. My informant was on the other end, "Bossman, she is Mrs. Amado Carrillo Fuentes!"

Great, fucking great, I just took one of the richest drug lords in Mexico's wife to meet God and she loved it. Like most drug lords, Amado Carrillo Fuentes was not a nice dude, and I am sure would be pretty pissed that his young wife got slayed in my hot tub, in the garden on my couch and well I treated her like my pinky toe and banged her on every piece of furniture I had and delivered the pecker paste. Amado controlled the Juárez Cartel after assassinating his boss Rafael Aguilar

Guajardo so no problem killing someone. Amado Carrillo became known as *"El Señor de Los Cielos"* or *"*The Lord of the Skies*"*, because of the large fleet of jets he used to transport drugs. He was also known for laundering money via Colombia, to finance this fleet. Now you understand why his wife was in Colombia.

So where do you go when you slept with a Drug Lord's wife. Home. I called the Country Attaché on his cell this time. "Big Poppy, I have an issue." I stated plainly.

"Knight, when don't you have an issue?!" I provided the 10-thousand-foot elevator speech.

"In my office in 30". I went to the Embassy met with Big Poppy Wilson. I knocked, "Knight, come on in and plop your ass in the comfy chair because it will be the only time your ass-hole won't hurt for about the next 6 months". Big Poppy always had a way to getting directly to the point. Big Poppy explained that he had informed the DCM, Headquarters and of course Pops!! "Listen, keep your head down and let me handle this."

"Roger."

Chapter 35

I WANT SOME CHICKEN

A few weeks later, nothing new on Super Model X and around 0100, on a cool night in Bogota the team in three armored suburbans, loaded with "equipment" from the secret side of the airport, streaked through the night headed to a new safe house where we were to set up operations. We would move safe houses on occasion to keep the Cartels guessing. We had located a safe house in western Bogota which is a secret place to hide people from the hostile actors (Cartels) and their actions against US Personnel, our Confidential Informants, and every-day Colombians.

Back home I would be getting ready for an early morning goose hunt and afternoon of black powder deer hunting, but here I was with my team, Shadow Strike. Passing a chicken shanty, I grabbed the radio and told the other 2 vehicles to proceed to the safe house.

"We are getting a midnight snack.", I belched over the radio. Bossman out.

We stopped short, I jumped out and made sure I was quiet as I slipped into the Shadows adjacent to the chicken shanty to get a good look and watched as the locals watched me. Not particular unnerving but not a hot brunette kneeling down in front of my pants either. As I moved through the shadows, fine filaments radiated with white gold from the fire pits that have been burning half the night. Inching closer, darkness around me began to splinter and break apart.

"Nothing stood out." I thought to myself but never forget about Mr. Murphy. I decided to enter on the right-hand side of the shanty, it kept me in the darkness, plus I could watch the other entrance.

As I entered, I was rudely interrupted by a gunman with an AK-47, typical jungle attire, bad attitude and looking right at me but I startled him. I fired the standard double tap, two rounds in quick succession and the pink mist blew out his back and dropped him to the floor. Bye Motherfucker, I thought but was rudely and immediately interrupted by two more gunmen. I just wanted some damn chicken as I let off another burst of .556 rounds and dropped both where they stood.

One I only hit once, so back to the firing range for ole 2 Crows, I guess. I slowly walked over, looked down and thought poor bastard, as a line of blood dripped down from his mouth. I fired another round to a face only a mother could love. Remember Gunny Sparks, "GentleMENS, anything worth shooting once is worth shooting twice, bullets are cheap but lives are expensive."

It is amazing how much blood a head shot generates not to mention my new crimson face paint with included blood, tissue and bone fragments, I glared at the old timers, and they gave me the 'well' look as I wiped fragments from my eyes.

"Well, what, Puss Nuts?!?" First things first.

"Abuela, eran parte del cartel?"

"Ella dijo que sí." she responded with a smile. I don't think she liked those sum bitches much either. Cartels would station personnel at these locations to work, intimidate, the locals and use them to gather intel.

"¿Había más" Negative was her answer, maybe she was a mind reader or afraid, but I placed an order but was immediately handed a large bag. I grabbed the chicken and potato offering, ordered more and turned to sit down and eat. Guinea and Knuckles were right there.

"What the fuck are you doing?" Guinea asked me as Knuckles scanned the area with his M16.

"Getting ready to sit down and eat some chicken." What the fuck did it look like I was doing?!

Knuckles asked if there were any others and told me the perimeter was being checked. I trusted the grandma so I wasn't worried.

"You fucking shoot three guys and they are laying right here and you sit down to eat some chicken."

"Yep, you guys want some." Quite frankly, I didn't see what the big fuss was about plus the green look on his face told me he wasn't about to have any chicken in the first place, the Candy Ass. Spearmint, if my sense of smell was correct.

"Guinea, calm down." Knuckles had his hand on his shoulder.

With a hard shrug and a jerk away motion, "Get the fuck off of me, you know he's missing something."

"Let's go to the colo." Knuckles pushed him in that direction.

After I was done, I gave grandma $300 greenbacks to take care of the mess, got the rest of my order and then left to see if I could get Guinea's panties untangled.

As I faded back into the shadow of the night, I turned to the old times and one more thing, "water your plants."

As we drove off back into the shadows of the cool night it did cross my mind as to what just happened - Grandma got a fireworks show, enough cash to live on for 6 months and three (3) dead tangos to clean up. Right or wrong the miniscule thought drifted off into the cool starry night. I did my good deed for the day, at least that is what I told myself. Plus, we still had to stand up the safe house before day light.

Did I just trade my passion? Now, was I fighting a personal war for greater glory?" Maybe, I thought to myself, as I stared out the window.

Chapter 36
DEPUTY CHIEF OF MISSION (DCM)

The time arrived when I got the call from Big Poppy that he needed to see me right away. If you have never had the privilege of getting sent home to meet with the Attorney General (angry by the way) of the United States of America, you just don't what living is all about. But I was making a name for myself and receive her Award for Valor so how mad could she be? I mean, right?

It had been several eeks since my involvement with Super Model X and surely, they have forgotten all about it.

"Pops???" I asked sitting across from Poppy.

Big Poppy looked at me "Yes, Sir. See Knight, your dad is in my chain of Command, I have direct orders to inform him every time you decide to screw the pooch, which in your fucking case is every week." Now, he was just bragging on me, we both knew it was every other week.

"What's next?" A visit to the Deputy Chief of Mission (DCM) since the replacement for the Ambassador had not yet arrived yet. Great, I am sure this will be a lovely time for everyone involved. I had four hours to get my story together.

A little background. At the Embassy, in a third world country, you live on an Island. It is your one safe place and reminds you of home. The Embassy held a happy hour every other Friday so we could feel like one big happy family and sing Kumbaya. Of course, I took it as a perfect opportunity to take advantage of the new arrivals; all the wild eyed young pretty things looking for adventure. Me and the guys are perfect tour guides for the uninitiated. However, there was one single lady that stood out from the rest and as I got to know her, I flirted with her on a constant basis, but I was getting nowhere. Kathy was exactly my type, petite, jet black hair, puppy dog eyes, and extremely intelligent. Remember, I first saw her in the hallway and asked her to join our Jews for Jesus club. Maybe when I was hitting on her, I should have thought that she had two staffers with her.

"Hello Beautiful, looking stunning as always," I winked.

"Knight, don't you ever give up?"

"Come on Kathy what's a little couch bouncing among friends."

"The way I hear it your couch is worn out not to mention stained," She said with a smirk.

"Now who would tell a lie like that?" I ask incredulously.

Kathy, cocked an eyebrow and gave me the 'Really' look and stated plainly, "THE whorehouse!"

As I turned to leave, "Knight, they are expecting you, they know your reputation (what the hell) so try not to be an asshole." Poppy causally mentioned. Wow, try not to be an ass-hole. I just didn't want to go home. I left the office and decided to take the stairs to see the DCM, I needed a few minutes to think. Wouldn't you know, who did I run into. Yep Peterman, the Dickhead.

"Well, well, well, Knight, Daddy isn't going to save you this time." He smirked.

"Peterman."

"It is Special Agent Blah blah blah the 16th"

"Peterman, thank god you don't have kids because it is quite obvious that stupidity runs in your family."

I went into the main office and was greeting by Brooklyn Brann, a beautiful lady from my neck of the woods in Virginia. Brooklyn was very intelligent and driven, the young lady was going be someone someday, I would bet on it.

"Monte, the King has returned." she greeted me with a smirk. "Good morning, lady, you look striking as always."

"King, you better save the bullshit for your visit." she winked at me. "Have a seat and relax, you might need the quiet time." Gee thanks.

"Got any coloring books?"

My ass had barely hit the seat when the phone rang, Brookie looked at me and nodded in the direction of the big double doors. I as I got close, the door opened, and I walked thru like a returning victorious champion waiting to be exulted and just like that the door shut behind me with a bang. Like a prison cell and I wonder if I could make a run for it if I needed to get out of here exit stage left. I noticed that the office had a nice assortment of plants and flowers. A large desk was directly in front of me with a very high back leather chair with the occupant facing the opposite direction so I couldn't see the person sittin there.

As I was standing at attention thinking about this puss nut and what he was going to pontificate about when the high back chair swiveled around and yep, all I could do was lower my head, gently shaking to the left and right muttered "and the laughs just keep ooooooooon coming."

Remember the smoking hottie I hit on every other Friday, yep it was Kathy. The DCM, damn if I can't pick them, Hey Pops guess what I did after school today? I am supposed to be a trained, Special Investigator.

Mr. Knight, Kathy addressed me as Mister, that's funny, it should have been Daddy but she had the upper hand, though for ever so briefly.

"Seems like you have been busy, with some......how should we say, extracurricular activities in addition to your normal job......wouldn't have included some couch bouncing would it?" Ahhhhh, well.

"Yes, maam it is a labor of love and I don't charge over time."

"Yeah." she was remotely curt.

"Your jacket is very impressive from the moment you stepped onto Quantico you have exceeded all the fitness reports, excelled at everything, received the Attorney Generals award and seem to piss your dad off at every turn."

"Ma'am, you see pops doesn't have a sense of humor and I would really appreciate if we didn't mention this, this unfortunate incidence."

"I already spoke to him this morning, nice man but he did want me to express his condolences!" I smiled and gave the WTF look.

I have read a preliminary report, Kathy explained that it appears that I was not at fault. Well, yeh haw, I did my job, got some fine ass and we knew the target and most likely could use her to infiltrate the Lord of the Skies Cartel. Where is my cookie? After a brief discussion, I was told I was being sent state side. I pleaded my case but she said you have to go home, see your dad and the Administrator and mostly a visit to the Ole Lady; The Attorney General of the United States at least she knew my name in a good way as well.

I was allowed to leave, dismissed actually. However, as I reached for the door, Kathy states, very confidently, I might add. "Knight, the joke is on you."

"Well, Miss Kathy, please retort."

"You see, everyone knew that you didn't know who I was. And that like every other half attractive female that steps foot on this compound I was a target for you."

"Wait, half attractive, at least give me some credit – you are hot."

"Yeah, ok, well I instructed everyone, if anyone told you who I was, they would be sent state side."Good to know Shadow certainly had my back, the bitches. "You are a very handsome man and in a different time and place, well, maybe, just maybe,

I might consider speaking with you." Consider? Hell, Kathy your crotch was leaking so bad for me, you could drown half the damn Embassy.

With a smile, "you are dismissed."

As I reached for the door, I stopped and turned around.

"You did say handsome? "

"Yes I did, you know what I think about you."

Glanced at my watch on my wrist, looked up at her raised eyebrow, "Well, I do have 2 ½ hours before I catch my flight."

"Get out." She did fight back a giggle as she said it.

"Yes ma 'ma Ms. DCM."

Now I love Kathy like a sister, we became close friends and have stayed in contact with her over the years and tracked her advancement throughout the Department of State (DoS). Never did get to hit that target but did make one hell of friend and I wouldn't trade that for anything.

Chapter 37

BACK AT HQ

Since I didn't have a house anymore in the United States, I had to consider my options. First, I could live with my parents again, I think Pops secretly wanted that, yeah right. I could go live on the Res but that was way to far away even though that would be option one for me. I could live with a friend or even and old girlfriend, yes course they still loved me. After you get MTL it is a livelong sentence of loving me. What can I say, I picked Mom and Pops.

From the first day, I could tell this was going to be a whole procedural process and The Office of Professional Responsibility (OPR), think Internal Affairs, was going to be involved. The word responsibility should be a dead giveaway that I was going to have issues here.

I was shuttled back and forth from my fourth-floor office in the East Building to the tenth-floor office in the west building, like I was a puppet at their beck and call. A nice Senior Agent Richard Haynes Collins was the guy running point for

OPR and Dick had my case, and he was determined to play goat rope fucking with yours truly.

See Dick would call me over and have me sit outside the locked door for a couple of hours, then come out and say, "Knight, we don't have time, go back to your office and wait till we call you."

"Ok, Dick."

"Knight, it is Senior Special Agent Collins."

"Thanks for the clarification, Dick."

"Keep on Knight, I will make your life Hell. "Oh, and Knight, Special Agent Pendergast sends his condolences."

"How is Willie? And his mom?"

"Out now."

"Yes Slur." I did a little checking and guess what? Yep, Dick and Peterman graduated last and second to last at West Point. Yep, facts and that explains a lot.

I get back to my office and sit down and guess who calls and says get over here, now! "Roger" I had to relieve myself first, stop by the cafeteria, get my car washed, get a pedicure so it took me a moment. I meander my way up to his office, ring the bell and announce my presence and take a seat. The door quickly opens and here is Dick.

"You are late."

"Heavy traffic on the stairs at lunch time, plus Sarah told me I had to wax her dolphins."

"Knight, you can't joke your way out of this, and I am going to get you kicked out and hopefully see you behind bars."

"Look Dick…."

"Its Agent Collins."

"Ok, Dick Collins."

"Shut the fuck up, I have had enough of your bullshit!" I think Dick was mentrating.

"I am sorry Dick, does something Vex thee?"

"Go, go back to your office, now and that's an order."

The cat versus mouse game went on for weeks. This dumb sum bitches just could not get it.

During that time, I was assigned to the Senior Staff Meeting every week. Now if I thought I was important I wasn't but that was oayk. I was a GS-13 and sat in the room with the Administrator, Deputy Administrator and the big 6 that were all Agents and not political appointees and great guys. Total respect for these guys who made a career of fighting criminals and making drug deals. I was often the backside of all the jokes. Roll Damn Tide.

Earlier Monday morning and everyone was talking about their weekend, and I was assigned to not leave my home and had armed guards to protect me, really but okay. I couldn't piss without them knowing and of course I asked for females. Yeah, yeah whatever.

We had a scandal or two that was discuss, SOD and stealing, Houston guy unloaded rounds into neighbor's dog only thing was he had to reload to make sure the dog was dead, or the bachelor party shootout in the street with Agents and bouncers, yeah I heard it all. But all came down to guys that support me and what everyone else did. Well, agent Knight did this, yeah but he also has a couple of major awards and so on and so on.

It came to a head when these warriors actually got mad at each other, and I thought they were going to throw down right there in the conference room of the twelfth floor West building. Great reporting for the Washington Times. The Administrator, hardcore New Yorker, who was the Police Commissioner cut that shit off. I was looking to dive under the table, I can only dodge some many raindrops at the same time, and this was Noah's Arc raining time.

"Everyone get the fuck out except Knight, NOW!" The Administrator barked. Well, well, the shit is going to get real.

Everyone left and I followed suit. "Knight, not you, sit down" as he looked at me. "Knight, what do you have to say"

"Sir, I think that...."

"Shut up Knight, I want to ask you a question."

"Yes Sir." standing back up at attention.

"Sit down, relax. Would you do it again" straight to the point, I respect that.

"Sir?"

"Don't look at me like I asked you if you were pumping the neighbor's cat." Well damn, this sum bitch has a sense of humor.

"Yes, Sir, in a heartbeat, I didn't know who she was, but she was as hot as a Rhino's crotch in August, Sir."

"After all you know, who she was and what she could mean to you, and you would still repeat the exercise."

"You god damn right I would, Sir and twice on Sunday."

2 CROWS *in the* SHADOWS

Well, that got him laughing. "Good boy, I like that."

"Thank you, Sir."

"Knight, Biggs told me to tell you. Play the card you were dealt if that means anything to you."

"Sir?"

"The-e-e card. Play it."

"Ah Yes."

"Dismissed."

"Yes Sir." As I was leaving, I heard him mumble, I love that fucking guy.

As I mentioned earlier, I had my picture taken with the Administrator on several occasions and he always smiles with me. Well, kinda smiled but it was with me because he sure as hell frowned with everyone else. I was asked plenty of times, why does he smile with you. Just lucky I guess but you guys know the truth.

Had just settled into my plush high back chair, staring out at the changing weather, dark clouds rumbling in as phone rings abruptly. "Knight, get your ass over to my office, NOW!" Dick states calmly...TOO controlled as I hear an undertone that rattles me as much as I let myself be rattled.

"Yes sir, Dick."

"It is Senior Agent." Click. Dial tone buzzing in my ear as I smile. I waited thirty minutes, and the phone was ringing of the hook, and of course I could see it was Dick and he was leaving voicemail after voicemail and seemed very agitated. I let him stew another hour or so and leisurely strolled to the west building and meandered my way up. I picked up the phone.

"Dick-k-k, Dicky, I am here-e-e," I say. (If it was after the Jack Nicholson movie. "I am home, Dear."

"Knight, I am frying your ass!" banging the phone in my ear again.

The door unlocks and Dick bows slightly from the waist, gestures that I should enter sweeping his arm expansively into the room, seemingly like I am a revered guest. Then erratically, "Get in the conference room, NOW! He now gesticulates wildly, jabbing his finger repeatedly towards the expensive rosewood table." Herman Miller, I surmise.

Even the smallest offices at the DEA have class. With him at my rear so close the hair on my neck prickles, I pick up the sensation of raw heat he is radiating. Well, guess who was there already seated? Yep, Peterman. I almost guffaw when I realize I am meeting with Dick and Peter, well, Peterman. There are no co-inky-dinks.

"Knight, sooo good to see you." Funny, the words were not matching the look on his face which said I was prey. I was almost, I said almost, taken aback.

"Willie, good to see you." I put forth my hand to shake but instead he looks down at a nearly foot high stack of paperwork before him and ignores my hand. Seems he has been up to some extensive researching. Is that all about me and my exploits I wonder?

With no ado he says, "Motherfucker, shut up. We got you red-handed this time." The comic racial slur, it seems noticed only by me. My years of watching Cowboys and 'Injuns'.

"Peterman, I heard you were colorblind."

"Yeah, so? quizzically.

Well, I guess you have a fantastic fucking time eating a bag of skittles, now, don't you?"

"Fuck you, Knight."

Dick enters from behind brushing my left flank rudely as he passes and we have a possible good cop, bad cop scenario getting ready to play out. But I surmise I am the good cop, outnumbered. He motions to his cohort to an axing hand sign as in halt and ceremoniously states "Several people in logistics have noticed some discrepancies in your paperwork that we need to review." Now, that tells me no Department Heads are involved with the paperwork so the discrepancies are from lower down the food chain where these clowns have been beating the bushes.

"Good to know."

They are now seated side by side like a fortification and indicate I am to seat myself across from them on the other side, where I will be blockaded in. Hmmm, the snare is laid. A snare being a thin wire noose set to lasso then trap animals viewed as pests or a threat, usually foxes or sometimes young coyotes. I look across the table where they have motioned me to sit. I see a pitcher of chilled water no evidence of ice so been sitting for a while and a glass, how thoughtful. Hmmm, does that mean thirsty work, like an interrogation? Also, a legal pad and felt tip...hmmm, taking notes and returning with answers to their queries. Next, a stack of papers matching the stack next to Peterman. I guess they intend we are to plow through together as we have our friendly visit. Teamwork, dontcha know?

I reflect back to days on the Res sitting cross-legged in front of the TV watching cartoons at Grammy's house. Dick and Peterman are reminding me of the animated characters, Heckle and Jeckle, a great series which starred two crows. Well, at that time I liked assuming they were crows, ya know. But actually, were yellow billed magpies. They played off each other, one formal and dignified with a British upper crust accent, the other with a Brooklyn swaggering accent, but both degenerating into jabbering looneys as Hijinx ensued.

Instead of seating myself directly across the table from them with my back against the wall, as planned...I pull a rolling chair from a small library table across the room and plant myself between them like a third bump on a log which 'kerfluffles' both, but then abruptly scoot my chair outward from the table toward the center of the room with one leg push, facing their backsides with my arms firmly gripping the chair arms like pistolas...so they both had to crank their necks sideways and backward to converse with me.

Now since they are both in chairs, they try to turn around in the chairs creating scraping and screeching sounds with the legs as they bump up and down until they face me, their backs blocking all the paperwork stacked on the table, their weapon of choice. This immediately gets the dynamic off balance. I am now the gunslinger, hands resting on my guns, and they are two townies caught off guard with no weapons. All that research work from the secretarial pool and hours of printing and meticulously collating now mute. A three-way faceoff. My trigger finger itching.

"Listen Knight," says Peterman rubbing his hands together in relish then reaching awkwardly backward to loudly thump the stack of papers as IF he is about to roll out the red carpet to my demise. From the looks of it, a long formal lashing was planned to ensue. As much as I would like to linger to savor the moment, let them lay out their chess pieces step by step and knock them off the board in one fell swoop, already done with this bs. I explode jolting both back in their chairs

"No, both you motherfuckers listen", as I raise out of the chair, towering over them with my 6' 3' frame. I slammed the card down on the table with a jarring jolt. They both crank necks back to look up at my scowl, and you cannot make this shit up...the storm rolls in and thunder crackles across the expanse of windows.

"Thank you, Great Spirit." I mutter under my breath.

Dick's face dropped seeing the card while, of course, Peterman had no clue.

"Knight, sit down." Dick looked over at Peterman and said, "Stand down."

"That's right, bitches, I lawyered up. Catch me if you can"

"What, wait. What, I don't understand." Peterman questioned.

"He has an attorney."

"That's right boys, so you two can go play blind-folded lawn darts and by the way, Peterman, you might have 99 problems but having some balls isn't one of them, now isn't it!" There! Left him with some dignity.

I break my stance, lifting off to shoot an air ball toward the end of the table, take three brisk long strides and stretch out pretending to catch said air ball. move toward the paper stack meant for me, swing around and scoop it up in a single motion under my arm, "Roll DAMN Tide!" let out a shout. Both have mouths aghast.

Now, I say, "Catch you on the flip-flop, thanks for the update." Slam door, take elevator up to pass paperwork off to the nosebleed section of DEA stratosphere. That was the end of that. They had to let me leave. They had no proof of any wrong-doing. There were being dicks for the sake of being dicks. Good for them. Both got picked last in kickball, AGAIN!

In retrospect, maybe they thought they were doing what was right, but they weren't. Neither ended their careers in a good fashion and neither got retirement. Within months powers that be and/or circumstances coalesced against them in a seemingly random chain of events. Nothing you could put your finger on. Team dynamics...who is to say? Survival of the strong? Poor sum bitches, you tried to make a drug deal with someone who didn't want what you had and wasn't afraid and you lost.

Chapter 38

OKLAHOMA CITY
"BENT BUT NOT BROKEN"

Wednesday, April 19, 1995

I have gone over this and over this and never really know what to say or how to address this one. I am cocky and demonstrative and know 'I can dodge raindrops' but this one hit home and still hits home every day since 1995 and 'when the Dragons come to roost', I get thunder struck.

I stood frozen in front of one of the multiple TVs and worldwide clock systems in our Command Center in the West Building. Global Clocks on the wall displaying times for almost every major city in the world; New York, London, Germany, Moscow, Tokyo and this list goes on and on.

I was witnessing one of the most horrific acts in my memory and aside from 9-11 nothing like this hit home. The Alfred P. Murrah Federal Building in Oklahoma City, Oklahoma was blown half apart and on fire. I didn't know at the time, but a massive homemade bomb composed of more than two tons of ammonium nitrate fertilizer and fuel oil concealed in a rental truck exploded. The building was later razed, and a park was built on the site. The bombing remained the deadliest terrorist assault on U.S. soil until the attacks on the World Trade Center in New York City and the Pentagon outside Washington, D.C., in 2001.

The total:
168 innocent people killed.
19 children in a day care center killed.
500+ injured.
Going about their daily lives.
An event that changed a nation forever.

A year later, during the time of construction fencing was installed all around the building site and people posted pictures of loved ones lost that day. There were birthday balloons, baby dolls, teddy bears and all sorts of gifts left for the lost but not forgotten children. Senseless loss of life.

I stood flat footed. I got sucker punched. But not for long, because shock soon turned to anger, and people were started to flock to the Command Center. The big six were mobilizing efforts around the world, along with all government agencies. We didn't know if it was foreign actors, a foreign government or any clue who could be behind this. I was on a plane within 8 hours headed for OKBOMB Ground Zero. I was not seeking justice; I was seeking revenge. Retribution. I had every intention of extracting a nation's pound of flesh from every mealy-mouthed window licking mother fucker that had any-thing to do with this.

Hitting the ground, there was mass confusion. We headed to what was left of the Murray building and DEA and others Ok City home office. As we got close, you could fully under-stand the sense of dread that filled the air. Buildings had win-dows cracked and other damage and, on we proceeded until windows were totally blown out. Getting more and more war torn as we closed in. Everything was blown apart, what the hell could have down this. The whole nation was in shock

At first my suspicions and that of others, wrongly focused on Middle Eastern terrorist groups especially since our dis-trainment of Iran. Attention quickly started to hone in on Timothy McVeigh—who had been arrested shortly after the explosion for a traffic violation—and his friend Terry Nichols. Both were former U.S. Army soldiers and were associated with the extreme right-wing and militant Patriot movement. Two days after the bombing and shortly before he was to be released for his traffic violation, McVeigh was identified and charged as a suspect, and Nichols later voluntarily surrendered to police. McVeigh was convicted on 11 counts of murder, conspiracy, and using a weapon of mass destruction and was executed in 2001—the first person executed for a federal crime in the United States since 1963. Nichols avoided the death penalty but was convicted of conspiracy and eight counts of involuntary manslaughter and sentenced to life in prison. Other associates were convicted of failing to inform authorities about their prior knowledge of the conspiracy, and some observers believed that still other participants were involved in the attack.

We lost five (5) people and a host of others to mental conditions like PTSD, alcohol and drug abuse and a multitude of other mental disorders that were hidden from view. I did not get revenge nor retribution, but I did witness an incredibly talented and dedicated group of Americans coming together with a common goal, justice. It taught me that violence, destruction, and death were not the only way and sometimes a helping hand is enough. Imagine that, a knuckle dragging heathen like me experiencing empathy and compassion. Do not get to comfortable thinking we are going to be whispering sweet nothings in each other's ears during a warm down out on a country road later.

Unfortunately, one of our agents, and my friend, survived the Oklahoma City bombing but was shot and killed in Bogota Colombia 6 months later in a nonsensical argument bar fight. Rest In Peace brother. 2 Crows was flying back to South America with a new focus and determination.

Chapter 39

THE ITALIAN CONNECTION

I landed in Bogota and went straight to the Embassy and straight to work and into business with Shadow strike. Checked in with Big Poppy and of course, my buddy Matt.

"Monte, welcome back, brother. I received word that you needed a country clearance and guessed you got a get out of jail free card."

"Matt, always a great day when I get to see you brother."

"How did it go?"

"Not as bad as what you might think." I explained to Matt about OPR, Dick and Peterman and of course the discussion with the Old Man.

"Really, seems everyone likes you."

I was sitting at my desk in Bogota on a Monday morning, Pamela had packed me lunch as usual yet, I was still hungry and it was only 0730 after a nice breakfast but I was pilfering my brown bag already. With a thunderous knock, Knuckles is standing in the doorframe, did this guy do anything quietly. "What's up?"

"Bossman, Intel has it that we might have an Italian connection that is running a freight train of coca from Santa Cruz to Italy via the Camorra express."

"Really, Italy has a lot of hot dark haired chicks Knuckles."

"Dude, really, you focus on a woman?"

"What?" I mentioned as I feigned shock and disbelief that he would question my motives.

"Does Guinea know?"

"Nope, I just got the info from last night's teletype via Interpol."

"Good can't wait to tell him his wop Genovese relatives in Sicily are mafioso drug dealers."

"Bossman, didn't his grandparents come from Italy?"

"Yeah, it was a little place called Udine in the upper eastern part of Italy."

The Bolivian Cartel, also designated as the Santa Cruz Cartel, is described as the 'most classy' cartel in the game, but also the most dangerous. They were very prim and proper, think high court functions in London.

Knuckles handed me the file and the first thing that stood out was the picture of a lady, Muzzolini and from the looks of her she fit into the classy type only with a side of Black Widow and should fit right in.

The most notorious cartel was run by Roberto Suarez, who was known as Bolivia's 'King of Cocaine' and worked with Pablo Escobar and the Medellin Cartel. The clans under Mr.

Suarez, are not very aggressive in expanding their turf, but they will not hesitate to attack a turf that is not well defended, and retaliate after being attacked. All the while thanking guests for attending one of their functions. Cocaine and heroin are their drugs of choice. Their low-ranking henchmen attack in dense waves, shooting from the hip, spray and pray that we see in every encounter with them, high casualties do not deter their attacks. You would think that with all the fat stacks of cash they have some of it would go to investing in target practice and firearms instruction. Don't get me wrong, I am glad they didn't.

The clans can put together up to 1000 kilograms of coca base and deliver them to Brazilian organized crime syndicates which ship it within the region and to Europe via Italy. This coca base, or cocaine paste, then feeds the "basuco" market. Basuco is like crack cocaine, a highly addictive form of the drug which is smoked. It is cheaper to produce than cocaine and has short-lived but intense highs, prompting addicts to engage in repeated and prolonged use, which ends up permanently damaging the user's health. Like the crack epidemic in the United States in the 1980s, that really gave gas to the rise of drug gangs on our streets and to the war on drugs.

Ichilo, in the suburbs of Santa Cruz, is one of the centers for coca base production, home to at least four of the more sophisticated drug clans. In an interview with the Bolivian TV program "Sin Letra Chica," a member of one of these clans said that his organization worked alongside another, and that between the two they had 600 members. In a good week the two clans produced up to 800 kilos of coca base, he added. Part of this coca base was transported to the Brazilian frontier and sold directly to Brazilian organized crime syndicates; another part was bought by Colombians, who process the base into cocaine. The source also made it clear that the police colonel in the nearby town of Yapancani was on the payroll of the drug traffickers.

Another example of a officials on the take, a very common practice in the 80s and 90s. Of course, it is Let's Make a Drug Deal. You take the cash and do our bidding and we let you live. You get something, we get something.

The Camorra is an Italian Mafia style criminal organization and criminal society that got its start in the Campania Region and Specially Naples. Think about it, Camorra has a society for drug scum bags and the Bolivian Cartel is high society for such as well. A marriage of dirt bags to scum bags made in heaven. It is one of the largest, if not the largest, they don't file taxes, so we are not sure how big, criminal organizations in Italy dating back to the 17th century or so. This isn't a god father style of pyramidal structure of say the Sicilian Mafia. The Camorra structure is divided into individual groups call Clans. Some Native American Tribes divide members into specific clans that have specific duties such as cleaning, protection, tribal affairs, you get the drift. You will have Capo or Boss, kinda like me with Shadow, except for Guinea the wop bitch – is the head of the clan where it could be as a few as ten or as many as a couple hundred all depending on the clans' power and structure. Consequently, as Camorra clans act independently, and are more prone to feuding among themselves.

The Camorra's main businesses are drug trafficking, racketeering, counterfeiting and money laundering. With most mafia affiliates it is not unusual for clans to infiltrate the politics of their respective areas. Anyone remember Marion Barry, the Washington DC Mayor who was arrested with his former girlfriend Hazal Diane "Rasheeda" Moor, in an FBI sting at the Vista International Hotel for crack cocaine use and possession. And the good citizens of DC decided to re-elect the sum bitch again. You have a crack head as a mayor and you wonder why DC is all Fucked Up Beyond All Repair, the true definition of FUBAR.

Since the early 1980s and its involvement in the drug trafficking business, the Camorra has acquired a strong presence in other European countries, particularly Spain. Usually, Camorra clans maintain close contacts with South American drug cartels, especially the Santa Crus Cartel, which facilitates the arrival of drugs in Europe. International Criminal Police Organization or Organisation internationale de police criminelle, commonly known as Interpol. It is an international organization that facilitates worldwide police cooperation and crime control. Headquartered in Lyon, France, it is the world's largest international police organization, with seven regional bureaus worldwide and a National Central Bureau in all 195 member states.

Interpol provides investigative support, expertise, and training to law enforcement worldwide, focusing on three major areas of transnational crime: terrorism, and organized crime. Its broad mandate covers virtually every kind of crime, including crimes against humanity, child trafficking, drug trafficking and production, political corruption, intellectual property infringement, and white-collar crime. The agency also facilitates cooperation among national law enforcement institutions through criminal databases and communications networks. Contrary to popular belief, Interpol is itself not a law enforcement agency.

First thing each morning we get communications from United States Embassies and Consulates, Military, other Intel Community folks, other countries including host countries and Interpol all in a classified format. The Secret Internet Protocol Router Network (SIPRNet) is "a system of interconnected computer networks used by the U.S. Department of Defense and the U.S. Department of State to transmit classified information (up to and including information classified SECRET) by packet switching over the 'completely secure' environment". It also provides services such as hypertext document access and electronic mail. Think of it as DoD's classified version of the civilian Internet and we get up every morning and read the daily news.

Knuckles who sleeps less than I do, is at the office at O'dark thirty and always has a very detailed summary report, because the vast amount of information has to be sorted out as to what interests us, or me in this case, and what doesn't. He is tedious like that, guess he has to be he does play with explosives.

"Interpol says that a young lady, Ms. Alexandra Muzzolini is visiting Santa Cruz on behalf of the Camorra."

"Camorra? The Italian Mafia is sending someone to Santa Cruz of all places."

"Interesting, didn't realize Alexandra was a common Italian name, what do we know about Ms. Muzzolini, and you did say Miss?"

"Yes Sir, Bossman, it is Miss." Here is an additional write up and some other pictures, I figured you would like the extra pictures." Now what was he trying to insinuate. "Her father is Orazio Muzzolini a notorious leader in Italy and was married to a woman believed to be from Costa Rica.

"Wow very nice, beautiful woman. Assemble the team for a 1300 pow wow." Ms. Muzzolini looks to be very interesting from her nonexistent rap sheet, striking good looks and stylish persona. I knew immediately I was going to designate this effort as Operation Bella. Bella translates to beautiful in Italian.

I got on the horn and was going to leave Big Poppy a message to inform him of what I had planned but the sum bitch answered the phone. Hadn't planned on that.

"Poppy, Shadow is headed to Santa Cruz."

"Knight, it usually works the other way around, that I tell you what the plan is. If you have a request, put in said request. I will be review and you receive permission to Go/No Go to take a flight outside of our host country and don't forget Peterman will review as well." Yeah, that guy is preoccupied.

"Guess you hadn't heard, the Administrator has other plans to Peterman."

"Knight, how the hell did you pull that off, never mind I don't want to know."

"Sir," yeah when I wanted something I had to bend the knee, if only for a second, but not both knees like Guinea.

"I have information that ties Santa Cruz to Italy that ties back to Cali and we need to do a sneak and peak."

"Ok, give me the writeup and I will let you know in a couple of days." Now, he should have spoken to Pop, because he knew damn well that the report would be written on toilet paper sitting on the toilet and delivered via a flush.

"Yes, you will have it by morning."

"Yeah, sure." Maybe he did know.

1300 arrived and we assembled in one of our conference rooms on the second floor away from everyone except Intelligence Officers and other non-DEA folks that supported us. Didn't want the brass and especially Asshat Peterman getting any word of this, knowing what we were planning until it was executed and successful. Better to beg for forgiveness than ask for permission.

"Gentlemen, and I use the term very loosely, and lady." Giving a slight bow to her highness. Again, with the finger. "We have been afforded an opportunity to visit beautiful Santa Cruz in the summertime."

"Hey Rodent, did you bring the shade, reference to sunscreen that is SPF50, so your black ass doesn't turn blurple like Gunny Sparks?" Barbie clipped as the team laughed.

"Barbie, I will bitch slap your ass back to the reservation."

"Skip, maybe you can give us a tour."

"Sure, just lead me to the land yacht."

Santa Cruz most days in the summers a mid-90's with a moderately hot wind with no lawn chair for the beach because there is no beach. Let's take a magic carpet ride to the desert.

"My initial impression of Ms. Muzzolini was just like Barbie, a BAB", In case you forgot, that's Bad Ass Bitch. I continued, "She is beautiful, apparently very resourceful, smart and elusive, she does not have an arrest record much less conviction or even a damn parking ticket."

"Bossman, I am sure this has absolutely nothing to do with Ms. Muzzolini being hot as if you wearing a gasoline suit running through hell!"

"Of course not." Not sure why I was deemed a misogynistic pig, but I knew they were just kidding. I think. Maybe. Yeah, no, they really were.

Knuckles started off, "This is Operation Bella." Of course, Barbie gave me a high eyebrow look, as he handed out the brief and started going over the objectives. Each team member had an assignment prior to leaving and once we had boots on the ground to make sure the objectives were met. Operation Bella was a 'sneak and peek' to gather the Intel we needed to bring down the Italian Connection.

First, we must investigate any type of narcotics conspiracy theories within Colombia and Bolivia, which we had a good local handle on, but now add in Brazil and Italy. We know government officials in these countries, in an official capacity, helped friends and colleagues to evade all United States counternarcotics efforts. We know that certain individuals attempted to learn the identity of a confidential informants who would provide authorities with information regarding cartel operations so it could be passed along to cartel contacts. In addition to providing intelligence to cartels, they would reportedly help steer investigations away from people and facilities. Further, they try to block progress on investigations into arrested individuals associated with the cartels to protect other members associated with the organization. As the Cartels grew in strength and size more and more people are recruited as agents for the most powerful and sophisticated drug cartels. Indeed, when one examines the reach and scope of these cartel's efforts to recruit agents inside every country, including the United States, to provide intelligence and act on the cartels' behalf, it becomes apparent that the cartels have demonstrated the ability to operate more like a foreign intelligence service than a traditional criminal organization.

For many years now, it has become apparent there are elite dynamics involved in of the cross-border illicit flow of people, drugs, weapons and cash. One of the most notable characteristics about this flow of contraband is its flexibility.

When smugglers encounter an obstacle to the flow of their product, they find ways to avoid it. For example, as the U. S. identified certain sectors and addressed them as High Intensity Drug Trafficking Area (HIDTA) was set up in that sector, the drug traffickers and human smugglers diverted a good portion of their volume around the bottleneck. In the US, they even created an extensive network of tunnels under any fence or close to cities to keep their contraband, and specifically profits flowing. Likewise, as maritime and air interdiction efforts between South America and Mexico have become more successful, Central America has become increasingly important to the flow of narcotics from South America to the United States. Now we add in Comara in Italy.

All this reflects how the drug-trafficking organizations have adjusted their method of shipment and their trafficking routes to avoid interdiction efforts and maintain the flow of narcotics around the world. Especially the biggest user in the world. Over the past few years, a great deal of public and government attention has focused on the U.S.-Mexican border. In response to this attention, the federal and border state governments in the United States have erected more barriers, installed an array of cameras, sensors and increased the manpower committed to securing the border. While these efforts certainly have not hermetically sealed the border, they do appear to be having some impact — an impact magnified by the effectiveness of interdiction efforts elsewhere along the narcotics supply chain. We decided to take a flight to Cochabamba Bolivia and helicopter into Santa Cruz to avoid detection at the airport.

Matt filled out the necessary paperwork and let the Santa Cruz office know and our plans were set in motion. Hopefully, we will make a drug deal.

Chapter 40

INBOUND SANTA CRUZ

Once all the coordination was completed, Matt always did a great job of this, like Radar in MASH. We were off to Santa Cruz and the nearest major airport El Trompillo. The International Airport is Viru Viru International, which has both international and domestic flights and is where Bella would be entering Bolivia. Once on the ground, our intelligence told us Bella and her entourage would be headed straight to Santa Cruz de la Sierra, the most expensive hotel in town. It featured an outdoor swimming pool, a garden, and a spa with a hot tub and sauna all the amenities a beautiful lady required.

We arrived in Santa Crus a couple days later and provided everything we needed. A safe house to avoid detection and all the transportation and equipment we needed for a nice relaxing vacation. We also got our own special guide, a young lady name Alejandra Villalta Roldman. Come on, do I even need to tell you how attractive this beauty from Costa Rica is. Yeah, Costa Rican and how she landed here I have no clue just glad she did. Ale had a heart of gold and is just as pretty on the inside as she is on the outside. We reconnected years later and became, well, that's another story. We needed to get the following in no particular order. Learn their patterns ahead of time and depending on how closely you know the person and their activities you come of with a plan. Get the gear we need to watch and/or record from afar. Remember don't advertise. The general rule when following is keep your distance, particularly if you are driving. Use mirrors, parking lots, public places to your advantage and a change of clothes and head gear whenever possible.

We were picked up at the airport in Cochabamba and climb on helicopters to take us to a designated drop off outside of Santa Cruz where we would be picked up by Dr. Brian Showman the Assistant Special Agent in Charge (ASAC) for Santa Cruz. Brian was one smart dude and had 3 PhDs to prove it. Me, I hear PhD and think Piled Higher and Deeper, but this guy was smart. Loved the Denver Broncos, why I don't know, and was one hell of a football coach. Now to look at the ponytail wearing, pasty white mother fucker you wouldn't think twice. Conjure up Donald Sutherland and that's Doc's twin. He loves hard core metal and would drop you with a shot between the eyes quicker than he could drink a diet root beer. Yeah, he liked that shit too.

We jumped off the bird and walked towards the waiting vehicles. "Bossman, heard you folks got lost and might need a lift." As Doc extended a hand and gave a shoulder bump followed by a back slap.

"Doc, good to see you brother, you still trying to coach?"

"Not here, they use a round football."

"Yeah, I would rather watch under water nose picking than soccer, unless it is women's soccer and hopefully that would be topless."

"Damn, dude somethings never change." A large grin stretches from ear to ear.

"What, Doc?" I look around quizzically.

"Yeah, he is still an asshole." Guinea had to open his fly trap.

"Facts." Out of the girl crew and my most avid support.

"Yep." Nods Skip.

"Loves dem Majestic Mammaries." Chimes in Rodent.

Good to know I have my whole teams supports me everywhere I go.

Doc drove us to the safe house and got us situated and we provided an overview of what we planned to do. Always remember Mr. Murphy. Doc was committed to helping us anyway he could. We settle in for the evening to relax by the pool, yep, the safe house had a pool, with some beer, stogies, and local cuisine. Living the dream but I was distracted thinking about Bella.

We got up in the morning and did some Physical Training, with the limited weight room a pool attached to the house. I needed to talk to Doc about how he allocated the funds for this. We got showered and dress as civilians and gathered everything we needed and headed out in separated directions to wait for the arrival of Ms. Bella herself. Her plane arrived precisely as Interpol had advised and we were on it. We were using radios to communicate, and Doc was at the Santa Cruz office playing Pig Pen and directing the actors. Rodent would be at the Airport awaiting her people to pick up the language and track them to the street, where we knew she had rented a couple of vehicles for her disposal.

"The Eagle has Landed."

"Great line." Doc responded.

Knuckles and Skip would keep their distance but follow until the hotel was in sight and hand off to Barbie and our Confidential Informant (CI), Raul Hernandez in the hotel lobby. After about 15 minutes most of which was the security detail doing their job and all the luggage that had to be de-planed and loaded up.

"The Eagle is flying high and headed in the right direction, over."

"Copy." We had setup a command-and-control center directly across the street from the hotel. Our Santa Cruz office had already bugged, with audio and visual equipment for the penthouse suite which we knew Bella's team had reserved for her. The top two floors were Ms. Mazzolini's for the month.

Bella arrived like she was the Mother Queen of Scotts with her security, entourage, and a bunch of other misfits in tow. She was immediately greeted by the hotel manager who escorted her to her room personally. On the way she ordered lunch and a Châteauneuf-du-Pape it's a nice Southern Rhône Red wine from France. Yes, I know my wines. It wasn't a 78 Margaux Margaux but it was lunch time.

They went to the suite and Bella immediately went to the bathroom for a shower, now see, the lady has class. Of course, others unpacked for her.

"Guinea, see that's class, plus next time you need to unpack my bags. Over."

"Suck it."

"I said Over."

"I said Suck It."

"Can't we all just get along, fellas." Doc mentioned.

The first day was normal chatter about shopping, a friend's birthday and getting a gift and maybe some meetings later in the week but for now, they all were are relaxing. The security was on the balcony which was large and had a small pool and hot tub, and at the front door on both floors and in the Lobby as well. For two days Bella didn't budge from the apartment. She had all her meals brought in, lounged around the pool, relaxed, read a lot and over all didn't do much of anything. No visitors, no phone calls just relaxing.

"How do I get a job like this?" Barbie queried.

"Marry rich." Doc shot back.

"I thought I was marrying you, Doc."

"I will take it under consideration." Could Doc be a little light in the loafers for not jumping on that.

"Wait, wait, wait." Skip added, sum bitch knew me too well.

"We can pretend, Barbie, with all the extracurricular activity you want." Ha, ha, ha.

"Sure, Bossman, I need my house cleaned."

"I can clean your pipes, upstairs and down," I couldn't hear it but I knew her eyes rolled, she shook her head and mouthed idiot.

On the third day, I had a chance to get close, probably too close in an eyeglasses and custom sunglasses store. Bella was alone, though security was close by but she and causally browsing. I entered and startled causally browsing myself. I was started when I heard a whisper, behind me and close to my ear.

"When something good happens to you, you would be foolish not to enrich your soul." All in perfect Spanish.

I was dumbfounded, "Excuse me?" I responded in Spanish, turning around. She was almost touching me and lowered her sunglasses. Bella's stunning hazel dark brown eyes were brighter than the stars at night and I was stunned and utterly speechless. I know, me speechless, well quite frankly yes.

She went on in English, "If you want beautiful lips, speak words of kindness, eyes are beautiful when they seek out the goodness in others, Mr. Knight." I think I heard that once in a poem I thought to myself. It immediately dawned on me, she was used by higher ups and protected for her gentle but wicked grace. Ms. Muzzolini was Invisible to everyone except the ones she wanted to see her, she was two distinct and separate people. Unfortunately, for her, I knew this game all too well.

"Mr. Knight?" I asked her.

"Yes, I know who you are, your reputation proceeds you!"

"My reputation, do tell, Ms…Mrs…."

"Ms. Muzzolini, I am widowed, but you knew that already so don't play games with me Montgomery."

Montgomery? Bitch, did you just call me Montgomery.

"Ma'am, I am sorry for your loss but only three people call me Montgomery, one is dead, one is my momma and you ain't the third one."

"I see, I did not mean to insult you Mr. Knight, would Monte be more appropriate?" I admit, I had to smirk at that one.

"How about Daddy?"

"Daddy?" as the look of confusion spread across her face. Yeah, never mind.

"Monte is fine."

"I am Alexandra, as I am sure you know."

"I do."

"I am not here for what you think, and I am not what you think either. If you mean a smoking hot drug dealer, well I think I am spot on.

"Alexandra, I don't presume to know much of anything, I was out for a stroll and the sun was bright so I thought I could use a new pair of sunglasses.

Alexandra smiles, "I see. Find anything interesting?"

"In fact, I did, very interesting." I think she digs me; I am the sassy kitten destroyer after all and remember I don't take prisoners. Well, they always have me in their hearts, but you already new that.

About this time, three of her 'assistants' closed in and surrounded us, or should I say me. They asked if I was bothering her in Italian but some words in Italian are the same. She looked at me and I am sure saw my expression change to war and quickly dismissed them. One thing I did notice behind them were two other fellas that were Hispanic and most likely Bolivian and part of the Cartel and not part the team that she arrived with.

Chapter 41

BOLIVIAN GAMES CONTINUE

Back at the safe house we were fortunate that Doc knew exactly who those two-star gazers were.

"They are two of Roberto Suarez's bouncers so to speak. Nasty dudes and really bodyguard assassins."

"Any particular reason they were assigned to her?" Barbie tenses her brow and honed in.

"We've never seen such a high-level person from Italy here, so we aren't sure." Interesting you assigned assassins as bodyguards.

"Here are the next steps, we will maintain our surveillance and Doc, see what CI intel you might be able to gather."

"Roger Bossman."

"And Doc, send the bill to Big Poppy."

"Roger, Roger."

We continued our surveillance and saw the occasional cartel traffic in and out of the hotel and they would also walk the streets flanked by all kinds of bodyguards to keep people from getting close and especially us. They were making drugs deals right in front of us, but we had nothing.

Interpol provided more Intel. Ale's father was assonated by the Camorra for some undisclosed breaking of a rule and her mother's whereabouts were unknown, but she was from Costa Rica. Seems Ale was forced into this position at a tender age by the higher ups in paying retribution for her father.

I decided to up the ante after two weeks of getting bits and pieces of conversations. On a warm, sunny Wednesday, that day seems to always have trouble associated with it, I the them team I am moving in to get a close. The teams' heads swiveled like synchronized swimmers and gave that look of WTF.

"Yeah, I want to speak to Ale."

"Ale, now its Ale?" Barbie quipped.

"Wait what-t-t?" Skip kinda barked.

"Bossman, you sure that's a good idea?" Doc followed the team's lead.

I got out the vehicle and moved across a crowded roadway, luckily traffic was stop and go. I proceeded to fall in line behind the bodyguards, who didn't even notice me at first. When they finally did notice, I was past them and right behind Ale.

"Good morning, Ale, I wanted to see if I might have a word?" I was surrounded very quickly by 5 guys who were trying to body me but at 6'3", I towered over all this guys. I glanced back behind them Knuckles and Rodent approached being tourist shoppers out for a stroll.

Ale waved off her men, and smiled, "Certainly Monte."

"Half Costa Rican and doing Dad's work?"

Again, a smile, "you certainly have been busy."

"Yeah, so you are not full-blooded Italian, and you probably aren't enjoying your visit here."

"As I mentioned earlier, I am not what you think."

"Then, let me help you, Ale."

Smiling, "Ale? And you are going to sweep me off my feet and hide me in America, is that the grand plan?" Surprise, surprise, I am Gomer Pyle, and I didn't think it that far through.

"Yep. That's my plan."

"Just like that?"

"Just like that. I can set the plan in motion, I will kidnap you so to speak. Next time you are seen make sure to wear a dark crimson lipstick to signal me that you want to proceed."

"You are crazier than they say."

"Just lies and fairy tales my dear."

"Have a good day, Monte." As she turned, she grazes me, slipping me a note and walked on with the rest of her crew thugs. One of the perks of the elites, a group henchman. I stood and watched the best part of her leave and like clockwork, she turned and glanced back and gave me a smile.

Everyone gathered back at the safe house and seated around the table sipping on their favorite beverage, most Jack and black. Doc doesn't drink and was standing.

"Bossman, what was that?"

"Doc, she doesn't want to be here, she doesn't like why she is here and wants out."

How the hell do you know that in a three-minute conversation?" Barbie concluded.

"I can smell it, plus she slipped me note."

I remember hunting on the Res in late October, walking on an old logging trail with my grandfather, it was sunny and warm, quiet, and peaceful. I was too young to carry a weapon at the time, so it was more a teaching moment. "Two Crows stop and smell."

"What is it granddaddy?" I said looking around.

"A snake is up ahead."

"How do you know; I can't smell anything?"

"Be patient."

We continued slowly and sure enough, in the middle of the path, warming itself between multicolored trees that were casting shadows, was a copperhead. My grandfather shot the snake and when we approached, he picked it up and said smell it. I did and recognized the smell immediately and had sensed it plenty of times and never knew a snake was so close. So, yeah, I could smell it. The fear Ale was casting in the wind. Over the years, I have taught a lot of people to recognize the smell a snake gives off.

"I think you might be smelling a certain time of month." Rodent had to chortles. "Wait, a note?"

Barbie, raised her typical eyebrow, "E-e-w-w, gross Rodent."

"Okay, Boss, even if you can smell her fear and read her thoughts what's the plan, kidnap an Italian citizen, who just happens to be mafia and in another country that just so happens not to be the United States."

"Yep." Not only that she wants her Mafioso mother in Italy, Aunt and two cousins, with bambinos on her get away ride along.

"Dude, have you lost your fucking mind, you are serious." Guinea said sternly.

"Obviously." both Knuckles and Skip announced.

"Jinks."

"Just how do you think Big Poppy and our Country Attache' will like those plans, not to mention your Pops?"

"Don't tell them until after she is seeking asylum." Well, it's a group rate! So, there's that.

"You are serious." Guinea looked at me in disbelieve.

"Bossman, come on this is international security shit, we could all go to jail."

"Listen if she comes to us to seeking asylum, we can get her to the Embassy in Laz Paz and hand her over to the Department of State, we would just be a taxi, so to speak."

"We have done enough for today, let's take this afternoon off and reconvene in the morning and come up with a plan. I have to speak to Matt, Big Poppy and headquarters. Just leave it to me."

"Roger, roger."

Chapter 42

EXTRACTING THE CONNECTION

We got the green light and Doc got all the intel we needed. Miss Sweet cheeks had an itinerary that a beaty queen should have. She would be staying the night at a Cartel safe house, yeah, those sum bitches had them too only a lot nicer with in ground pools, hot tubs, well you get the picture.

As we drove through the moonless night, passing all the run-down homes with half rusted metal siding, tin roof shanties with bars on the windows and barbed wire along any fence or pathway. The streets were empty and peaceful. We slowed to a stop a block in a half from the luxury home, Guinea, Barbie, Skip and I jumped out and moved through the shadows and approached a non-descriptive apartment building that Ale had arranged for a large gather for tomorrow. A party to celebrate the drug deal the Italians had agreed to with the Santa Cruz Cartel. I had other plans, and since I didn't receive an invite, I decided we were going to crash the party and be the party pooper.

As we approached there wasn't anyone outside the gate. Good so far, but always keep Mr. Murphy in mind. We got to the eastern most corner and hoisted Barbie up enough to get a look see. No, I didn't grab her ass, well maybe just a little feel. No one, she gave the signal and clambered over the wall and one by one we followed. Carrying handguns with silencers, except Knuckles who had a M4 just in case we needed to be mobile, agile, and hostile. Our counterparts at Interpol coordinated parallel plans in Italy. Since it was unexpected, it should go without a hiccup assuring there would be no time for retaliation or an assassination.

The entrance was on the backside of the building, and we could see two bad guys, standing and smoking cigarettes and not really paying any attention. Doom on you mother fuckers. I gave the signal and Guinea and Barbie let off double taps, with silencers and both collapsed to the ground. Remember, ammo is cheap and lives are expensive. We rushed forward, drug them out of view, pulled off their jackets and hats. Skip and I put on the stinky taco smelling garments and started moving forward. I pressed the button and told whomever, in my best vernacular Spanish, "I want some coffee and take a dump". Click, click, went the door and we were in.

We start our ascent to the fourth floor where we knew Ale was staying. We moved with cat like reflexes as we climb the stairs. I was a little shocked when a tango was coming down the stairs, I guess to relieve the sentinels. I double tapped him, and he fell with a loud thud to the floor and soon pouring crimson red. We froze. We could hear a door open and see the light castigating down the stairs.

We upped our pace, we were at the bottom of the steps when he saw us, but too late, I double tapped his ass in the head and moved to the open door. Skip moved the body and quietly laid him on the floor as I made it past the doorway and immediately was met a bad guy with a knife. I immediately flinched backwards and instinctively caught the knife with both hands at his wrist as the bad guy thrust towards my stomach. I stepped under, rotating my back to him and thrust hard toward my left side, drove his own knife into him as hard as I could. I let go of the knife, grabbed the back of his head, dropped to my sexy butt and making sure to snap his neck. As I was getting back to my feet, I could see muzzle flashes and some yelling before everything went silent. I entered the living room and there was Ale, all dressed, carry a bag, ready to go.

"Hey hot chick, need a lift?" as I looked her up and down.

"Senior Knight now might be the time to run." she mentioned with one eyebrow raised.

Quick radio call and we were headed down the steps and running toward the gates when the gates blew open, we were in business. Doc and the remaining crew, plus two other trucks with armed personnel were standing ready.

"Someone said you folks needed a lift." Doc yelled smiling.

"Sure, as hell do." as Ale jumped into the backseat followed by me and everyone was loaded up and trucking before anyone even knew what happened, ewe radioed to find out the parallel Italian extraction went down as a smooth as a double cappuccino, heavy on the cream.

We sped down the street and that's when I could feel the familiar warm stickiness. I looked down, pulled up my shirt enough to see a small portion of my intestine sticking out, I pushed it back in, undid my tactical belt repositioned it over the wound and pulled tight.

Ale looked at me, "Are you hurt?"

"Just a flesh wound, I am fine."

"Let me see."

"I am fine."

Ale leaned forward and tapped Doc on the should, "Monte is hurt."

"What? Bossman you alright?"

"Only a flesh wound, Doc, keep the pedal down, brother."

Barbie turned from her shotgun position and said, "let me see" as Doc turned on the overhead light.

"Damn, boss, are you shot."

"Nope, the first guy got me with his pig sticker, but I am fine, and turn the light off."

It took about 40 minutes, but we got Ale safely to the bird.

"I can't thank you enough for what you have done." Ale said as she hugged me.

"All in a day's work." I shrugged.

"You are a hero, my hero."

I looked at her and smiled, "I am no one's hero, I live in a world where there are no sensible rules."

Ale gave me a hug and a kiss and headed to a bird that would whisk her away to La Pas where the State Department was waiting, and she would be sent to Miami and then destination unknown. We got her family out of Italy and Santa Cruz and the treasure trove of information earned the team another Attorney Generals Award.

I had to have surgery, again, to fix my intestines and it meant I would be back on bed rest and light duty for at least a month. Not to mention, no MTL because you use your stomach muscles when you thrust.

Chapter 43

CAST YOUR OWN SHADOW

Checking my watch, I knew the time was approaching for the raid, that Guinea was going to lead in my absence. The stiches had been removed for several weeks but my stomach was still sore but then I did get to view my own intestines and stuff them back into my own gut. Another story for another day.

"Guinea, time for you to cast your own shadow now, brother." were the last words I said to him as he turned towards the yap, yapping bird ready to take off.

Before climbing to hop on, he turned and yelled, "Fais Do Do, Bossman." and gave me the thumbs up with a goofy grin. About damn time he recognized my authority.

While I stood watching the birds take flight, I thought about fall on the Res, when the leaves begin to change and float to the earth in all their brilliance of red, golden and brown in a last display of life. As they blanket Mother Earth, an emptiness in their absence echoes in the towering trees that once bore the colorful ghosts. Whispering lightly to those looking for answers. How absent I felt. The longing I felt, to walk the high grass, to hunt quail with my grandfather, and his dog Susie, on our sacred tribal lands, to step back in time.

I went back to my office, sat down and methodically plot out he next mission for the team. Time slowly ticked by, minute after minute, hour after hour and while still ruminating only inconsequential chatter on the radio.

Suddenly, all Hell broke loose. "Two crows! TWO CROWS" Lamar Coles screamed from the doorway.

"What?" Jolted into present time.

"Command Center, NOW!!"

We scrambled down the long corridor and up two flights of stairs, my gut reminding me to slow down, which I promptly ignored. and bound thru the locked door and immediately turn right. We are met by two armed marines; flash the credentials and we were immediately garnered access. Inside was a large conference room, arrayed with computers, TVs, Satellite communications equipment and the voices of obviously stressed personnel on the sat comms. I learned that Guineas and the gang were under attack and the force was sizable and were not spraying and praying. I was in the Pigpen, our command center and the normal killers were Big Bird, and Rubber Duck circling in the air above.

"Right now, no kidding, Visibility zero." Shouted alarmed voices hovering over the scene.

"Big Bird and Rubber Duck, sit rep, over."

"Receiving fire all around......Receiving all kinds of god damn fire on right hand flank and scattered from three sides, this ain't no picnic."

"Lots of smoke and sporadic fire skyward at us, larger force than anticipated."

"Patchy crossfire is steadily growing from patchy to heavier and heavier and closer and closer the enemy closing towards our position."

Big Bird and Rubber Duck, were armed with the standard 60 Cals are skyward and providing cover, for now.

"Guinea, Boss Hog and Steel Rain are inbound hot, throw red smoke, over."

"Roger, Pig Pen."

Boss Hog and Steel Rain, on the other hand were H1-C or Huey Hogs, outfitted with 40mm nose cannons and rockets but no flex gun system, was inbound hot. Now, they were only there for observation and training purposes, right? Remember that.

"Rodent, see if you can get to that outbuilding and lay down some fire." Thumbs up and he bolted. "Barbie, fall back and watch the right flank." Guinea quipped.

"Copy."

"Pig Pen, we are holding but Bravo is pinned down on our right-hand side. Several wounded, over."

A grenade is lobbed onto the first storage building providing cover and most everyone halted like deer in headlights, guys bailed in all directions. While the grenade is sitting there crackling, Guinea always a fast-thinking sum bitch with no break between receiving a transmission and action...runs across and scoops up the grenade like a Boston Red Socks shortstop and hurls that bitch to first base and back where it came from.

Guys scatter, bodies winging in all directions, all hell unleashed, putting hands over necks for protection...tick tock, tick tock, tick tock, tick tock, tick tock, tick tock. The grenade, burst in mid-air and this seems to cause a moment of hesitation in the action. The sum bitches have grenades. Logic can be twisted like a pretzel when operative plans go awry especially when little makes sense in the first place but calm minds rule if only in retrospect.

"Pig Pen, Guinea's position is marked with red smoke, enemy position is 285 degrees and 50 meters, and 90 degrees at 200 meters."

"Danger close, how copy?"

"Guinea, Boss Hog is on your six, inbound."

"Red smoke, where the hell are you at now."

"Get your heads down, boys."

"Get these fuckers, Boss."

"Gotcha, rolling in and drop off 5 or 6 rockets on target area. Give me 3."

"1, 2, 3 off."

"Copy, right on...............Still heavy fire, would like to work that area over again."

"Roger, roger, banking and reapproach."

"Still heavy fire, looks like these sum bitches have gotten to 45 degrees 60 meters."

"We've been hit, Pigpen we've been hit, Big Bird over."

Silence.

"Duck is banking for crop dusting with the 40 mike, mike, to your right, over."

Silence.

"Dusting is commencing on target...........Banking."

Silence.

"I believe if you eval your right the tangos have been cleared out, have a nice day."

"Rubber Duck, get eyes on Big Bird."

Silence.

"Roger, looks like it wasn't light automatic weapons, grenade launcher or 37mike mike but think we were too close for that. Big Bird is riddled with shit."

"Jesus Christ, Duck track Big Bird, over."

"Pig Pen, got eyes on Big and he's got smoke trailing and holes right up to his nether region and golf balls busted his ride, over."

"Rubber Duck flyover spray remaining on target and track Big Bird home."

"Tracking."

"Boss my right side has slowed, fix my left."

"Coming hard left, danger close, everyone dips and duct."

I had heard enough of this shit, I spun and pick up the phone and called depot.

"I need 2 Hogs immediately and any shooters available, Bossman out."

"Knight, what do you think you are doing?" Big Poppy spoofed.

"The Intel sucked again." As I was sprinting out of the room. Charging out the door, I told the marines, "I need some off duty misguided children and any other shooter support HOT." and I continued on.

"Yes Sir."

I had time to pick up tactical vest, weapon and four other half wounded warriors as we hit the door. By the time I got to the Hogs, the pilots had the rotors rolling, just like the Tide before a big game. Just by chance two greenies, four seals, three Christians (why these guys were on board, only the Lord knows but I wasn't complaining) and four jar heads along with six DEA guys that wanted in on the drug deal. Oh, and a Sargent first class. We split 10 on one and 10 on the other.

"Hey pencil dick, what the fuck took you so long?" Black 4 yapped

"I thought you were still nursing your L squared (sprained left labia)," I responded as I jumped on.

"Figured that splinter you received was going to keep you laid up for weeks." one of my new besties Mikey Z chimed in.

"Glad to see we have the Lord on our side with your heavenly presence." Directed at the Christians.

We were airborne in seconds and moving at full speed in less than 30 seconds for a 30-minute ride that might as well have been 30 days. My mind was frantically questioning the operational details searching for flaws as the self-blame was at hand. Had traded my passion for glory? In the pursuit of pleasure and forsaken reason? Was peril to escape a haunting memory or did I feel relief only when the impending trouble arrive?

Let's get drunk and screw was grating on every last nerve, red flashed to green. Alpha left and Bravo Right and let's make sure this drug deal ends badly for these sum bitches. Bellowing smoke identified our landing zone a mile away and we all knew that this was a real deal fire fight with a larger force that was determined not to let go of the strangle hold of the major manufacturing facility.

"Guinea, two more birds are in bound hot, help is on the way."

Silence.

"Prepare for strafe." We came in low and fast and hit the air brakes as we let rockets and spray from the 40 go. Bank and came in behind the line. We came in fast and prepared for our Parachute Landing Fall, see I knew this would come in handy one day.

"Ruff Rider inbound times two with shooter support, drop red for confirmation, over."

Silence.

"Ruff Rider inbound times two, over."

"Rider, put us down" I shouted into the radio."

"Roger, inbound." as we quickly touched down.

"Go, go, go, go." Black 4 screamed.

The ground radio was silent.

"Guinea, Guinea come in." I could hear, as I dismounted Transmission has stopped.

When we hit the ground and spread out and moved to the sound of now sporadic fire. A team left and B Team Right and Black 4, the three Christians and I went straight up the ole bunghole. It wasn't thirty seconds, and we were getting buzz cuts from the Hogs spraying the 40mm and letting loose rockets on the Bolivian snow-white defenders again. Now that really got their attention.

By the time we were moving the right-side fire had slowed from the shit show I had heard some time ago, but the left was on fire. The Christians instinctively moved towards the heat with a hand signal to me and Black 4 followed in pursuit. Moving closer, I was struck, and jack hammered backwards, ass overhead and flat on my back, my wind was knocked out of me. Took a second but realized I dodged another rain drop but my weapon wasn't so lucky a round or two had splintered the butt stock. Fired a burst and it was still in working order.

The right side was fully engulfed, but it was the good guys, this time, administering the boot to said backside. A loud BOOM that shook the ground could only mean one thing. Someone exploded the kerosine in several hundred barrels and it had to be C4. The smoke reminded me of pictures of Nagasaki. Big and black rising to the heavens.

It took what seemed like a lifetime, but when the shooting stopped, we all just sat there looking around. People were down all over, some of ours but mostly theirs.

"Pig Pen, we need multiple medivacs." I heard someone talking on a radio.

"Inbound already."

I looked at several bodies lying on the ground I saw Nathan Javaras face up, eyes open. I put my hand on his chest and ask for the Great Spirit to guide him home.

"Great Spirit, you called this warrior home. Bless him and let him sit at the Tribal Council with his fore fathers, for he is a warrior and he died fighting for justice." I stood and looked around at the carnage, another body lying in front of me to the left with a radio blown to bits laying just out of reach.

I felt a hand on my shoulder and turned, it was a bloody faced Barbie, barely walking with obvious shrapnel wounds. "Glad, you could make the party," she half smiled and collapsed in my arms.

"Barbie, be quiet, help is on the way, I have you."

"Nathan saved me, he saved my life. Where is he?"

"I don't know, just relax now," as I laid her down.

Unfortunately, her gaze caught what I was staring at, and she let out a God awful "N-N-Nooo-o-o-o-o!" and buried her head into my chest. I held onto her for a brief second as I looked over my shoulder. I knew that I had stared into the fire already, I saw through it and knew the sacred field was before me again. I laid Barbie down, and I walked to the body, kneeled, hesitated, and felt for a pulse. Nothing. I rolled the lifeless body over, only to look into dead panned eyes staring back at me. A large sucking chest wound meant no way to save him and he was already walking the spirit path, he was gone.

I laid my head on his chest.

Chapter 44

IT'S FINALLY OVER

Let me say, there's more to tell and I'll get it all out one day: how the DEA snookered Congress, how we slew more *sicarios* (hitmen), how we tracked down Escobar, and how a lover's wiles helped me win the trust of the Colombian people. While among these people, they helped me send grunts gunning after their persistent bane—the cartel-men. All of it being an ill-fated campaign to bring to the people of South America the peace they imagined, and which so much of the rest of the world already had.

By now you know the story of 2 Crows in the Shadows. The events which took place over the years shaped our lives. As we served, we walked tall and assumed we cast a 10-foot shadow and were bullet proof or in my case felt I could 'dodge raindrops' as a young man. We took an oath to defend this great country 'against both foreign and domestic foes' and relished the role. But you already know all this.

As time progressed, we settled into our lives. Some stayed in the Military, FBI, CIA, DEA and had great careers. Others left and entered back into civilian life, most became husbands, dads, leading ordinary lives, at least on the outside.

In retrospect, though I couldn't see it at the time, the trajectory of my life was spiraling downward. This little thing called PTSD, the Roosting Dragons, ruled my life. It was a destructive path that had no boundaries though my mind continually pushed it aside. The Dragons were undeterred and came both in wake and sleep causing a state of chronic agitation, hypervigilance, and exhaustion. In talking with my Docs, this can lead to delusional thinking, loss of time and even paranoia. PTSD led my buddy Patrick to put a bullet through his head, just to relieve the pain, guilt and despair. And Clint literally and intentionally drank himself to death, even though he vowed to never pickup or to use a weapon again. RIP my brothers, your war is over.

You see when one takes up arms to serve ones Country, and uses lethal force against Enemies of the State, the moral compass we are raised with does not forgive these transgressions. Therein, the beginning of the real battle lines.

To anyone and everyone that has or is suffering from PTSD whether through combat, your job, domestic abuse, an accident or whatever it may be. YOU ARE NOT ALONE. There is help. There are many avenues to lead you through and out the other side. I list some at the back of this text. Do not ever feel ashamed for asking for help. Take that outstretched hand and someday your recovery will allow you to reach out and give back to others. Both getting help and giving help is a salve, the key being to open your heart and admit you are merely mortal. Keep the faith and never give up.

I would be lying if I said that I have never thought about ending the Roosting Dragons. Even held a cocked weapon and thought just do it; the pain will be over for myself and everyone around me but the image of my daughters, Makenna, Karsyn and Elise, standing in front of my casket as I did at my own father's funeral prevented that. Thank the Great Spirit, for all those who suffered so much and stood with me before I moved through the chaos in my mind back into the bright light of life and the idea of what I needed to endure and to make more of my life for my three daughters, family. and friends and last but not necessarily least myself.

Exiting my service, I started drinking and it became too much over the years and then psychopath tendencies arose again. My lack of empathy for what I did and was doing left a path of destruction in my wake. I destroyed the things that mattered most, relationships with my wife, kids, family, and friends. If I could take it all back of course I would, but I can't and I will live with that and will do penance the rest of my life. For the first time, I was stricken by something I couldn't control. No matter how much I tried, I lied, I pretended, I had met my match and I was helpless against it.

I went into a tailspin that took months to snap out of and only because I stared death in the face and for the very first time, I was afraid. Afraid to move, to think too much, over think it, or not enough, do nothing, do too much, so I just existed, stalled in time and place.

Thankfully and maybe mercifully, on 29 March 2021, I received the greatest gift I never, ever wanted, I died. 2 Crows in the Shadows was in a motorcycle accident and died during a liver transplant operation and so did my past. It radically changed my course in life. I had three surgeries and three sets of chest compressions over 10 days. I saw the other side and was given a second chance. You see, we believe that once you leave this life, you have completed what the Great Spirit set forth for you, you will take another path in the afterlife. When the demons were cast from heaven, they were not allowed a second chance but the warriors that fought against them and became protectors in in this life, get a second chance. I was allowed to have my demons cast from me and I could see the truth and I could see the light.

Today, it is simply 2 Crows or Monte, I am no longer in the Shadows because that person died along with it the demons that lived and haunted me there. I want to thank the Great Spirit for allowing me to continue in this life and for the little good that I did and forgive me for all the bad. Now, I try to be a good friend, a great father and help everyone I can. It is a work in progress. I hope that everyone will make a habit of not holding someone's past against them. Especially when they have worked hard to grow and change into a better person, allow them to show up as that person.

"MaTa MaCiLan Ni Ma TiuPia.
NaMe Kwax Ni MaTiu."

Ninj O'Ha Wa Sok

"Don't remember the man of the past.
See the man of the future."

2 Crows

Coming Soon: 2 Crows Rising